He looked like every girl's dream and their chaperons' worst nightmare.

Even the blue coat, fawn breeches and top-boots of a country gentleman did nothing to detract from the danger signalled by his sardonic mouth and fathomless dark eyes. Add in curling dark hair as black as a raven's wing, and it was little wonder she had been momentarily dazed, she told herself.

She could envisage him on the quarterdeck of a privateer, or grimly determined as he charged into battle like a latter-day Achilles, but tamed by velvet and ermine and sitting in the House of Lords? Something told her he would hate such ceremonial splendour. The very thought of it made her smile as she came out of her reverie to greet the latest Earl of Carnwood.

'So the prodigal returns,' he remarked, with a smile that did little to soften his stern expression.

Dear Reader

I can't resist spending time with stubborn, irresistible heroes and feisty, intelligent heroines who are just made for each other, if only they would realise it. No wonder I have loved losing myself in Mills & Boon's compelling romances ever since I discovered them through reading the wonderful Sophie Weston's first book, and loving it so much I just had to find more. Then Mills & Boon began publishing historical novels, and I was well and truly hooked. Since then I have always known I can enjoy the luxury of forgetting my worries for a while as their romances take me into a different world, and somehow things never seem quite so bad when I come back to earth!

I finally found the confidence to write the stories that had been whizzing round my head for years, and distracting me at all the wrong times, and somehow there was never any risk of them being other than historical romances. Today I still love reading other authors' books, and the more I learn about writing, the more I marvel at their skill and ability in transporting us readers to exotic locations on deeply emotional journeys.

Beginning a very different journey as an author has made me realise how much expertise goes into producing books that seem effortless, so in their centenary year I would like to dedicate this book to those wonderful Mills & Boon romance writers, past and present, and to the unsung editors who patiently hone their work so we can all dream a little when we need to.

Elizabeth

A LESS THAN PERFECT LADY

Elizabeth Beacon

MILLS & BOON®

Pure reading pleasure™

First published in Great Britain 2008
Large Print edition 2008
Harlequin Mills & Boon Limited,
Eton House, 18-24 Paradise Road, Richmond, Surrey TW9 1SR

ISBN: 978 0 263 20170 3

Set in Times Roman 16 on 17¾ pt.
42-1008-78044

Printed and bound in Great Britain
by Antony Rowe Ltd, Chippenham, Wiltshire

Elizabeth Beacon lives in the beautiful English West Country, and is finally putting her insatiable curiosity about the past and her love of words to good use. After leaving school at sixteen, Elizabeth was sure she had blown her academic career by not paying much heed to lessons other than English and History, because she was reading historical novels under her desk! Imagine her surprise (and that of her long-suffering former teachers) when she graduated with an honours degree in English Literature as a fairly mature student twelve years later, and, as an undergraduate, a course in creative writing made her think she might one day put her fertile imagination to good use as well.

After many stalled attempts to be sensible, Elizabeth has realised her ambition to write historical romances at last, and hopes anyone else who nurses an unlikely dream will take encouragement from her story and pursue it.

Over the years Elizabeth has worked in her family's horticultural business, become a teacher who sympathised too much with students who didn't want to concentrate either, worked as a secretary and, briefly, tried to be a civil servant. She is now happily ensconced behind her computer, when not trying to exhaust her bouncy rescue dog with as many walks as the inexhaustible Lurcher can finagle. Elizabeth can't bring herself to call researching the wonderfully diverse, scandalous Regency period and creating charismatic heroes and feisty heroines work, and she is waiting for someone to find out how much fun she is having and tell her to stop it.

Recent novels by the same author:

AN INNOCENT COURTESAN
HOUSEMAID HEIRESS

Chapter One

The Honourable Mrs Miranda Braxton considered the visitor's view of Wychwood Court, and found it even more imposing than she remembered. Through a veil of drizzle, the golden stones of the great Tudor mansion looked warm and welcoming after her five-year exile and she shifted in her seat to peer at it even more intently. It was impossible not to think of the folly of youth as she recalled how blithely she had left all this for the mirage Nevin Braxton had proved to be.

All she needed to do this time was hold on to her composure and keep out of the way of Aunt Clarissa and her Cousin Celia for the week she would be permitted to stay. Why Grandfather had decreed her attendance at the final reading of his will was beyond her, considering he had made it very clear that she would never be allowed to darken his doors again. It wasn't his door any more, so he had cunningly kept to the letter of his decree, she supposed. Yet, considering that his heir was the son of a man Grandfather hated, he must be spinning in his grave at the arrival of so many cuckoos in his precious nest!

Even in north Wales she had heard whispers that the Carnwood heir was doing well for himself in the City. She had permitted herself a secret smile at how poorly that news would go down at Wychwood. Aunt Clarissa would hate the fact that he was tainting the noble Alstone name with so strong a whiff of trade, even if he *was* rumoured to have grown very rich doing so. Miranda wondered what her aunt thought the family fortunes were founded on, and spared a moment to consider the ridiculous hypocrisy of the higher echelons of polite society.

'Just like his lordship to have his will read all these months after he died. He always was a contrary old curmudgeon,' Leah, Miranda's maid and companion, remarked as the coach began to slow. 'Looks just the same as ever though, doesn't it?' she ended gruffly, and Miranda could see now that Leah had missed this lovely place as much as she had herself.

'Yes, it does.'

'It'll be different inside, I dare say, what with there being a new earl and everything. Lady Clarissa will be in a right tweak about that, just when she'd finally got your grandfather trained, so to speak.'

'I really hope you won't, Leah.'

'Won't what?' her friend asked innocently, for friend she had been since they were children. Never mind the supposed gulf between mistress and maid—if not for Leah, where would Miranda be now?

'Speak your mind.'

'And why shouldn't I?'

Leah had long ago decided not to be the sort of maid who was seen and not heard. Miranda reflected that their five years of living in such an unusual household was unlikely to convince her friend to change. 'Because it might help keep the peace,' she replied wearily.

'Hah! Some things aren't worth keeping.'

'Whether or not that's true, this household has naught to do with me nowadays and I'll thank you to remember it,' she insisted.

'It's your home, Miss Miranda.'

'No, it was my home,' she replied calmly enough. She might have yearned desperately for Wychwood when she found it closed to her for good, but her darling godmother had given her a new home, and one she loved and appreciated. At Nightingale House she had learnt much she would never have found out as the pampered grand-daughter of an earl, yet she had to admit to herself that Wychwood Court would always be some-thing more to her than a grand manor. If she was given to extravagant flights of fancy, she would call it the home of her heart, and it was as closed to her now as it had been five years ago.

'His lordship should never have sent you away,' Leah grumbled on.

'No, he was quite right to do so. He had more important things to consider than a wayward young idiot with more hair than sense.'

'Nothing should have been more important to him than his own flesh and blood.'

'Precisely,' Miranda returned smartly, as the hired carriage drew up at the front door of her old home.

As the steps were lowered and she stepped down on to the gravel, she hoped the two very good reasons for her five-year exile were safely en-sconced at their select seminary in Bath and that nobody had insisted on them being present at such a sad and solemn occasion.

'It would not have been suitable for me to come

home, Leah,' she said quietly. 'I have two little sisters who would have been tainted by association, and you know very well I am happy with Lady Rhys.'

'You haven't been that since the day you left,' Leah replied with a mulish expression that warned Miranda there was very little point arguing. But Miranda was more convinced than ever that Grandfather had been right to make her stay away, lest her example continuously remind everyone just what Alstone girls were capable of.

Even so, she felt the tears she had promised herself not to shed threaten as she looked up to survey her old home, and met the coldest and most cynical pair of brown eyes she had ever had the misfortune to encounter instead. Her latest detractor had been standing so still she had not noticed him, until his stony gaze fell on her and revealed his contempt. She didn't know what she had done to offend him. Still, he looked like just the sort of enemy she would have travelled far to avoid, she decided, with a shudder that she sincerely hoped he was too far away to notice.

Far too optimistic a notion! His sharp stare seemed to bore through her across the famous entrance to her one-time home. Yet even knowing that she was staring could not make her remember she was a lady and look away. No need to worry about that anyway, when the wretched man's hostile gaze met hers with no concession to good manners. She contrarily felt as if a series of little fires had spontaneously taken hold at every nerve end.

He looked like every girl's dream and their chaperons' worst nightmare. Even the blue coat, fawn breeches and top-boots of a country gentleman did nothing to detract from the danger signalled by his sardonic mouth and fathomless dark eyes. Add in curling dark hair as black as a raven's wing and it was little wonder she had been momentarily dazed, she told herself.

She could envision him on the quarterdeck of a privateer, or grimly determined as he charged into battle like a latter-day Achilles, but tamed by velvet and ermine and sitting in the House of Lords? Something told her he would hate such ceremonial splendour. The very thought of it made her smile as she came out of her reverie to greet the latest Earl of Carnwood.

'So the prodigal returns,' he remarked with an smile that did little to soften his stern expression.

He descended the steps with a grace that reminded Miranda of a self-assured predator and one with every confidence in his power over his prey, she decided as she forced herself to stand her ground. The new earl had long legs and a leanly muscular build that would no doubt be a match for any athlete. There was something wholly untamed about him. Once upon a time his feral assurance and hunter's eyes would have drawn her to him like a moth to a flame. Every inch of him was a challenge to any female in possession of her senses, and the rebellious, headstrong Miranda Alstone she had thought long dead was urgently reminding her she still had a full set of those.

'Sir?' she said stiffly, cross with him for scouting her delusion that she was in full control of both mind and body nowadays.

'Madam?' he replied blandly, offering no excuse for his intent summary of her face and person, just as if she was the next item on his bill of fare and he wasn't quite sure if he was too fastidious to gobble her up or not.

Suppressing a shiver that should have been one of revulsion, but fell loweringly short, she assured herself that she had the right to expect better from the man who was now head of her family. Eyeing him warily as he stepped down to her, she concluded there was very little point in trying to shame him into politeness. If the mix of hunger and fury in his dark eyes was anything to go by, he certainly hadn't much intention of acting the gracious host towards his latest guest and she might as well resign herself to a very uncomfortable week.

'We have not been introduced,' she said, unusually flustered as she took an involuntary step backwards.

He frowned impatiently at such an irrelevance. As the new earl and therefore her little sisters' guardian, he had good reason to be wary of her. In fact, rumour must have told him far too much about the stormy petrel come to pollute the family nest for her to feel at all comfortable in his company. She supposed he almost had a duty to dislike her visit. After all, Grandfather had refused to receive her and, once upon a time, he had loved her.

'Since you show no signs of remedying the situation, I take it you must be the Seventh Earl of Carnwood?' Miranda said quietly as they stood and sized each other up like adversaries before a battle.

'Indeed, and it's always a pleasure to acquire such a beautiful relative, Mrs Braxton,' he replied with a wolfish smile.

'Is it, indeed? What a delight to welcome such a flatterer to the family, my lord,' she replied, having no intention of being 'acquired' whatsoever.

She ought to be used to the scurrilous opinion so-called gentlemen seemed to have of her morals and instincts by now, but somehow his failure to see past the obvious was more of a betrayal than all the others put together. Which really was quite ridiculous; she had only just met him and after this week they would never meet again, with any luck at all. Straightening her spine and raising her chin in defiance of him, and her shady reputation, she stood back a little to look directly into those impudent, angry eyes and defy his ridiculous prejudices.

'I make a point of telling the truth when circumstances allow, madam,' he informed her smoothly enough, the sardonic glint in his dark eyes informing her that he considered she wouldn't recognise honesty if it slapped her.

Blazing defiance of whatever judgements he had formed out of gossip and misanthropy back at him, she let her generous mouth curl in a very slight sneer and gave him one of her best downing looks. She had learnt a battery of them over the years. Malicious tongues hounded her even in the remote Welsh valley where her godmother lived. Relentless gossip had led far too many apparent gentlemen to try their luck with a female with such a shady past, but rebuffing them in no uncertain terms had been child's play compared to outfacing this wolf in wolf's clothing.

'You must have a goodly supply of enemies,

Lord Carnwood,' she parried calmly enough. 'Few people relish hearing the unvarnished facts about themselves, being such erring creatures as we are. Pray, how do you tell truth from lies?' she went on with spurious innocence.

'By uncovering more accurate information,' he returned without a blink and she frowned at the implication that he knew more about her than the malice and rumour that usually passed as knowledge.

Unease gnawed at her hard-won assurance as she considered parts of her past even she could not fully recall. Nobody but Nevin Braxton had known all the sordid details of their life together, and at least he was beyond telling anyone of them now. No, his lordship had better look elsewhere for his sport; she had no intention of escaping one petty tyrant to replace him with a worse one. Even the fact that he had provoked memories of that time in her life was quite sufficient to make her hate him, thank you very much!

'That is sometimes a next-door-to-impossible task,' she challenged his boast confidently enough.

'I usually find a way,' he told her, and it sounded halfway between a threat and a promise.

'Then the moment I feel the need to have my prejudices confirmed, I shall come to you for advice, my lord. For now, though, the wind is getting up and we have had a long journey. I fear that Leah and I will catch an ague if we stand here for much longer like exhibits at a fair.'

'How remiss of me, you must make allowances for my ignorance of polite society.'

'To do that I would have to believe it ignorance and not disregard, my lord.'

'Would you, Mrs Braxton? How singular of you,' he parried swiftly, and if she had been in the slightest bit inclined to underestimate her foe she would have considered herself fairly warned by such an effortless counter-attack.

Trying to find a bright side to a very large thundercloud, she decided that, while she might deplore his manners and despise his prejudice, he would make a fierce protector to any lucky soul he considered worth protecting. Hopefully her little sisters would be among that number and nobody would ever have the chance to lure them into the sort of ridiculous follies she had so unthinkingly committed herself.

Something young and silly in her yearned to be one of the select band Lord Carnwood cared about, until she looked up and met his flinty scrutiny once more as he marched up the wide steps at her side. Trust him to manage to watch her every step into his lair without tripping over his own feet, she mused with savagely controlled composure. Stiffening her backbone, she forced herself to casually glance away as if his fierce gaze meant nothing to her.

Getting to the top of the steps without falling flat on her face would be defence enough for now and, once she had rested and washed off the travel stains, she would counter-attack so strongly he would leave her be for the rest of her stay. Well, she silently amended as they at last reached the wide front door, since she was to be a guest under his roof she could hope he could tell from her chilly manner that she was not interested in rogues of any variety. She had taken her fill of them at a very early age and, be they weak and bullying like Nevin, or strong and arrogant as the new Earl of Carnwood, she wanted no more of them.

'Miranda! You have grown so thin and drawn I hardly recognised you.' A light soprano voice cut through the tense silence between the master of the house and his reluctant guest. Miranda was shocked to find she was rather disappointed to have their hostile tête-à-tête cut short.

His lordship was even more dangerous than she had thought, she decided, and resolved to become as close to invisible as made no difference for the next few days. Fighting with him had made her feel more alive than she had been in five years, and some things were better left dormant. For now she dare not take her eyes off her old enemy to consider her new one, for she knew of old how sharp-eyed Mrs Cecilia Grant was. Her cousin even managed to add to the grace and elegance of Wychwood's famous Marble Hall, making even the exquisite sculpture of the goddess Diana posed behind her look clumsy, but Miranda shivered at the coldness in her eyes.

Celia was six years older than her, of course, and might be considered almost at her last prayers by a blind idiot. No doubt it would take a duke, or some well-placed dynamite, to shift her from Wychwood now. Already there was a possessive glint in her grey eyes as they dwelt significantly on his lordship's broad-shouldered figure and then swung back to Miranda. Point taken, Miranda privately conceded with a bland smile.

She knew perfectly well that any warmth in her cousin's smile was there for the Earl's benefit. She and Celia were hardly likely to pretend affection for each other at this late stage. Anyway, from what she had seen so far, Celia and the new master of Wychwood would suit each other very well indeed. At least if they were safely wed to each other they wouldn't make two more deserving people miserable for the rest of their lives.

'Good day, Cousin Cecilia,' Miranda greeted her relative cautiously, wondering if Bonaparte himself might not receive a warmer welcome here than she had thus far.

'Miranda,' the lady replied coolly, as if they had seen each other but yesterday and not much enjoyed the experience.

'How do you go on?'

'Much as I ever did,' Celia replied, looking pardonably pleased.

'So I see,' Miranda acknowledged, not at all surprised when the courtesy was not returned. 'I trust my aunt enjoys her usual excellent health?'

'Mama seems to have recovered from her loss at last, and the new earl has relieved us of a multitude of cares.'

She sent a melting look in his direction as Miranda watched cynically. Since Celia seemed to be looking for a second husband the wonder must be that she hadn't yet found one, and the arrival of his lordship must have been a gift from the gods.

'Managing the household alone has put great strain on us both,' Celia went on in the die-away voice that had always made Miranda long to box her ears.

'I'm quite sure it has,' she replied blandly, impressed with her own restraint even if nobody else was.

She even managed not to smile when she heard Leah's loudly expressive sniff at such a shameless lie. Anyone who knew them would realise Celia and her mother enjoyed holding sway at the Court, while doing very little actual work. Maybe something of her thoughts showed in her face despite such self-restraint, though, for Celia's gaze grew even stonier as she let it dwell on Miranda's apparently insignificant form. Luckily she was too ladylike to sniff and just let her expression tell Lord Carnwood of her gallantly suppressed outrage. No doubt he shared it and when they were alone they could commiserate with each other on having to own to such a disreputable connection.

'Mama is taking tea in the state drawing room,' Celia prompted, a steely glint in her grey eyes.

From her satisfied expression Celia knew she was calling up a formidable reserve force, and Miranda had to admit it was a masterstroke. A summons to Lady Clarissa's favourite haunt had struck terror into her youthful heart once upon a time. Yet if Aunt Clarissa and Celia thought she was still the insecure girl who had left Wychwood five years ago they were in for a shock. She would not have survived marriage to Nevin Braxton with her sanity intact if she had remained so dependent on the approval of others for her peace of mind.

Miranda met her cousin's cool gaze and gave her a slight nod of acknowledgement and, as Celia's lips tightened as far as she ever allowed them to in mixed company, she knew her message had been received.

'Some refreshment would be most welcome after such a protracted journey,' she coolly informed the space between her reluctant reception committee.

'How remiss of us not to offer it sooner,' the Earl remarked with an irony that would have done Beau Brummell himself proud, then he stood aside to let the ladies precede him with all the *ton*nish elegance he had previously disclaimed.

She spared them an openly considering look as they closed ranks behind her, then swept across the expanse of polished marble with a deliberately exaggerated grace. She could almost feel his arrogant lordship's gaze lingering on her swaying hips and the supple flow of her long legs. Let him think what he pleased. The rest of the world seemed determined to do so anyway, and she refused to allow him to be any different. To distract herself from those two sets of condemning eyes fixed on her unsatisfactory person, she let herself consider them as cousins and found them as dissimilar to each other as they were to her. Celia hated the fact that she had not inherited the famous dark blue Alstone eyes, but the new Earl didn't have them either.

He took after the founders of the family fortune in looks and doubtless in ruthless ambition as well. Miranda recalled the legend that every time a dark-haired, dark-eyed Alstone became head of the family, he either brought disaster or extraordinary blessings to Wychwood in his wake. Whichever it was to be, nobody should expect a peaceful time of it, but, for the new earl's advent to be a personal disaster, he would first have to acquire an importance in her life she refused to grant him.

'I must bid my aunt a good day before I get rid of my dirt,' she said cheerfully enough.

Celia looked as if she would have been quite happy to sacrifice her company and his lordship frowned and veered off towards the library, ordering Coppice the butler to deny him to callers, before he went into that vast room and closed the door emphatically behind him. Miranda somehow managed not to laugh at her cousin's shocked expression. His blatant refusal of a tête-à-tête with Celia, while the inconvenient new arrival was shuffled off on to Lady Clarissa, almost put the two cousins on a level footing for once.

Chapter Two

'Cousin Christopher is always busy when he's been to London on business,' Celia remarked distantly.

Where once the very mention of the word 'business' would have had Celia raising her aristocratic nose with distaste, it seemed that a belted earl and head of the Alstone clan could soil his hands with work and still gain her blessing.

'How long are you intending to stay?' Celia went on, getting down to business now there was no need to pretend even the slightest welcome.

'Not long, springtime is busy in Snowdonia.'

'I hope Lady Rhys doesn't expect you to help her shepherds?'

Luckily Miranda had learnt the value of self-restraint, and knew nothing would infuriate Celia more than seeing her barbs go astray.

'My godmother would have me be a lady of

such leisure I would be bored to the edge of reason if I listened to her,' she said with a fond smile.

'Then she cannot know you.'

'Five years is quite long enough a time to know a person when you live with them day after day,' Miranda replied, hanging on to her temper with something of an effort.

'Perhaps not long enough,' Celia insisted maliciously.

'We knew one another very well before I went to reside with her, thanks to my holidays at Nightingale House,' Miranda argued serenely.

'She always was foolishly indulgent with her charity cases,' Celia said, hoping to spark Miranda's temper as she had so skilfully in the old days.

Luckily, Miranda thought with a coolly ironic smile, she had learnt a great deal of self-control since then. 'That's why none of us takes advantage of her generosity, or likes to hear her traduced,' she countered instead.

'The opinion of jailbirds, street urchins and fallen women is unlikely to influence persons of quality. Nor is a shabby widow hidden away on a remote estate without the blessings of civilisation of much interest to her peers,' Celia went on undaunted.

'My godmama will doubtless be delighted to hear it,' Miranda returned blandly and was delighted to see a flush of temper tint her cousin's cheeks.

'Of course, if you stay away from her isolated little valley for long, you will not remain similarly uninteresting,' she snapped.

'How unfortunate for me,' Miranda replied smoothly, deciding not to tell Celia she intended returning to her new life as soon as possible just now.

'Yes, it would be.'

'That sounded almost like a threat, Cousin Cecilia, how very clumsy of you,' she murmured as they entered the grand saloon together. 'Ah, Aunt Clarissa, I can see that you are enjoying your usual good health.'

'Niece,' her least favourite relative greeted her with no obvious enthusiasm, as if she was acknowledging some unpleasant condition she was justly ashamed of. 'You're sadly worn looking and far too thin.'

'Then I shall eat well and take more rest while I am here,' she returned blandly, and welcomed the look of fury building in the stony gaze.

Fury was a far better reaction than the gloating look they had shared whenever they succeeded in pointing up her faults in the old days. Yet despite it, they managed to exchange a few stiff courtesies with their unwelcome visitor. Miranda knew it wasn't fondness that had prompted their reluctant politeness, but the entrance of Coppice and his minions with the tea tray. Casting her old friend a grateful look for his strategy, Miranda left them to their tea with no regrets on either side. With that duty done, at least she could relax until dinner and her next skirmish with her less-than-loving relatives.

'A word with you, if you please, Mrs Braxton,' a deep voice demanded as she hurried toward the staircase.

Miranda bade a silent farewell to the interlude of peace and quiet she had been promising herself and spun on her heel with a social smile she hoped would confound him. It made no impression on him whatsoever. The Earl of Carnwood was already marching toward the library without even looking behind to see if she was following. Arrogant boor, she categorised crossly, even as she obediently trailed in his wake.

A warning shiver ran down her spine as soon as she found herself alone with the new earl for the first time. For some reason she felt as breathless and shaken as if she had suddenly run full tilt into a stone wall someone had thrown up without telling her, and it didn't chime well with her picture of herself nowadays as self-contained and even a little cold. Trying to control her peculiar reaction to a stranger who seemed oddly familiar, she drew heavily on the lessons the last five years had taught her.

Maybe he was even more intimidating now than he had seemed outside, but hard looks and accusations could only hurt if she let them. Yet he managed to exude an air of power, just held in check by the demands of civilisation. It must prove an enormous asset to him in his business dealings she decided, and the fine hairs on the back of her neck stood up in some sort of warning. But no, she was immune to adventurers, she reiterated fiercely to herself, and hoped her lips hadn't moved in time with her thoughts.

A shudder shook her as she met his dark eyes again and decided a wise woman would walk away right now, before anything irrevocable could happen. Once upon a time she had run headlong towards damnation with a confident smile on her silly young face, but she had acquired a little wisdom from her youthful follies. In which case, why was she having such trouble controlling this urge to tremble at the very sight of the new Earl of Carnwood?

Somewhere in her most feverish dreams she had met the dark eyes of a fallen angel somewhat akin to him, and that was what was doing the damage to her defences now. Her dream hero had been all power and intensity too, but she had fantasised him as her other half. Unfortunately he had been an illusion, produced by a sick mind and suffering body at her darkest hour, and my Lord Carnwood was much too real for comfort.

Miranda watched warily as he let the silence stretch and her nerves along with it. He took her mind off his piratical looks when he seemed to consider what he had to say to her before turning about and shutting the door behind them.

Despite its lofty proportions, the new earl dominated the huge room effortlessly and she felt as if she had unwarily entered a trap. She stiffened her backbone and told herself he would not intimidate her so easily, but she wasn't entirely convinced she was right. Reminding herself of her godmother's motto that knowing your enemy took you halfway to taming them, she wondered if anyone could know this one. He let silence echo around the large room with the slow tick of the elaborate French clock on the mantelpiece and she made a cautious survey of him, looking for any weakness to exploit when battle finally commenced.

He had high cheekbones and a Roman nose, but

a surprisingly sensitive mouth offset the haughty cast of his features, and surely it was made for better things than clamping into the hard line it took on now? She shivered and resisted the temp-tation to cross her arms over her body in self-defence. Her predominant sensation was one of cold isolation, as if he had deliberately excluded her from the generosity of that firm mouth and whatever gentleness he might be capable of.

'We have not met before, have we?' she asked, puzzled by a feeling of familiarity with this stranger.

'I should recall it, even if you did not, ma'am,' he replied with apparent uninterest. 'Being admitted to the charmed circle of the Earl of Carnwood's close family would have been memorable for such a rough creature as I was in my youth. Perhaps we should cite an elusive family resemblance in support of your obvious bewilderment?'

Despite the sickening lurch of her heartbeat when she recalled where certain gaps in her memory fitted, Miranda held his gaze and pre-tended her knees were not threatening to wobble like a jelly. No, she would not forget the new Earl of Carnwood. She doubted anyone could, however hard they tried.

'You do look a little like Wicked Rupert Alstone,' she agreed lightly.

'Should I be flattered by the likeness?'

'Not unless you have a taste for ruthless piracy and riotous living, in which case you would probably consider him a prince among men. If not, we must hope I'm mistaken. Sir Rupert was a *very* bad apple.'

'I dare say you must be, then,' he said with a cynical smile that told her he was unsure of her soundness. 'But you must not keep my lord-ing me, Mrs Braxton. I would prefer being simply your Cousin Christopher, if you will be my Cousin Miranda in return?'

'Then of course we must be cousins, my lord.'

She doubted he had ever been simply anything, but it sounded such a comfortable notion. Not kissing cousins, but distant ones in every way? Oh, yes, that would do very well.

'That's settled then, Cousin, and I bid you welcome to your old home and my new one,' he said with an elegant bow.

'Thank you, I look forward to reacquainting myself with it.'

'I'm quite sure that you do,' he replied and this time there was no mistaking the cynicism in his smile.

Did he think she was planning to run off with the family silver, for heaven's sake? A picture of herself staggering out of the house weighed down with clanking booty at the end of her stay almost made her smile.

'I do not intend to stay any longer than necessary,' she sought to reassure him, but if his formidable frown was anything to go by, she didn't succeed.

'I believe my predecessor ordered that you remain a week,' he argued.

'I am of age and a widow, and thus in command of my own destiny.'

'Yes, and just look what you have done with it,' he snapped.

'Which has nothing whatsoever to do with you,' she said with apparent calmness; it was that or throw the nearest ledger at his ridiculously handsome head.

'I am head of the family now.'

'Congratulations, no doubt you will enjoy wielding your authority over them, but luckily you have none over me.'

'Your annuity comes from the family trusts, I believe?' he asked in a voice that was suddenly silky with unspoken threat.

'And I hope you are not thinking of using that fact against me like the villain in a poorly contrived melodrama?' she returned scornfully.

'Anything to put a brake on your folly,' he ground out as if tried to the very edge of his meagre stock of patience.

If Miranda had not known better, she might have considered him a man driven to extremis by some deeply hidden passion, but surely an hour's acquaintance wasn't enough to raise his hackles so thoroughly?

'My conduct is none of your business, my lord,' she objected and suddenly she wanted to commit every sin in the calendar just to spite him.

'Of course it is,' he replied, more formidable than ever as he stepped closer and seemed to tower over her like a Titan.

'If I choose to dance naked on every gaming table in Mayfair, you could do nothing about it and you know it.'

'Try it and you'll very rapidly discover your mistake,' he gritted through clenched teeth, and she actually heard herself squeak with surprise when he clipped her into his furious embrace, as she discovered too late that she had goaded the predator in him just a little too far.

Possession, fury and sheer need blazed back at her as she stared up at him in wonder, waiting for her own rage to catch up with shock. It *was* shock that held her immobile, of course it was. To be helpless in the arms of a man whose strength and power far outran her own was a nightmare. Or at least it would be as soon as her mind took over from her senses. Then she would turn stiff and outraged in his arms, instead of lying passive and even a little intrigued against his muscular torso like some swooning idiot.

'I won't allow it,' he informed her tersely, just before he did just what her silly senses wanted and bowed his dark head to take her mouth with his.

And take he did. She stood bewildered in his arms and gave right back with a generosity part of her screamed was the biggest mistake of a long line of them. Nothing that had gone before had armoured her against this, she realised, even as her mouth softened and then yielded to his and she let her senses drown in him.

His kiss felt almost desperate; hungry with more than mere lust, as if he had been starving for this for a long time. Ignoring the cynical inner voice that whispered she was living in cloud cuckoo land, she felt his tongue circle her suddenly pouting lips and then effortlessly persuade them to part and let him inside. Right in the heart of her something softened and glowed into dangerous life. The essence of her femininity was still there after all, she discovered, unsure whether to be shocked or fascinated as her body revelled in his touch as it never had before.

Not even Nevin Braxton had managed to destroy her, she suddenly knew, as another man's mouth melted the ice her husband had put about her deepest desires. Christopher Alstone groaned at her passionate response while she exulted in it; knowing he had freed something locked down and lost at the heart of her. Yet if she was not to regret it, the annoying voice of returning common sense informed her, she must stop him before this went much too far for both of them.

Then he plundered even deeper and his tongue danced with hers and her curiosity sparked dangerously to life as well. What would it be like to know the extremities of passion with such a man? Every instinct told her there would be nothing of compulsion or horror in such mutual need. From what seemed like a long distance she heard herself groan, not in disgust, but because she wanted more, closer, deeper. A hand she did not even know was free until then wandered round to the nape of his neck and rubbed at his silky curls, left just a little too long for the strict dictates of fashion. The scent of him, fresh air, good soap and aroused male, filled her lungs and she felt almost as if she was becoming part of him, as if fate had a hand in a joining far more intimate and just as inevitable.

'No!' she gasped as the prospect shook every resolution she had formed the day she finally got free of her husband.

Their gazes clashed as they took in what had happened, and what might have, if she hadn't awoken to the possibility she was about to be made the Earl of Carnwood's mistress. Oh, the humiliation that would have been, when passion was spent and both parties realised what they had done to satisfy it. All she had learnt from Nevin was that humiliation and much worse, not the jag and drag of frustration and regret not making love with Christopher Alstone had left her with.

'No,' he confirmed.

'Then release me?' she asked and let her eyes drift to where his long-fingered brown hand rested on the curve of her slender waist.

He dropped his hand as if she had burnt him, and hectic colour burnt along his high cheekbones as he stepped away. His dark gaze became guarded even as hers sought the reassurance that she rarely asked for nowadays. If she hadn't seen those long, strong fingers shake just once before he clenched them into fists at his sides, she might have thought him as un-affected as he was suddenly trying to appear.

'Please accept my apologies,' he finally managed, although his voice sounded gruff and somewhat rusty.

Eyeing him as dubiously as he was watching her, Miranda dipped him a perfunctory curtsy and forced herself not to make an undignified bolt for freedom. Then she cursed herself for not escaping as his grip on her wrist stopped her in her tracks.

'Have a care, Cousin Miranda,' he warned in a deadly undertone, 'if I hear gossip of this I'll have you put out of the park gates, will or no will.'

'How dare you?' she whispered back fiercely, heartbeat racing at the angry mixture of excitement and fury his touch and those contrary words aroused.

'I dare what I must to protect my own,' he rasped. 'Your sisters are in my care now, and you will behave yourself for their sake.'

She gave him a haughty glare and thought dark thoughts about his future well-being. Yet for some silly reason her mind kept presenting her with an image of him, eyes warm and hungry for her and everything about her, and she didn't even like him, for heaven's sake!

'You don't know me, sir, and you never will.'

'Don't underestimate me, Mrs Braxton. Force

me to hold up your life to public scrutiny and you'll very soon regret it.'

The unease that constantly stalked her pooled in her stomach and threatened to turn her physically sick, but she braved his flinty gaze again despite it, if only because she would not be stared at as if she was something unsavoury on his boots.

'Do you make a habit of relying on second-hand judgements, my lord?'

'No, I rely on experience,' he told her with an impassive stare she flinched away from understanding.

Yet even while he was condemning her, his long fingers soothed her tense wrist and she was shaken by a tremor of forbidden excitement very different from the effect he was striving for. The memory of that kiss was not just in her reeling mind, it was imprinted on her body, spinning between one drunken sense and the next.

'Behave yourself and you can have your week, my dear,' he went on, 'you can hardly wreak your usual havoc in so short a time.'

'As Grandfather's will insisted I was to be given house-room before his estate was finally distributed, you must offer me welcome, my lord, and I am certainly not your dear.'

'I always have a choice, madam.'

'Choose to let me go and you might get your dinner on time, then.'

He dropped her hand with unflattering haste and thrust his own into his coat pocket as if she had scalded him, and she saw some of the vulnerability and driven passion he had shown in that kiss.

'Go on, then,' he rasped, almost as if he was in pain. 'I dare say you plan your every entrance you make for maximum effect.'

'I long ago made it a rule never to be predictable. A trait you might do well to mimic, my lord, if you plan to make a success of *your* new life.'

'Nothing you do could surprise me, madam,' he warned with a smile that did not reach his eyes.

Then he bowed a brief and not particularly polite farewell, before picking up one of the ledgers stacked on the nearby desk as if he had dismissed her from his thoughts.

Telling herself she was glad to forsake the company of so boorish and prejudiced a man, Miranda left the room without another word. If so small a piece of self-restraint was all it took to assure him of his own omnipotence, he was a man of straw after all. Outside the fine mahogany doors she blinked determinedly a few times, telling herself that the threat of tears stinging her eyes was purely the product of tiredness and ill temper. She *would* not let him spoil this brief homecoming, and even Christopher Alstone could not police her thoughts.

Chapter Three

Kit waited a few moments to make sure she had really gone before he threw down the ledger he had been staring at as if it was written in hieroglyphs and poured himself a brandy to brood over. He might have given vent to a grim laugh if he could indeed read Miranda's mind. After all, he couldn't govern his own dreams, let alone her thoughts. The last half-hour had proved that, when it came to Miranda Alstone, he had no sense at all.

Restless night-visions of her had haunted him for five long years, even when he managed to dismiss her from his waking thoughts. Indeed, they had an annoying habit of plaguing him with ridiculous fantasies about a woman he had encountered once and never managed to forget, try as he might. Well, now he had made bad worse, and how could he finally persuade her to take him to her bed and slake this ridiculous, ill-begotten, urgent need of her when she was a guest under his new roof?

The knowledge that she was totally oblivious to their one fateful meeting all those years ago made him want to throw something to vent his volcanic fury, lest it boil out at the most inappropriate moment and scald those who didn't deserve it. He made himself lean back in his chair and reassemble the cool self-command he had learnt so painfully. Let one passion in and another might ruin all, he assured himself, and that kiss had nearly changed everything.

Yet he couldn't help wondering how the Honourable Mrs Braxton would react if he stormed up to her room right now and took what should have been his five years ago. He smiled wryly as he anticipated the spirited refusal such tactics would meet with. A base part of him might be in thrall to the lovely witch, but wasn't that very spirit the reason he wanted her so stubbornly? He had never forced a woman in his life and didn't intend to start now, so he sat in the chair by the fire to remember her, standing proud and defiant in that stinking tavern on Bristol docks as if it was yesterday.

Five years ago Kit Stone had let his hair grow and forgot to shave now and again as he adopted the language and habits of the street. A man of his upbringing developed many unfair advantages over his competitors. Maybe he should be thankful for the years when he had to scavenge, beg and steal to feed and clothe himself and his sisters. Or maybe he should just carry on hating his noble relatives for leaving them all to go to the devil, along with the drunken gambler who had fathered them.

Thanks to Bevis Alstone's decline and fall, it didn't take long for his son to establish himself as a shady dealer in whatever came his way, once he had traced the two rogues who had corrupted or murdered his crew and stolen his cargo. After a day spent finagling customers and suppliers out of as much as he could get, he usually spent the evening drinking and dicing in one of the lowest dives on the docks while watching and waiting. At least the man he had drunk with that night had almost played fair, which was all a half-honest man could ask after all.

'Gen'lmen…' a voice rose over the hubbub in the stinking tavern '…got a proposition for you.'

Seeing who was making it, the customers went back to gaming, drinking and whoring with a contemptuous shrug and a snarled curse or two. Kit's gaze lingered thoughtfully on the ravaged figure at the door that must lead upstairs. The man's face, under that unkempt golden beard, must have been handsome before drink and dissipation put their stamp on him, and his voice had the polished edge of a gentleman, even if the rest of him fell well short of the mark. A man with nothing to lose, he deduced, and wondered if he was on to a lead after all.

'Last time 'e wanted to 'awk a goldmine,' his fellow gambler told Kit with a dismissive shrug. 'Told 'im to take it up to Clifton where there's flats a-plenty to catch.'

Kit's well-honed instincts told him there was something odd about that particular drunkard. Business and pleasure carried on around him, but when the sot reappeared, the woman at his side took Kit's breath away, and stopped the clamour in the tavern between one second and the next.

Smoky lamplight highlighted a heavy mass of silky hair that was neither gold, brown nor red, but a rich mix of all three as it lay loose on her shoulders and framed a face made for a far better setting— Olympus, perhaps? Kit blinked and tried to believe rum and lust were riding him, but when he opened his eyes the goddess was still there, looking back at him as eagerly as he was staring at her.

He might have been flattered, if not for something strange in that lapis-lazuli gaze of hers that

part of him wanted to lose himself in and not count
the cost. They would be bewitching he decided,
even if the rest of her didn't match their vivid glory.
Yet half-closed eyelids and velvety black pupils
woke him from a daydream, and told him she
didn't see him for the narcotic ruling her.
Apparently his Venus of the dockyards was far
from untouched by the corruption around her after
all.

'Drugged to stop 'er runnin', poor soul,' the
barmaid murmured, as she placed another glass of
rum on the table beside him.

Did she think he'd pay well for a harlot fresh to
her trade and thus keep the irascible landlady
happy for once? Or was that simple pity for
whatever indignity his goddess was about to
suffer? He'd been a cynic practically since he
learned to talk, but something in Venus's demea-
nour told him not so long ago she had been more
innocent than he had ever been in his life.

'Tol' you I had a prop'sition,' the man slurred out
with unstoppable determination. 'Wife sale,' he
concluded triumphantly. 'That's how you peasants
do it, don' see why it won' work for me.'

Luckily for him, too much attention was on the
woman at his side for him to suffer for those
reckless words, at least for now.

'C'mon, gen'lmen, what am I bid? Ah,' he said owlishly, his finger just hitting the side of his nose, 'need to see more of the goods, eh?'

The girl stared serenely at Kit as if the sight of him negated the avid eyes and eagerly licked lips around her. Then her husband tore her high-necked gown from neck to navel, revealing her snowy breasts, rising proud above her chemise, and she looked for a moment as if reality was about to descend.

Kit's hands tightened involuntarily into fists even now as he thought of the casual way that miserable drunkard had torn even that fragile pro-tection aside to expose more than any woman should have to in company. Yet at the time Kit's gaze had clung hungrily to her coral-peaked nipples despite his fury, and his loins had tightened viciously. He might have been filled with revulsion by the whole sordid business, but he had still been racked with such lust he became almost a stranger to himself. Unsure if he was more furious with himself for behaving like an over-excited lout, or her for being the siren he wanted above all others, he was still in thrall to Venus.

He had reminded himself that he was a success-ful man now, and when he wanted a woman he kept a willing one in luxury. Yet he met the densely blue eyes of his goddess and nearly fell headlong into her blurred reality. When her gaze faltered she had looked very young all of a sudden. He watched her sway and correct herself to stand as far away from the sot at her side as she could with his cruel fingers biting into her arm like fetters.

When Kit looked again, he decided he must have been wrong about her age after all, for her fathomless eyes were full of dazed sensuality as they met his. He felt heat shoot through him. The bidding was up to ten pounds when his brain finally persuaded his senses to pay attention and he knew that, whatever she was, he was going to have her tonight and that was that. No other man deserved her, and certainly none present tonight were capable of seeing she had a seduction fit for a goddess.

'That's giving her away. Fine-looking woman, even if has go' tongue like an asp,' the vendor claimed rather foolishly, but his audience scarcely heard him.

'Twelve,' an eager young tar shouted.

'Twenty!' the ship's master Kit had been pursuing all week offered, and greedily feasted his eyes on mysteries only Kit should be allowed to see.

The rating fell back, disappointment written all over his tanned young face.

'Thirty!' Kit heard himself shout above the din. The room went silent as a new tension filled the air. Kit knew he had been right in thinking this was the hideaway of at least one of the rogues he was after. It obviously took a brave man, or a fool, to challenge him here. He was certainly the latter, he decided wryly, as weeks of careful work went begging for the sake of a bought woman he intended having in his bed for many nights to come.

'Any more f'r any more,' her contemptible keeper bawled cheerfully.

'Fifty,' the master snapped, and Kit guessed he had already spent most of his ill-gotten gains after murdering half Kit's crew and suborning the rest.

'Sixty guineas,' he countered quietly and his rival's shoulders slumped, until he remembered how to lie again.

'Seventy!'

'If you got that much gelt you'll pay yer shot fust, Toby Rigg,' the landlady bawled from her vast chair by the fire. 'Pay me what's owed afore you bids for my drabs, or don't expect me to 'ide you next time Lloyds men come arter you.'

'Shut your loose mouth, you'll be paid when I'm good and ready.'

'You'll 'and over me money now or soon wish as you 'ad,' the woman rapped out implacably and her three burly sons gathered around her to discourage any counter-threats he might care to make.

'You'll 'ave it ten times over, when I gets my proper share.'

'That fine gentleman you sets such store by is long gone, my lad, or I'm a Chinese; which I ain't nor never will be. So we'll take them seventy yellow boys on account, eh, m'lads?'

'He's coming back, I tell thee, and I'll be a rich man when 'e does.'

'You'm a damn fool, and I wants me money,' the lady of the house informed him implacably.

'Sold to the pirate captain!' the goddess husked.

Taking advantage of the startled silence, his friend the barmaid pushed the goddess toward him.

'Got it on you, Captain?' she asked saucily.

Trying to resist the sensuous appeal of warm and curvaceous woman as the goddess snuggled into his arms and instinctively hid her nakedness against his broad chest, Kit decided it was time they got out fast. Sooner or later the inevitable brawl would break out, and even a man of his background would be helpless to protect her from random violence.

'I'll split the twenty I have got with you if you get us out of here with a whole skin. The rest when we get back to my ship.'

'Ten guineas now?' she bargained, and casually clouted an over-eager customer with a pewter plate.

Kit handed her his purse, certain he would shortly regret it. Of course he had wriggled out of far tighter spots, but not encumbered by a half-conscious goddess.

'Here's for you, lads,' the wench shouted and threw a couple of gold pieces and all the silver high in the air so that it scattered round the room.

As fighting broke out, she grabbed the swaying Venus by her other arm and towed her away from the wife-seller who was now striving vainly against the surging crowd. Shouldering open the one stout door in the place, Kit gasped in air that might have seemed rank if he hadn't just spent hours in a stinking tavern.

The cooler air felled his goddess like a hammer blow. Cursing bitterly, and not sure if he was more furious with her or himself, he swung her over his shoulder and started to run. He stood little chance of avoiding pursuit, so he had no choice but to run for his ship when the door behind them opened so abruptly Kit was surprised the bang didn't shake the wretched place apart.

'Run to the *Ellen May,*' he gasped to the tavern wench.

The so-called husband was straw in the wind,

but Kit's rival in the bidding was a hardy rogue. Burdened with a drugged woman, Kit knew he would need a wonder to avoid a fearsome beating, especially when his tavern wench melted into the night. Nobody was more shocked than Kit when a rich contralto voice bellowed out, 'Ahoy there, *Ellen May!*' at the top of a very healthy pair of lungs. 'Help us, oh, God help us!' she managed in an ever-weakening voice.

'Well done, Venus,' he gasped

At the very least she had won them a few seconds' grace as his pursuers tried to remember where and what the *Ellen May* might be. Kit took advantage of everyone to spurt towards the sturdy sloop, but he knew he wouldn't do it when taverns along the dock emptied and their patrons joined in for the thrill of the chase. He had betrayed his lost crew and now would very likely be torn to shreds while his dockside Venus fell victim to the mob.

Then came the relentless beat of a drum and regular treads on the cobbles, a disciplined body of men approaching at a sort of running march and the warning cry, 'The Press! The stinking Press!' spread along the waterfront.

The dock emptied even faster than it had filled and Kit was left panting and spent, helpless to defend himself or the beauty in his arms. Years at sea loomed ahead of him, and heaven knew what fate his Venus would meet at the press gangs' brutal hands. It wasn't the hard work and indignity, he decided, but the loss of all he had fought so hard to make from nothing that galled him. His blue-blooded relatives would be proved right and Christopher Alstone would come to nothing, just like his father and grandfather before him.

'Damned high-nosed Alstones,' he rasped as he sank to his knees on the cobbles, and his fair burden stirred across his broad shoulders and moaned in what sounded like despair, 'whole pack of them can rot in hell!'

'Already there,' he thought he heard her murmur.

Then Venus had somehow found the strength to stand and was swaying uncertainly on her own two feet when the tavern wench appeared out of the shadows and tugged at her hand again. For a moment they sketched a pantomime of urgency and reluctance as the half-naked beauty clung to his shoulder, and then she let go and was gone just as if she had never been. Winded and shocked as any silly beau out on the strut in the wrong place at the wrong time, Kit glared into the darkness and saw nothing but inky shadows and silent menace. She had left him to the mercies of the press-gang!

The memory stung anew as he came back to the present. She couldn't have known his ship's master had made as much noise and commotion as he could and fooled the crowd into fleeing from him and his crew. Somehow it still stung that he had rescued his Venus from an appalling fate and then she had blithely left him to his fate without a backward look. Then there was the fact that it had taken him so long to forget the wretched female the first time round, and now he would have to set himself to doing it all over again.

When he had steeled himself to do his duty as host and welcome his latest cousin back to the fold, he had been in danger of letting Venus fell him twice as he was transported back to that filthy dock, on his knees and almost in despair. Instead of the hoyden he had expected Mrs Miranda Braxton to be, given her fabled elopement and disgrace, he had looked down and seen his tavern goddess instead. He had even managed to convince himself he must be mistaken, until the sight of the so-called tavern wench standing bold as brass beside her, daring him to say he knew her, scotched that hope for ever.

The open and friendly smile that had curved Mrs Miranda Braxton's lush mouth upward had almost charmed him all over again, until fury roared through him like a tornado. Then an image of the composed and lovely widow superimposed itself over that of his wild young Venus, with her heavy eyes and sensual smile, and desire had torn through him in a merciless fever. How he got through the next few minutes without either strangling the wretched female, or throwing her over his shoulder and carrying her off to the lofty luxury of his bedchamber, he couldn't say even now.

Staring grimly into the glowing fire, Kit unconsciously tightened his grip on the brandy glass until the fine glass snapped and blood and spirit mingled when he opened his hand at last. So much for the fine control he had once prided himself on. Now all he had to do was to overcome this need to seize the witch and carry her off to some isolated lair where no one else would find them and he might be free of her spell at long last.

Even as he considered forgetting her, his lips curled into a sensual smile as he fantasised about Mrs Miranda Braxton, lying sated and sleepy-eyed in his bed. If he couldn't force oblivion on his raging desire for her, he would see her so, he vowed to himself. Then he rang the bell to confess at least some of his folly and have his wound fussed over with due ceremony before the blood ruined the carpet. Oh, yes, he decided while he was waiting for the inevitable fuss to die down, before she left Wychwood the incomparable Miranda would be emphatically his and then he could set about learning to forget her once and for all.

Only denial had made her memory so potent that every woman he bedded was measured against an impossible standard of beauty. Well, this time his revenge would be sweet and very complete and Miranda Alstone would be his mistress before she left Wychwood. He had seen something of his own driven desire in her blue gaze before she veiled it and left the room with such offended dignity that he could not but admire her anew. The lovely Miranda did not want to want him, but she couldn't quite help herself and eventually that desire would seal her fate.

That kiss should be a warning to him to let her go, for it had rocked his certainties and demolished all his defences. He should leave her strictly alone, but the yearning to feel her writhe in ecstasy beneath him all night long was powerful, and how the devil could he let her go back to her isolated Welsh valley once he had experienced such a luxury of the senses?

He decided Kit Stone was as big an idiot now

as he had been that night he first cursed her loss so harshly. Then he had been one huge ache of frustrated passion, but this time he wouldn't burn alone. Their first kiss had told him it wouldn't take much persuasion to tip Mrs Miranda Braxton from cool sceptic into warm and very willing lover and he longed for that abandoned little sensualist as if he had only lost her yesterday, instead of five years ago.

There was a bright fire burning in the grate of Miranda's old room and Leah was waiting with the promised tea. For one dangerous moment Miranda felt as if she was truly home. Then, remembering how effectively his new lordship dealt with such unworthy souls as herself, she shivered and wondered for a wistful, wasted moment what it might be like inside the magic circle she knew by instinct he would cast about those he loved.

'I thought you were in a great hurry to put off your travelling attire,' her maid chided, before falling significantly silent.

Surely Leah didn't think she had lingered below out of some insane desire to cultivate the new earl's interest?

'I am,' she insisted calmly and eased off her half-boots with a sigh of relief to prove it. Rubbing her feet to get some warmth back into them, she sank down in front of the fire and wriggled her cold toes in the welcome heat.

'Ladies don't sit on the floor,' Leah rebuked mildly, before saying with apparent carelessness, 'His new lordship's a very handsome gentleman, don't you think?'

'If you admire that kind of dark, damn-your-eyes looks.'

'As any sane female would.'

'Then you'd better write me off as insane,' Miranda told her firmly, recognising the calculation in her friend's eyes, 'his lordship will need to work a little harder to win my appreciation.'

'Maybe,' murmured Leah in an infuriatingly smug undertone and Miranda only just suppressed the urge to throw something at her.

'Having behaved madly once over a handsome face, I have no plans to repeat the mistake,' she said lightly instead, 'and if I ever take another husband, I intend to make a dear friend of him first.'

'That sounds a shrewd enough notion.'

'Well, so it is.'

'And awful dull, Miss Miranda.'

Part of her wanted to agree, but the Miranda of recent years overrode it, and wondered if there was a man alive who could persuade her to take another tilt at matrimony. Of course his lordship had no such honourable intent, or he wouldn't have fallen on her like a hungry wolf. Even the thought of being more than friends with Christopher Alstone sent such a shudder down her spine that it convulsed her whole being and left her fighting a heady sense of promise. Experience told her it was a mirage, yet still her lips throbbed at the memory of his wicked mouth teasing and demanding there.

She moved a little closer to the fire and rubbed her feet in the hope that the movement would disguise her reaction to the very thought of being intimate with so much untamed masculinity from her shrewd maid.

'Much depends on one's expectations, I suppose, but have you found out all that's happened since we left yet?' she asked.

'Even I need more than half an hour for that, Miss Miranda.'

'You must be more tired than I thought,' she said lightly, then insisted Leah went downstairs and took tea with the other upper servants in the housekeeper's room. 'For you'll be busy enough later on and might as well indulge in a good gossip while you can.'

Protesting that she *never* gossiped, Leah went all the same and Miranda settled in the armchair by the fire with a sigh of relief. Obviously she was deeply attracted to the new earl, whether she liked it or not, and she was fairly sure that she didn't. All hope of finding happiness with a man like him had died the night she eloped with Nevin, for she would never be his mistress and he would never ask her to be anything more. Heaven knew she had received enough dishonourable offers over the last few years to steel herself against another one, but this time, unfortunately, she would be fighting herself as well as the importunate gentleman in question.

Chapter Four

At least Miranda had had no illusions that there would be a true welcome awaiting her in the home of her ancestors when she set out on the long journey from Nightingale House, so she really shouldn't be disappointed. Yet nothing could have prepared her for meeting the new Lord Carnwood, and suddenly she longed for her little sisters with a familiar pain she knew could never be soothed. Although she knew in her heart they were better off away from her, and from Wychwood at such a time, they were the only living Alstones she cared a snap of her fingers for.

Trying to think of them instead of a certain darkly handsome nobleman, she attempted to rest after that tedious journey in preparation for the ordeal dinner would certainly be. Every time she closed her eyes, images of a certain arrogantly handsome nobleman imprinted itself on her mind. All in all, it was a relief when Leah came back to begin the tedious task of dressing her mistress for a formal dinner.

'His lordship's expecting the lawyer at any minute and Mr Coppice was instructed to tell everyone not to stand on ceremony. Her ladyship will have something to say about that, I dare say,' Leah observed as she set about the task of subduing Miranda's hair to some sort of order.

'The sky will fall before my aunt allows her standards to drop,' Miranda replied wry as the fiery mass stubbornly crackled and curled even under Leah's skilled fingers.

'Good, I'm not having that high-nosed maid of Miss Celia's looking down her nose as if I'm incapable of turning you out properly.'

With a militant expression Leah finally wound her mistress's hair into a neat chignon and secured it firmly, allowing only one or two curls to escape and kiss her brow. Then she triumphantly produced the beautifully pressed lilac silk gown that Miranda's godmother had insisted on having made up by her London dressmaker when Miranda put off her blacks and went into half-mourning for a man who had ignored her for the last five years of his life.

After Leah had gone to so much trouble to iron it, she could hardly refuse to wear the cunningly cut gown, but once it was on Miranda was beset by doubts. For some reason Lady Rhys would never be persuaded it was better for her goddaughter to dress quietly and do nothing to attract undue attention to herself, and this time she had clearly been determined on the opposite effect.

'Nonsense,' Lady Rhys had said brusquely when Miranda protested the gown clung a little too lovingly to her curves. 'Hiding a fine figure and a lovely face like yours behind black crepe and that wretched cap is nigh on criminal. Kindly consider us poor souls who have to look at you for a change.'

Miranda cautiously surveyed the end result in the full-length pier glass she had once vainly insisted on owning, so she could survey her younger self with misplaced complacency. She froze as she recalled what a vain fool she had once been. Reminding herself stalwartly that a great deal of water had flowed under the bridge since then, she turned away to pick up the dark shawl she would surely need in Wychwood's lofty hallways.

'I look very fine,' she admitted flatly. Leah just sighed and stood back to critically survey her mistress.

'That you do. Time you put some flesh on your bones, though. The gowns you left behind here would go round you twice.'

'You don't mean they're still here?'

'In the clothes press, just as if you left yesterday. I don't know how I am supposed to fit all your current ones in. Not that you have half enough of them to clothe a lady of fashion.'

'Just as well I am not such a delicately useless article, then,' Miranda replied stalwartly, but she found the notion that her grandfather had ordered her room kept as she left it less comforting than she would have expected.

So much love had been wasted in stubborn pride on both sides that she felt tears threaten, before she reminded herself she could not afford to indulge in sentiment. She had her aunt and cousin and a far more significant foe to outface in his new lordship before she could even think of doing that.

'Do with my old gowns as you think best, Leah,' she ordered. 'I'm a different person from the one I was then, as well as a thinner one.'

'I could take them in for you—fashions haven't changed that much,' Leah offered, in the teeth of her own interests. After all, discarded gowns were usually regarded as ladies' maids' perks.

'No, I don't care to be reminded of the past,' Miranda refused with a shudder.

'Mumchance in this place.'

'True enough, but I want no extra reminders of my past folly and they are a young girl's gowns, so get rid of them for me, would you, please?'

'Of course, Miss Miranda.'

'Thank you. You have always been a better friend to me than I deserve,' Miranda admitted ruefully.

'Nonsense, now get along out of my way, do. If I'm ever to get your things unpacked and stowed away, I need to clear the shelves straight away.'

Miranda thought of the quantities of over-trimmed gowns she had once thought essential for her comfort, and marvelled at such vanity.

'Thank you,' she said sincerely, mighty relieved to be spared the task herself, 'and don't wait up. We've both travelled interminably these last few days, so just this once pray don't argue with me.'

'If you promise to ring if you need me,' Leah cautioned.

'I will,' she lied serenely. 'Now go and charm Reuben out of his wits again and forget about your duty for once.'

'A breath of fresh air before supper might just do me good, after being cooped up like a broody hen for days.'

'I dare say it might, but don't break his heart.'

From what she had seen earlier, the youthful head groom had matured into a very well-looking man during the years she and Leah had been away from Wychwood. Miranda knew her maid too well to mistake the gleam of interest in her eyes when they dwelt upon the suitably dazzled Reuben.

'Just so long as you take care not to get yours broke either,' Leah cautioned shrewdly.

'I'll guard it like the crown jewels,' Miranda said with heartfelt ardour. Not that Nevin had exactly broken hers; more trampled on her pride and then smashed any remains to dust.

Kit allowed himself the luxury of lurking in the shadows for a moment as he watched the former darling of Wychwood descend the stairs like a fallen queen. The multicoloured mane he remembered so well was subdued and pulled back from a heart-shaped face that was now a little too calm and controlled, as if she had been chastened by life into hiding whatever emotions animated her. Those blue, blue eyes would still steal a man's soul away if he only let it slip, but look closer and you could see a deep wariness. Impatient of just looking after so many years of not being able to touch, he emerged from the darkness and stood in the open space at the foot of the stairs, waiting for the beautiful Mrs Braxton to step into his web.

As Miranda descended the last few steps her heart thumped a tattoo she was thankful only she could hear at the sight of him waiting for her. She was conscious that the cunningly cut lilac gown emphasised the sway of her hips, the swish of silk against her long legs seemed very loud in the stillness and she felt that her figure was outlined rather too emphatically by the soft fabric that clung lovingly to every movement. For some reason she longed for him to see beyond the gifts nature had lavished on her, but knew it was too much to ask. Miranda tried to hide whatever regrets she felt from his sharp eyes.

In evening dress he looked even more magnificent. An immaculate black coat fit his broad-shouldered figure superbly, knee breeches and stockings only emphasised his leanly muscled legs. His snowy linen made his dark eyes and hawkish features more arresting than ever. She stepped down beside him at last, just in time to see a flare of heat flash through his dark brown eyes before he ruthlessly controlled it. It was just as well that she was a woman of the world, she told herself, for no unfledged girl could have stood her ground in the face of such an untamed rake.

'We are both very fine tonight, are we not?' she asked calmly enough.

'As fivepence,' the earl replied blandly and offered her his hand.

Stiffening her backbone yet again, she laid her gloved hand in his. Through the soft kid she felt his strength and sensuality threaten her self-imposed isolation. She stamped hard on the promise that threatened to surge into life between them once more. She could do this, Miranda assured herself, and raised her chin to challenge any resolution he might have to the contrary.

'You're even lovelier than rumour reported you,' Lord Carnwood informed her and raised her hand to his lips with apparent sincerity, drat him.

The depth and range of his quiet voice reflected the mighty physique that produced it, but somehow she managed to blame the frosty night for a shiver that ran through her like quicksilver. She couldn't possibly be feeling the warmth and threat his mouth promised through her supple glove.

'Am I? Reputations often lie, don't you think?' she challenged him.

'I always form my own opinions, Mrs Braxton, and once they are made I rarely find need to change them.'

'Then I must argue for more flexibility of mind.

It is the gift of great men, and should be cultivated by the mightiest of us. After all, Rumour seldom deals well with her victims, does she, Lord Carnwood?'

'You may argue for whatever you please of course, ma'am, but we're all at the mercy of our reputations, I fear, although I suppose we can prove whether or not they are deserved by our actions.'

'Excellent, so pray let us join my aunt and set about witnessing that theory in practice, Cousin Christopher.'

With the very tips of her fingers brushing his offered arm, she let him lead her down the lofty hall to the state drawing room Lady Clarissa insisted on using, however few of them were assembled for dinner. Knocked off balance by the ridiculous urge to tremble at the contact of his firm flesh under her over-sensitive fingers, Miranda felt her composure waver for a perilous moment. She slanted a furtive look at the new earl's impassive face and almost succumbed to an urgent desire to turn tail and bolt back to her room, declaring herself too tired to face this ordeal so soon after her journey.

'Do the Reverend and Mrs Townley join us tonight?' she asked more or less at random.

'Not unless they have abandoned their new living.'

'I suppose it's foolish of me to think all will be as it was after so long.'

'Not so very long, surely, Cousin?' he replied with a quirk of his eyebrows that told her he thought she had been angling for that very compliment.

'When a lady has as many years in her dish as I have, she eschews exact calculation, my lord.'

'Nonsense, my dear. You can't be much more than seven and twenty,' he baited her with a touch of his initial hostility, as if he found her assumption of the air of a bored society beauty distinctly irritating.

While he was cross with her, at least he would not be slanting her any more of those disturbingly perceptive glances from his sharp dark eyes. 'I could even be a little bit less,' she said with a bland smile and hoped he had waited in vain for an indignant glare when he set her age five years beyond reality.

'Age is largely irrelevant when experience is added into the equation,' he replied cynically.

'Now there, my lord, you are quite wrong. Age is never irrelevant and you may ask any woman between eight and eighty for corroboration of that particular truth.'

'Thank you, I'll take your word for it.'

'My, that will be a novelty,' she returned smartly and thought she had won that round, until she saw his mouth lift in a sardonic smile and knew it had just been a skirmish he thought too unimportant to contest.

By the end of it, though, they had reached the drawing-room doors and the butler nodded regally to the head footman, who solemnly opened the double doors as if admitting supplicants to the royal presence.

'The Honourable Mrs Braxton and his lordship, the Earl of Carnwood, your ladyship,' the butler announced, and Miranda wondered how long the man of power beside her would tolerate being announced as if he were a guest in his own home.

Lady Clarissa waved a regal acknowledgement from the largest and most comfortable chair in the room, staring at the newcomers in a fashion that would have been considered distinctly ill bred in a lesser aristocrat. Then a frown twitched her brows together, probably in vexation at the sight of her scapegrace niece dressed so finely and standing at the side of the heir as if she belonged there, so Miranda just smiled blandly under her basilisk glare.

Celia adhered determinedly to her sofa, while somehow finding the energy to smile a languid greeting at the new Lord Carnwood. She ignored Miranda regally, obviously satisfied that her warning needed no repetition despite Miranda's position at his new lordship's side.

'Niece,' Lady Clarissa acknowledged flatly, 'you may kiss me now you are not travel-stained.'

'Why, thank you, Aunt Clarissa.' Miranda placed a peck on the cold cheek offered to her like a royal favour. 'As I remarked earlier, you look well.'

'I cannot return the compliment, but I suppose it is not possible to live the sort of life you do and not have it show in one's face.'

'What a fast existence you do credit me with, Aunt Clarissa,' Miranda replied lightly.

'You know perfectly well what I mean,' Lady Clarissa barked. 'I will not put up with your impudence now, my girl, any more than I did six years ago. If I hear any more of it, I shall pack you off back to Nightingale House, and good riddance.'

'I believe it is five years since I lived here, not six, and I am not here now by your invitation, but my grandfather's, so you will just have to ignore me for the next few hours, will you not? After so many years of practice, I dare say it will come easily enough.'

'Impudent hussy! If I had my way, you would

never have darkened these doors again. I cannot imagine what Papa was thinking of, ordering you must be here before a word of that section of his will could be read.'

'Neither can I, but I plan to restrain my curiosity until a more appropriate time.' Miranda couldn't be sorry for answering back, even when her ladyship was powered by fury to actually rise and ring the bell herself.

'Mrs Braxton will be taking dinner in her bed-chamber,' she announced as the doors opened too rapidly for anyone to doubt the butler had been well within earshot.

'Don't trouble yourself, Coppice,' Lord Carnwood intervened coolly. 'Mrs Braxton is far too conscious of the extra work it would cause the staff to put them to so much trouble. Lady Clarissa overestimates the tiring effects of her long journey on her niece's excellent constitution, do you not, ma'am?'

Lady Clarissa's chilly grey eyes locked with the Earl's fathomless dark ones, then fell before a more implacable will than even her stubborn one. 'Apparently,' she conceded as if it might choke her. 'You may go, Coppice, unless dinner is ready?'

'Not quite, my lady.'

'Then you had better find out what is delaying both Cook and our guests, had you not?'

Lord Carnwood let that ungracious order pass. From the look Coppice sent him and the faint shake of his dark head, Miranda doubted it would be carried out anyway.

As the doors shut behind Coppice, Lady Clarissa glared at her erring niece with a venom that would have set the gauche Miranda of five years ago trembling in her satin evening shoes. Now she returned her aunt's hard look with an insincere smile, before subsiding on to a gilt chair at a healthy distance from the roaring fire.

Celia continued to stare into the fire as if she was lost in a world of her own. Miranda draped herself across the chair in imitation of a notorious beauty she had met scandalising a neighbour's party she once attended with her grandfather, before she became notorious herself, of course. Having been given a bad name, she might as well hang herself in style.

Ignoring both Celia and the artistically draped Miranda, Lord Carnwood engaged Lady Clarissa in stilted conversation. Miranda was annoyed to find that she was so attuned to the dark timbres of his voice, even across the formality of this great room, that she missed not a single word he said.

It was a relief to hear voices in the hall just before the doors opened to admit her grandfather's middle-aged lawyer, along with a handsome couple possibly ten years older than she was herself. When she was introduced to the Reverend Draycott and his lively wife, Miranda soon decided she preferred them to the stuffy couple who had inhabited Wychwood Rectory when she was a girl. She detected none of the sour disapproval she would have met from the Reverend and Mrs Townley for her sins, so she sincerely hoped they were not ignorant of them.

The Earl of Carnwood greeted his guests genially, but Lady Clarissa managed only a stiff nod in the lawyer's direction as Celia pretended to be lost in a world of her own. Unable to watch another greeted as uncivilly as she had been herself, Miranda gave him a warm smile.

'Mr Poulson, I hope you are recovered from your journey?'

'As much as can be expected at my age,' the rotund little man replied with a self-deprecating smile. 'Fancy you remembering my name after all these years, Mrs Braxton.'

'Since you used to give us children peppermint drops whenever you came to visit Grandpapa, I was very unlikely to forget it, sir.'

'So I did! Those were happier times for us all, were they not?'

'Indeed they were—would that we had them back again.'

For a brief minute Miranda allowed herself the indulgence of the might have been. If only her brother had not caught an epidemic fever at school, and come home so weakened he had to be accompanied by a tutor. If only she had listened to Grandfather's fierce pronouncements on her infatuation with Nevin Braxton, said tutor, and, above all, if only Jack had not died weeks after her defection. Of all her regrets, that was the heaviest of all, she realised now—it far outran the thought that, if Jack had been here, she would not have to steel herself to avoid Christopher Alstone's eye whenever possible.

'Regrets, Mrs Braxton?' he questioned her softly now, his deep voice hard with distrust again for some odd reason.

'Memories, my lord,' she replied briefly, determined not to let his suspicion incise Jack's wicked smile from her mind.

'A commodity I patently cannot share. How are you, sir? It was an ill day for travelling today, was it not?'

'That it was, my lord. I freely admit that these days I much prefer my chambers to the open road.'

'Maybe one day we will be able to travel like birds instead of it taking us days to get from one side of the country to the other,' Miranda mused.

'Like flying pigs, Cousin?' Kit asked impatiently.

'Not quite, but equally unlikely, I am afraid.'

'A pleasant idea though, my dear madam,' Mr Poulson put in with a fatherly smile of encouragement, seemingly oblivious to the suppressed tension between his companions. 'It would certainly save a good deal of time on dirty roads.'

'If only we could invent machines to direct all those balloons people spend so much time watching launched, maybe your idea would be possible, Cousin Miranda,' his lordship admitted.

'Until that happy day, I suppose we will just have to make do with mud and inconvenience like everyone else, my lord.'

'Indeed, and you have had a longer and harder trek than the rest of us, if I am not mistaken.'

'And I doubt that you often are, my lord,' she replied rather waspishly and felt the lawyer's shrewd gaze on them both this time.

He seemed to gauge the undercurrent of awareness that ran between the new earl and his scapegrace cousin and momentarily looked puzzled and then oddly pleased. Miranda ordered herself to be more circumspect in future, but something kept her standing at his lordship's side, pretending to be sociable all the same.

'I thought we had agreed to be cousins,' he chided when Mr Poulson's attention was diverted by the new vicar of Wychwood.

'Do you mean to acknowledge me as such in public then, my lord?' she asked mockingly. 'I'm probably beneath your touch, as well as us being connected to you only in the third or fourth degree.'

'And it would make such a change for your branch of the family to note the existence of mine, would it not?'

She covered her bemusement at his peculiar statement with a social smile, for Grandfather had been rebuffed in the harshest of terms when he tried to send his cousin Bevis Alstone's son and daughters to school instead of settling Bevis's vintner's bill as demanded.

'Are we to celebrate our newly established kinship, or mourn it, do you think?' she asked lightly.

'I shall withhold judgement.'

'Shall you indeed, cousin? How very refreshing to meet a gentleman who refuses to rely on the prejudices of others to form his opinions.'

'You can be certain of one thing, Cousin Miranda, I long ago made it a rule to trust my own prejudices ahead of any others.'

There was no mistaking the heat in his dark gaze as he let it dwell on her discreetly displayed curves for a little too long, but she chose to pretend ignorance and gave him a sweetly insincere smile. 'How unenlightened of you,' she said lightly, 'so pray excuse me while I look up prejudice in my grandfather's copy of Dr Johnson's famous dictionary, Cousin. Does it come before or after proof, I wonder?'

'Oh, dear, that tutor of yours really wasn't very good, was he? Before, of course.'

'Then should I not appeal to Mr Poulson? I believe it is customary to present all the evidence before the court forms a judgement?'

'Or so we are told,' he replied sardonically.

'Then I rest my case, my lord,' she told him.

'Cousin,' he corrected abruptly.

'Very well, but Cousin what, pray?

'I suspect you know very well my name is Christopher,' he said and silently dared her to remark on the fact that it was a very common Alstone forename, and probably given to him in defiance of his father's family rather than to please them.

She felt a sneaking compassion for the little boy he must once have been, forced to live with the consequences of Bevis Alstone's drinking, gambling and whoring. Cut off by his family,

Bevis must have been an appalling parent. Miranda forced herself not to look for the vulnerable boy in the hard man his son had become. It was far simpler to think of him as just another man of the world, not the complex creature he really was.

Chapter Five

Coppice opened the doors and warily informed the company that dinner was served. As the senior and most socially distinguished woman present, Lady Clarissa went in on Lord Carnwood's arm. Miranda told herself she was well pleased to be next to Mr Poulson and opposite the new vicar. Lady Clarissa took the foot of the table and had to content herself with insisting Celia took precedence over the vicar's wife and had the other seat by the new Earl.

'Surely we don't need to stand on ceremony?' Miranda asked rashly, used to informality presiding over state at her godmother's table.

'Indeed not,' Lord Carnwood agreed. 'Coppice? See that a round dining table is installed in the Blue Parlour by tomorrow night,' he ordered with the air of easy command that Miranda had already noted the servants obeyed without a second thought. 'We shall take our meals there whenever there are less than a dozen of us to dinner in future, and meet beforehand in the Countess's Sitting Room, not the State Drawing Room.'

'Very good, my lord,' Coppice replied, a faint smile lifting his thin lips.

'I do not approve of such shabby-genteel arrangements!' Lady Clarissa announced regally.

'Very well. Coppice, will you see that Lady Clarissa is served in here every evening? I doubt the rest of us will disturb her at such a distance.'

Coppice wisely said nothing, but Miranda thought she caught a twinkle in his eye as he waited impassively on events.

'Well, I shall enjoy the novelty,' Celia said, with a hard look for her bridling parent.

Ambition for her daughter narrowly beat Lady Clarissa's pride. 'Very well, let it be so,' she said grandly and nobody bothered to point out that it would be so, whether she liked it or not.

After that Miranda was not the only one to concentrate on her excellent dinner and her thoughts. Deciding that her aunt would always be a mystery to her, she turned to her dinner companion in the hope of setting an innocuous hum of conversation going.

'How did your journey really go, Mr Poulson?'

'In truth, I would rather not travel at this time of year, Mrs Braxton. The roads are naught but a sea of mud and the beds at the inn I stayed in last night were decidedly damp,' the little lawyer told her indignantly.

'How very distressing for you,' she said soothingly, thinking ruefully of her desperate journey to Lady Rhys's remote home five years ago, when she and Leah slept fitfully on top of a swaying accommodation coach to stretch their small store of money.

'Still, we must all suffer in the line of duty now and again,' the little lawyer said piously, 'but how was your own journey, ma'am?'

'Uneventful,' she said cheerfully, 'and worth it to experience the benefits of Cook's skills again. Have you tried her baked trout, sir?'

'It almost blots out the memory of those sheets,' he replied with a self-deprecating smile.

While he set to with a will, Miranda surreptitiously watched their dining companions. Mr Draycott was being condescended to by her aunt while she regally ignored his wife, presumably because Mrs Draycott was very pretty and must not interfere with Celia's fascination of the Earl. She saw Mrs Draycott meet her husband's gaze with rueful amusement and wondered how it felt to love like that after years of marriage. Her own delusions of love had barely outlasted the ceremony over the anvil, and how she wished she had possessed a little more patience and discernment.

Ironic, was it not, that a woman supposedly experienced in the arts of love knew virtually nothing about that tender passion? Luckily Celia's polite titter distracted her just then and reminded her of another conundrum. Considering her cousin rarely did anything on impulse, her hasty wedding to a mere lieutenant of Foot Guards was a puzzle in itself. Surely Celia hadn't married for true love?

Miranda frowned and wondered why she thought her cousin incapable of such untidy emotions. She had never met the gallant lieutenant, of course, and the poor man had been dead within weeks of their hasty London wedding. There had been no seven-month pregnancy to tell of illicit passion, unlikely as such weakness seemed on the part of her icily lovely cousin. Yet Grandfather must have disapproved, or Celia would have been married from Wychwood with as much splendour as Lady Clarissa could contrive.

'This beef is as good as any I ever tasted, Mrs Braxton,' Mr Poulson said with a hint of reproach as he eyed her untasted portion.

'My appetite seems to have deserted me,' she admitted.

'Indeed, this must be an ordeal,' he said with quiet sympathy.

Touched by such understanding, she sought to reassure him. 'I have grown a very thick skin of late years,' she assured him with a mischievous smile. 'And my old friends below stairs seem pleased to see me.'

At last it was time for the ladies to retire to the barn-like State Drawing Room while the gentlemen enjoyed their port in peace. It wouldn't be a riotous interlude, Miranda decided, considering the company. Yet she would rather have endured the earl's jibes than join her aunt, Celia and a vicar's wife who must disapprove of her on principle. She bore it stoically for a while, then excused herself, fearing that if she stayed she might say something scandalous just to live down to their expectations.

Opening the door of the library cautiously, in case his lordship had sneaked back into it when her back was turned, she sniffed the familiar scents of books and lavender polish. Closing her eyes, she could almost fool herself that Grandfather would be sitting in his favourite chair by the fire, absorbed in his beloved Homer and a glass of fine cognac. Of course the chair was empty when she opened them and she allowed herself a sigh of regret at not seeing him so one last time.

'Don't tell me you're looking for a book, Mrs Braxton?' the new Earl asked disbelievingly and Miranda cursed herself for leaving the door open—although she supposed she could hardly shut him out of his own library.

'Then I won't, my lord,' she told him equably and tried to move round him; the dull safety of the State Drawing Room suddenly seeming appealing after all.

'Off to charm the little lawyer out of his wits again?' he asked sardonically as she turned to leave.

'Don't be ridiculous, Mr Poulson was a friend of my grandfather's.'

'You're right and I'm sorry.'

'I beg your pardon, my lord, I think my ears must be deceiving me,' she said, genuinely shocked to hear his admission.

'We have got off on the wrong foot, Cousin Miranda. I apologise for my harsh words and inexcusable actions.'

'Thank you,' she replied, too dazed by this turnabout to say anything clever.

'Which doesn't mean we have to become bosom bows, or suddenly trust one another with our deepest secrets,' he replied with a lopsided smile that nearly made her knees melt.

'I think that most unlikely, but I can assure you that I am nowhere near as bad as rumour accounts me, my lord.'

'Cousin,' he corrected and his eyes were sceptical again and his smile a matter of form.

Thus far and no further, his expression seemed to say, and she told herself to be glad of it. He was nothing like the gentle picture she had built up over the years of a man she could slowly trust with her secrets and her heart, after knowing him for many months, if not years.

'We should not be alone in here,' she said defensively.

'I know, I was about to go outside and blow a cloud when I heard you. Perhaps I had better do so, before your aunt finds us absent without leave.'

'Which would never do,' she replied with a cool smile. After their earlier scene in this room, she didn't altogether trust his mellow mood.

'Indeed not,' he said with a rigidly correct bow, and let himself out of one of the long windows to indulge in his occasional penchant for cigarillos.

* * *

Kit had reconsidered his impulse to do anything in his power to bed Miranda Braxton at last. During dinner he had secretly watched her try to mitigate the failings in her aunt and cousins' hospitality, and finally acknowledged to himself that she possessed the instincts of a true lady. Having reached that disappointing conclusion, he had then forced himself to consider her past like a rational human being instead of a lust-ridden fool.

In truth, Braxton had subjected her to such degradation and horror that it revolted every instinct Kit possessed. He had spent most of his early years somehow scratching together the means to keep his little sisters out of the very trap Braxton had knowingly, even gleefully, sprung on his own wife. For five years he had thought her a fallen beauty, cunning enough to work the age-old trick of selling herself to the highest bidder then letting her pimp in to rob and attack their victim, before or after the fool had taken his pleasure. It had been obvious, until he had looked down at his Venus and seen her pretend to be a virtuous widow more sinned against than sinning.

Only tonight had the heat of betrayal finally faded and cold reality taken its place. Braxton had tried to sell his wife into a life Kit wouldn't wish on his worst enemy. The wanton cruelty of that action could overcome Kit's wish to see Miranda as a noble houri, flitting from conquest to conquest with no thought for her victims. Then he could have taken his pleasure of her and moved on as thoughtlessly as the harlot he suddenly imagined her would have done. Given that he had finally worked out the truth, that lusty scenario must be forgotten.

Remembering their passionate kiss now he was acutely uncomfortable. There had been a peculiar innocence to her lips, as if she was surprised to be wooed rather than forced. No, there could be no more of that, for it would lead to places he refused to go. A mistress could arouse his passion and even affection—as such he could have kept her and not cared if he liked her a little too well. Unfortunately, ladies expected marriage instead of a *carte blanche,* even ladies like Mrs Miranda Braxton.

He couldn't wed a headstrong beauty whose wildly rebellious nature had already precipitated her into one hasty marriage. After all, he had long ago decided to wed for reason and not emotion. An excess of that had led his mother to marry a man who cared for the green baize tables and the wine bottle more than he ever did about her or her children, and he had no intention of following her down that particular road to damnation.

So Kit strode about the shadowed terrace and thought about the excuse for a man Miranda Alstone had married and, if his fists tightened until his slender cigarillo was in danger of ending up mangled and burning him in the process, that was because he loathed cruelty and injustice. He forced himself to relax his tensed muscles and tried to ignore his sudden suspicion that Miranda Braxton would always rouse strong feelings in him. Emotion fogged judgement and he had no use for such folly.

No, a lifetime of suspiciously watching every man who so much as looked at his wife held no attraction for him. All he had to do was endure the next week without disaster and then he could avoid her until one of them was safely wed and out of reach. Something told him that if they ever spent too long together the consequences would be inevitable, and catastrophic. Having settled that conundrum in his mind, he returned to the over-gilded barn Lady Clarissa had best enjoy presiding over one last time, and made himself endure the rest of a dull evening just to prove himself right. Resisting the extraordinary beauty of his newest relative would get easier, he told himself stubbornly, as the evening at last wound to a weary end at long last and the Draycotts went home.

He took his candle and headed off to his bedchamber, after assuring himself Lady Clarissa had not lodged either of his guests in the lumber room. Kit threw himself into the chair by the fire in the master bedroom and sighed heavily. He would do it, he reassured himself. After all, he and his childhood friend Ben Shaw had risen from the worst slums in London and wrought a fortune out of nothing but will power, so he had a goodly stock of that commodity. Overcoming a craving for a lady of dubious reputation and spectacular beauty should be easy enough after that Herculean task, so long as he avoided her more steadfastly in future.

As he tossed and turned through a very uncomfortable night with only half a dozen doors between him and temptation, he kept repeating that assertion in the hope it might one day be true. Yet when he eventually slept uneasily, his dreams were haunted by a dockside Venus who watched him with reproachful eyes as if he had disappointed her hopes and dreams all over again.

After marrying Nevin Braxton, Miranda had thought herself immune to the baser passions, like a person who had survived a life-threatening disease and was protected against it for life. Therefore she was shocked to spend a restless night, thinking far too often of renegade earls too handsome and dangerous for her peace of mind.

There was, she reassured herself, nothing tender in the Earl of Carnwood's hot gaze that might woo her from her determination never to succumb to her wayward emotions again. He wanted her only in the most elemental way a man wanted a woman, to slake his lust. It was instinct and nothing more, she decided, and she hadn't resisted so many dishonourable proposals to end up as a bed-warmer for her grandfather's successor. Next time she laid eyes on him she would be armoured against him, immune to his fallen angel smile and that fathomless dark gaze she suspected could even make a harlot blush.

The trouble was, she knew perfectly well that a base part of her might well thrill to his wicked attentions if he ever renewed them. Even as she permitted that maverick thought to enter her mind, a current of fiery heat ran through her. Well, his lordship and the abandoned female he seemed to bring into being would be doomed to disappointment.

She would never yield to passion without love

again, and had to scotch the idea that, with that heady emotion added to the mix, no female on earth would be able to resist the new Earl of Carnwood's dishonourable intentions. It was a ridiculous idea; he had shown his true feelings for her first on the steps when she arrived and in the library. Even if she had the right to love him, she wouldn't let herself do so and he would never become entangled with the likes of her on any serious level. It was a ridiculous idea born of tiredness. She had laid eyes on him for the first time today, after all, and even in the old days it had taken her longer to fall in love with a handsome face.

Tomorrow, she promised herself, after the will had been read and her presence was no longer required, she would leave if she had to travel all night. She doubted anyone here would sincerely protest her going, except one or two of the staff dear to her from her childhood. Miranda fully intended Leah to stay behind with Reuben and her family. She refused to spoil her oldest friend's romance twice and, however sorely she would miss Leah's stalwart support, it was time she finally learnt to stand alone. All she had to do was avoid the arrogant new Earl of Carnwood for the scant time she intended to remain and all would be well again.

* * *

Waking at the outrageous hour of ten o'clock the next morning, Miranda hurriedly washed and donned a plain cambric morning gown she could put on without Leah's help. She hadn't come to Wychwood expecting to impress, so she couldn't complain if she failed to do so thus far. Determined not to let it matter what the current occupants thought of her, she donned sensible shoes so she could walk in the garden and wondered where the new Earl of Carnwood was this morning so she could avoid him. All in all, she couldn't be safely back at Nightingale House too soon. Even he shouldn't be able to trouble her across such a distance.

'You're awake at long last then, Miss Miranda! Why didn't you ring or at least wait for me to come and help you dress?' Leah exclaimed as she bustled in to find Miranda both up and clothed.

Suppressing a wicked impulse to reply that, if she was not awake she had a serious problem with sleep walking, Miranda meekly agreed that she was, and had indeed erred in managing for herself.

'How on earth did you get all my gowns pressed so quickly?' she asked as a diversionary tactic. 'You must have been at it half the evening.'

'You were sleeping like the dead when I brought the rest back this morning, and the laundry maid did your muslins. At least she knows her job, not like that wall-eyed baggage Lady Rhys employs solely out of the goodness of her heart.'

'She has always seemed skilled enough to me. Tell me how you found Reuben last night, pray?'

'Just as he always was of course, how else would he be?'

'Elated, I suppose. He has waited five years for you to come home after all. Not many men would be so patient.'

'Good things are worth waiting for,' her maid said smugly and Miranda concluded that their reunion had gone well, despite her refusal to admit it.

'You should never have left here, Leah. If you had only stayed when I left, you and Reuben would have had a home and children by now.'

'I always wanted to see the world, remember? I thought that would mean going to London when you were presented and spending a few years away after you were wed, but I got my wish anyway and I don't regret it.'

'Even if the back-streets of Bristol and an unconventional household in a remote Welsh valley were hardly what you or your family expected?'

'Travel broadens the mind.'

'Then ours must be very wide by now. Still, I have kept you two apart for too long.'

'Now I've seen and done more than I ever would have if I'd stopped here, and wished I was somewhere else, Reuben and I will run a lot better in harness. I'd have grown into a right shrew.'

'Who says you haven't anyway?'

Leah bared her teeth in a mock snarl and brusquely ordered her mistress to go downstairs and eat some breakfast. 'For I can't be expected to run up and down all them stairs when you're quite capable of taking yourself off and bothering someone else.'

'Good morning, Miss Miranda,' Coppice greeted, as he ghosted into the morning room with a fresh pot of coffee. 'As you ate so little of your dinner last night, Cook prepared your favourite breakfast from the old days.'

'Warm rolls and honey?'

He nodded benevolently and Miranda suppressed the urge to hug him. Such familiarity would never do for one of Coppice's stately dignity, but at least the servants had welcomed the prodigal even if the family looked on her as a very mixed blessing.

'His lordship has arranged for the family to meet

Mr Poulson in the library at a half after eleven,' Coppice informed her apologetically.

'Thank you, I will endeavour not to keep them all waiting.'

With another nod that conveyed a good deal of sympathy, the butler left the room and Miranda contemplated the sunny morning with a jaundiced eye. It would be hard to leave Wychwood on such a day, but leave it she must. If she stayed the earl might believe she was tacitly accepting the idea that he could, and would, suborn her to his bed sooner or later.

She didn't trust his lordship's change of heart, either. Gentlemen were well known to be mellowed by fine port or brandy and she dare not let her guard down. Forcing herself to chew every bite of her roll and savour every last sip of her excellent coffee, she decided she was too restless to skulk about the house until the appointed hour and went outside to walk off some nervous energy. She had not gone two paces along the yew walk when she realised her mistake, but by then it was too late to turn tail and scurry back into the house without giving herself away.

'Good morning, my lord,' she greeted the very gentleman she had been trying hard to avoid as if she hadn't a care in the world. 'A very fine one it is as well, is it not?'

'Quite beautiful, Mrs Braxton,' he replied as he stopped to greet her. Doubtless he meant her to be flustered with the fact that his eyes were fixed on her face while he made that agreement.

'Who would believe we should wake to such a fine day when yesterday was so overcast?' she asked with just as double-edged a meaning, for he would soon find that two could play at that game.

'I can't but wonder if such brilliance is too intense to last,' he countered with a lazy good humour.

'Then surely that makes you a pessimist of the worst kind, my lord?'

'Do you think so, cousin?'

'Yes, to a stranger like myself it seems you prefer clouds to sunshine and tempests to placid breezes and soft airs,' she persisted gamely with the analogy, just as if his steady dark gaze wasn't causing havoc with her determination to be cool and self-contained in his company.

'At least I know where I am when the elements are doing their worst,' he returned blandly.

'What a glum thought to mar such a fair morning, Lord Carnwood. Must we always seek to prefer the worst in life, just in case disappointment spoils the best?'

'You are an optimist then, Mrs Braxton?'

'How could I not be in this sunshine?' she parried, unsure of herself under the surface sophistication of their double-edged conversation now it had become personal again.

'Then perhaps you would introduce me to my gardens while we enjoy it? I doubt if even Lady Clarissa could disapprove of so public an encounter.'

'She disapproves of everything I do. Luckily I'm no longer ruled by her opinions. I'll risk her displeasure if you will.'

No sooner were the words out of her mouth than she cursed her unruly tongue. She had no wish to spend half an hour strolling round the gardens with her reluctant host. She had, she told herself sternly, no wish to spend any time with him alone whatsoever, so why was she not marching back into the house with her nose in the air at this very moment?

Never mind, soon she would be leaving for home and would avoid his disturbing, distrustful presence for the rest of her life. She might miss the fire in his bitter chocolate eyes and be haunted by the memory of her lips yielding under his cynical, knowing mouth, but that was a secret she could happily keep for the rest of her life. The silly little fool she had once been, the one who naïvely believed in heroes and happy ever after, was dead and done with after all, and she no more trusted those impulses now than she did the unpredictable creature at her side.

Chapter Six

'I'm surprised you trust yourself in my company after I behaved like a boor yesterday,' Kit finally said abruptly.

'You did apologise. How could I not accept it when I'm a guest under your roof?'

'Consider reproach piled on reproach, Cousin. I should point out that we are not currently under that roof,' he pointed out with a wry smile that did far too much damage to her resolution to keep him firmly at arm's length.

'The gardens are yours as much as the rest. You will have to play the honourable host here if you mean to be so at all.'

'Of course, you can write yesterday off to my less-than-honourable beginnings, Cousin. I have finally remembered that I have risen above them.'

'Yet how very convenient you seem to find them,'

Miranda mused and won herself a formidable frown that told her she had hit on a truth. 'But I have not seen the pleasure gardens for too long and my mother always loved them, so why not?'

'I have only managed to spend the odd day here during the last six months, and even those were taken up with decisions about the house and estate. I have seen enough to know the grounds have been neglected since your grandfather lost his heir.'

'Poor Grandfather.'

'I doubt you expect me to be hypocrite enough to agree, but I was going on very well without it all,' he said, ushering her through the gate into the wilderness as ceremoniously as if she were a perfect lady.

'Forgive me if I think you a dissembler, Cousin. Wychwood is a jewel worth coveting, even if you possessed fabulous wealth of your own.'

'I didn't say I was blind or a fool, Miranda, just that I was content with what I have by my own efforts.'

Miranda eyed the excellent cut of his dark green coat, the fine fit of his topboots and the snowy purity of his linen. He wore it all with such unselfconscious ease that she had no doubt he had become accustomed to such luxuries long before her grandfather's death.

'Cousin Miranda,' she corrected him absently. 'I admire your industry,' she added truthfully.

'Then you're one of the few of your kind who do.'

'If you're looking to me to confirm your prejudices, you'll be sadly disappointed. I never made my come-out and probably know less about the *haut ton* than you do yourself.'

'Do you regret it?' he asked unexpectedly.

'What girl would not?' she asked lightly, but, seeing his intent look, tried to be a little more honest as they paused by the sundial in the winter garden. 'I regret the loss of my grandfather's affection and friendships I never made. I didn't appreciate what I had until it was irretrievably lost, but at least it taught me that for most of us respect and affection have to be earned, not demanded as a right.'

'I should not care to think of my own sisters left unprotected by those who should care for them as you must have been.'

'I'm relieved to hear it. I didn't know you had any sisters, my lord.'

'I suspect you thought me sprung from Vulcan's workshop fully formed,' he said with a rueful smile that gave her such a jolt she suddenly realised how close they were standing and hastily stepped back.

'It would account for your steely determination, I suppose,' she said lightly, avoiding his suddenly intent gaze. 'I asked you about your family, I believe, my lord?'

'Then I have to tell you that they are now very happily settled with a respectable husband apiece and matching braces of children. It's my belief they are competing to forget our less-than-happy beginnings in wedded bliss,' he returned lightly, allowing her to set the pace of their conversation and confounding her all over again.

'And you love them a great deal.' At least there was no hint of wistfulness in her steady voice, but Miranda felt a dangerous lurch of self-pity when she saw that love soften his firm mouth into a reminiscent smile.

'I do indeed,' he admitted.

'I think them very lucky, then, to be so loved by both their brother and their husbands.'

'There was a time when I would have profoundly disagreed with you, but, yes, I think that they are sincerely content now.'

'I am glad for them.'

He looked surprised and his eyes were still softened by the feeling mention of his sisters had brought with it. He gazed down into her face for a few moments as she waited for she knew not what.

'I really think you are. What a remarkable female you are turning out to be, Mrs Braxton,' he finally informed her softly.

'Yes, how very remarkable that I should wish two people who must have gone through a great deal of hardship in their childhood well, is it not?'

'When you have never met them it is.'

'You refine too much on a careless comment,' she told him defensively.

'Maybe I do,' he agreed politely enough, then seemed to remember his resolution not to seduce her after all, for all intimacy suddenly drained out of their conversation.

'Where is this famous medieval tower I have heard so much about?' he demanded in an impersonal tone she should have mentally applauded, but somehow could not.

'By the lake,' she replied, hoping to show him that hoary relic and return to the house as soon as possible. 'It was part of the original stronghold the Alstones built when they were little more than thieves and pirates. Apparently the gentleman who laid out the pleasure gardens went into such raptures at finding a genuine gothic edifice, he insisted on its restoration. According to local legend it's haunted, probably by our great-great-grandfather as the man nearly bankrupted him with his fanciful ideas.'

'Then the place is part of our history, I suppose.'

'Yes, it's always a good idea not to forget we come from a long line of freebooters and robber barons,' she replied lightly.

'You are very well informed about them. I probably know more about the royal House of Hanover than I do about my own.'

'That's because I once had a governess with a passion for history and we read some of the family papers together. Why must gentlemen always assume females lack interest in aught but fashion and gossip?' she asked, determined to keep this conversation as impersonal as possible.

'Personally it's because I have visited Almack's Club and a few balls with my sisters. Little wonder after that if I now believe ladies live for both.'

'Well, I have never experienced such delights, but surely society isn't quite that empty-headed.'

'No, at times it just seems so, but you didn't miss much. It seemed to me that the general run of young society misses are intent only on catching a suitably rich and well-connected husband.'

'The new Earl of Carnwood being at the top of all their lists, I suppose?' she teased and won a reluctant laugh from him.

Laughter changed him, making him even more

handsome and lending his fascinating eyes warmth. She almost wished they were still enemies, for he was even more dangerous this way than he had been when he glared and stormed at her. She was wondering if it was worth annoying him somehow when she had only hours left at Wychwood, when she caught a flutter of movement out of the corner of her eye.

For once she turned thankfully to face Celia, drifting towards them with languid determination. Even, so she caught a distinct glint of masculine admiration in the Earl's dark eyes and had to smother an unworthy hope that her beautiful cousin would trip on one of those filmy shawls and fall flat on her patrician nose. He was even more dangerous than she thought, Miranda cautioned herself, and greeted Celia with a smile she regally ignored.

'Good morning, I saw you from my window and thought we could take our morning walk all together,' she greeted his lordship.

He bowed and wished her an impersonal good morning before dropping behind the ladies, as there was no room for three to walk abreast. Celia dawdled along languorously, giving the new earl plenty of time to view her shapely curves. At this rate they wouldn't reach the tower before it was time for the will to be read, Miranda decided im-

patiently. She quickened her step, hoping to walk
on alone. Yet at his lordship's suggestion that he
and Miranda went ahead, Celia discovered she
could move fast after all.

'Anyone would think you two were having a
race,' Celia said archly when she had breath to
spare.

'I never could stand sauntering along,' Miranda
declared, suddenly finding Celia's artifice utterly
infuriating for some reason.

'No, you were always sadly headstrong.'

'I was, wasn't I?' Miranda gritted, dangerously
close to letting her temper ride her under the goad
of Celia's constant carping.

'Is this it?' his lordship asked, eyeing all that
remained of the original home of their ancestors:
a few crumbling stone arches and the two storeys
of the keep that had been re-roofed and fitted
with overly pretty gothic windows, now peeling
and rotten.

'Very disappointing, is it not?' Miranda asked,
knowing she was being diverted from Celia's
constant needling and not sure just why.

'The sooner it finishes falling down the better,'
he replied with disgust at such a sorry spectacle.

'Oh, no!' Celia protested in a rare show of spon-
taneous emotion.

'It's a travesty of its former self, unless I am very much mistaken. It would be better out of the way and a summerhouse that could at least be used set in its place,' he insisted.

Celia looked as if she might possibly faint at such a radical idea. 'If it ever goes, they say the Alstones will fall with it.'

'"They say" a great deal, and I have little patience with them. Soon it must either be shored up or pulled down. I have no mind to have it fall on my guests—I should consider that very back luck indeed.'

'No! It must not be touched,' Celia insisted, a hint of her mama's regal manner spoiling her die-away air.

'I have little patience with stories dreamed up to frighten the gullible,' his lordship insisted.

Interested to see how her cousin would avoid arguing with a man she wanted to charm, Miranda was disgusted with them both when Celia tripped artistically and lurched toward him to cling like a limpet, and he let her.

Miranda chose to move away and inspect the folly, noting that ivy had nearly covered the rough stone walls and frowning at the chaos Grandfather had permitted to go unchecked these last five years.

'It looks dangerous,' Kit observed, frowning at

the unstable structure as he carefully ignored Celia's attempts to corner his attention. 'I must set the local masons to make it safe or pull it down.'

'None of them will come here,' Celia told him, actually standing away from him of her own accord in shock. '*They* know it must be left alone.'

'Then I suppose I shall have to pay them more.'

'Celia's right, the villagers are fearful,' Miranda reluctantly admitted.

'Well, it must be made safe, one way or the other,' he insisted.

'You cannot do the job yourself,' Celia gasped and Miranda wasn't sure now if she was more shocked at the thought of the tower being touched, or a gentleman, nay, a nobleman, performing such physical labours.

'If I have to, Mrs Grant,' he confirmed impatiently.

'But that would be madness, and completely ungentlemanly.'

'Would it? I'll still risk it, as I have been so for most of my life,' he informed Celia with a sardonic smile she seemed to find bewildering.

'You will be cursed if you take it down, and what about the succession?' she persisted.

Miranda began to think the old tower was something of a mania for Celia to risk offending an unmarried earl over it.

'What about it?' he said dismissively and it looked for a moment as if Celia might really faint for once at such blasphemy. 'I dare say there's another junior branch of the Alstone tree somewhere, and I'll be cursed in earnest if I allow a few crumbling lumps of stone to endanger my friends. It must be dealt with,' he insisted.

'But not today,' Miranda put in, playing the peacemaker for once.

'No, Mrs Braxton, not today,' he agreed with a smile so warm it gained him a suspicious frown from Celia.

Iron determination hardened her usually misty grey eyes, but Miranda was too busy fighting the heat that threatened to turn her into a blushing idiot every time he softened his eagle-like gaze, and smiled with his eyes in that enervating fashion, to note it.

Kit glanced thoughtfully at the sylph-like widow, however, and wondered how far Mrs Grant would go to gain her own ends. He was surprised to conclude she would stop short of very little and, with her true character in the open, the lady reminded him uncomfortably of her dam. His expression was carefully blank as he let Celia monopolise him on the way back to the great house that he doubted he would ever call home. He might have been secretly appreciating Miranda's fine figure as she stalked ahead of them, but luckily he was too skilled a hunter to let one woman gauge his preoccupation with another.

'I have always found Cousin Miranda the most exhausting of company,' Mrs Grant observed when Miranda was lost to sight at last.

'Yet I doubt she is ever boring,' he replied distractedly, then cursed himself as he saw the hard glitter in his companion's eyes.

'A few days' worth of her energy and high spirits always try Mama's health most severely,' she said, her voice so soft it nearly faded into the light spring breeze.

Could that observation be construed as a warning? he wondered. Impatient with his predecessor for allowing his daughter to insinuate herself so deep into his household, Kit began to plot her expulsion and that of her daughter, before he found himself caught by the tricksy female.

'We had best get this will read as soon as may be,' he said, with every intention of ending this houseparty very quickly.

Once his predecessor's estate was wound up, he would forget Miranda Braxton and find a convenient countess. There must be no more lapses like this morning's, when he met her and couldn't walk away. Yesterday he had silently cursed her for being his long-lost Venus, but today he cursed himself for wishing she was that Venus, not a lady he must protect from villains with dishonourable intentions such as himself.

'I shall be glad to see everything settled at long last,' Celia agreed with a smile that gave him a clue to her own expectations.

'Then we will meet again shortly, Mrs Grant,' Kit replied, with a bow that dislodged her clinging fingers when they finally reached the garden door.

With some relief, Kit resorted to his suite to change and consider the immediate future. He donned the dark coat and sober breeches and boots laid out ready and sat down at his predecessor's desk to pen a letter to one Benedict Shaw, his business partner. Kit's hopes of rapidly getting back to work quickly were receding. A good businessman had a nose for trouble, and his was telling him there was more here than he had thought.

He sat back in his chair and considered past, present and future. It was high time he found out more about Miranda Alstone's ill-fated elopement than she would ever tell him, for this morning had taught him that nothing about his role as head of the family was as simple as he had believed it to be.

* * *

In his professional capacity, Mr Poulson pushed his spectacles up his nose and looked disapprovingly at his late client's last will and testament.

'This document,' he observed, shaking his grey head and looking mournfully at the fine parchment in front of him, 'really is most irregular. If only his late lordship had asked for my advice, something far more conventional could have been contrived.'

'It is legal, I suppose, or none of us would be here,' Kit observed, lazily stretching his legs in front of him as he tried to accommodate his height to the chair Lady Clarissa had left him, after seizing more comfortable ones for herself and her daughter.

Seeing her eye his long limbs as if they caused her personal affront, he stretched an elegantly booted foot to kick a burning log back into the grate and met her gaze with a challenge in his own.

'Yes, it is quite within legal bounds, my lord, if not what you would call an entirely proper legal document.'

'I doubt if any of us would be so rash as to call it anything of the kind, being largely unacquainted with the finer by-ways of your profession, but if the thing is lawful, then we must abide by it.'

Mr Poulson raised his eyebrows and looked askance at the sheet of paper, as if it might explode if not watched carefully.

'You had best hear what it has to say before you admit that, my lord,' he observed drily.

'Then let's have the burden of it, man,' Kit said impatiently.

Lady Clarissa sniffed eloquently and Celia wrapped one of her myriad of shawls a little closer about her languid person. Miranda stared out of the same stand of bay windows that lit the Earl's bed-chamber above, and fervently wished the whole business over and done with. Her grandfather had made it clear that she would receive nothing from him if she married Nevin Braxton. The surprising news that she was a beneficiary of her grandfather's will had forced her to revisit her old home, but she expected little more than the proverbial shilling.

'You all understand that the late Earl insisted none of you could be apprised of the contents of this section of the will until six months after his death, when you were out of strict mourning? I am sure you are all eager to see matters resolved at last,' Mr Poulson announced solemnly.

Miranda was reminded of a showman, a very ex-clusive and highly educated one, of course, but still a performer of some skill and renown. He looked over his spectacles at his spellbound audience and she had a most inappropriate urge to laugh. She could not, of course, as she had no intention of spoiling Mr Poulson's show.

'My grandfather's conditions would seem to have been met, sir, so we might as well get on with it and return to our daily lives as soon as possible,' she encouraged him with a smile of support, one outsider to another.

'You are very blunt, niece.' Lady Clarissa could not seem to help herself rebuking Miranda out of sheer habit. 'You always were outspoken to a fault, and neither time nor your godmama have done much to improve you.'

'Thank you, Aunt. As you are always willing to express yourself so openly, I can only cite you as an excellent example for a niece to cultivate.'

'I cannot think why Papa wanted such a mannerless hussy present. The sooner this distasteful business is over, the better, so you may rejoin that outlandish Eiliane Rhys the sooner.'

If Miranda ever had the slightest doubt that her aunt hated her, it could not have withstood the chilling dislike in Lady Clarissa's stony gaze now. She stiffened her backbone and reminded herself that she was grown woman, not a girl to be easily put in her place.

'The hospitality, or lack of it, at Wychwood Court is mine to command, Lady Clarissa,' Lord Carnwood intervened, before Miranda could launch the spirited defence of her godmother trembling on her tongue. 'You would not be wise to make assumptions about where I choose to bestow it.'

Miranda was more aware than ever that he was no idle aristocrat, but a tried and tested man of affairs, even if Aunt Clarissa was silly enough to think she could bluff and bully him into accepting her dominance. For a moment it seemed as if her ladyship might counter-attack, but luckily she possessed some discernment about where and when to vent her spleen.

'Of course, nephew, that is your privilege,' she conceded majestically, as if he was at fault for assuming she suffered from such presumption.

'You once informed me that our connection was so remote it did not warrant your acknowledgement of it, Lady Clarissa. Now, I suggest you proceed with this business, Poulson, before this charming family gathering descends further into farce.'

Celia's attempts to look unconcerned puzzled Miranda. Sir Horace Ennersley had been a very rich man, possibly the only quality his noble second wife had considered acceptable about the henpecked baronet in his lifetime. Surely the obscure Lieutenant Grant had not lived long enough to run through Celia's generous dowry? And what expenses could the weary widow have incurred in the wilds of rural Derbyshire?

None at all, if her grandfather's periodic outbursts on the subject of bloodsucking hangers-on were to be believed—darts that had glanced off Celia's armour as easily as they did from her mother's conviction that she ought to have been her father's sole heiress. Telling herself she would soon be out of the range of Celia's darts and her aunt's arrogance, Miranda concentrated on the little lawyer's rather pleasant voice as he read out Grandfather's last message to the world.

'To my heir, Christopher Martin Thurrold Alstone, I leave Wychwood Court, Wiston Manor in the county of Shropshire with their demesnes and incomes unencumbered, along with my blessing, which he does not need, and my apologies, which I doubt he will accept. To my granddaughters Katherine Margaret Alstone and Isabella Penelope Alstone I leave my Irish and Scottish estates respectively, as well as their rightful share of their parents' fortunes, as specified in my son and daughter-in-law's own wills. They will become the responsibility of my heir upon my death and I sincerely hope they give him less trouble than their elder sister did me.'

Mr Poulson paused, but no comment was forthcoming. Miranda had expected nothing else and gave the kindly little lawyer a faint shrug to indicate her acceptance, so he ploughed doggedly on.

'My London properties, the Northumbrian estates and all the lands and properties in Leicestershire inherited by second wife, my joint stock holdings and interests in the shipping firm known as Stone and Shaw, I bequeath as a marriage portion to whichever of my granddaughters has the good sense to persuade said Christopher Martin Thurrold Alstone to marry her within three months of the reading of this will. If none of them meets that challenge, said monies and properties will be divided between my granddaughters and my heir at the end of that period, so long as a serious attempt at accommodating my wishes has been made in the judgement of my old friend and lawyer, Matthew John Poulson.'

Enjoying the effect of this unusual testament by now, Mr Poulson looked round his spellbound audience and coughed, keeping them waiting for more while he took a long slow drink from the wineglass his host thoughtfully passed to him.

'To even the odds, I leave my granddaughter, Miranda Rosalind Alstone, now known as

Braxton, her share of her parents' estates and my late mother's house in Bath on condition that she never marries another tutor, music master, or drawing instructor and remains at Wychwood Court for the period of at least one month after the reading of this will.

'This is my last will and testament. If any member of my family tries to have it set aside, my lawyers are instructed to exact a strict accounting for fifteen years' board, lodgings, dressmakers' bills and her other endless expenses from my daughter, the Dowager Lady Ennersley, and demand repayment immediately. To said daughter and her child Cecilia Georgiana Grant I leave my blessing in the hope that they will learn to count *their* blessings more carefully in future.'

Mr Poulson sat back in his chair and eyed the new Earl speculatively. If anything, Miranda thought his lordship had looked amused by the extraordinary bequests, until it came to the condition about him marrying either herself or Celia. Grandfather must have intended to live a few years longer, as so mean a choice could not have been his intention. Still, Christopher Alstone would probably enter marriage in the same mercenary spirit as Celia, so they ought to suit each other very well.

Chapter Seven

Trying to ignore a pang of something very close to bitter regret, Miranda ordered herself sternly not to be a ninny. She even managed to look serene instead of overwhelmed as she contemplated financial security for the first time in five years. It settled something ruffled and abandoned within her that Grandfather had left her provided for after all, but no doubt his lordship was already finding her guilty of trying to lure him into matrimony.

Well, he would be disappointed. She could think of nothing worse than to end up wed to a man who thought her some kind of amateur harlot, always looking about her for the best chance of an easy life. If she wanted one of those she would certainly not entertain the notion of marrying an arrogant, mistrustful, handsome and misguided idiot. So it was just as well she never intended marrying again.

Even so, she wasn't ready to become a Bath Quiz just yet. The fine house in which the Dowager Countess of Carnwood had spent her declining years would command an excellent rent. It suddenly occurred to her that she could probably afford to live wherever she chose now, or at least she could after her month was up. London, if she could find any lady rash enough to lend her respectability, and perhaps Brighton in the summer, or maybe a genteel cottage in the country where she could keep spaniels and a pony cart and forget the past?

No, some things could not, and should not, be forgotten. She would go back to her new home and help Lady Rhys support her worthy causes. She looked about her and tried not to wish for the moon, for nowhere could be home to her as Wychwood Court had been in her youth. Yet not even to stay here was she willing to sell herself into matrimony, even if her prospective husband didn't regard her as a fool or a trollop, or both.

'That is the sum of the bequests, my lord. You will be aware of the legacies to servants of long standing, old friends and remote family members, since the first part of the will that dealt with them was fully disclosed after the old lord's death.'

'Ridiculous, he was obviously not of sound mind and the will must be set aside immediately,' Lady Clarissa finally announced disgustedly. 'As his only surviving child, I must be his principal heir.'

'You must be aware of the consequences if you try to challenge your father's will, my lady,' the lawyer observed coolly, many years of being over-looked and condescended to denying the possibility of any softening of his shrewd gaze now.

'Of course you must not dream of doing so, Mama,' Celia admonished with a thread of steel running through her soft voice. 'We could not subject the family name to unsavoury gossip.'

Or lose themselves a very great deal of money, of course, but Celia always did put a rosy gloss on her own self-interest. Pointing that trait out now would hardly help her little sisters' position in the household when Celia became Lady Carnwood, so Miranda bit her tongue and looked away.

Of course, the new earl would not wed a woman such as herself, but a shiver of something warm and forbidden ran through Miranda at the very thought of spending a lifetime of nights at his lordship's mercy. Would he be a tender lover, or driven by hot desire and the need to keep her so occupied even he could not believe she would stray? No! Not to be thought of, she would not spend her life at the side of a man who would not, could not, trust her. Before long it would become more of a hell on earth than her first marriage had proved to be, for something told her she would come to care far too much for Christopher Alstone's good opinion if she let herself.

'If that is all?' Celia asked with iron composure.

Miranda had to admire her cousin's panache. Celia looked as if she had heard a slightly amusing story told by a rather wearisome acquaintance, instead of a chilling rebuff from beyond the grave.

'Indeed it is, Mrs Grant,' the little lawyer replied with what Miranda considered excusable satisfaction.

He had produced a fine performance, and, given the script Grandfather had left behind, it would have caused a sensation outside these four walls. Miranda hoped word of it would not leak out, for if she had to watch Celia snare the new earl she didn't want to hear a blow-by-blow account of how matters stood between them every time she set foot outside the door. Neither did she want any foolishness to develop about her own prospects of becoming the next countess. The new earl would never wed a woman whose shady past might trip him up at any moment, so Celia it must be.

'If you will excuse us then, Cousin?' the lady herself said with such an air of graceful concern Miranda almost clapped. 'Poor Mama is quite overset.'

'Of course,' he agreed, obviously glad to see her ladyship quit the room before the inevitable storm broke.

'Miranda's return has been such a strain on Mama's nerves,' Celia explained as if the fact pained her.

Miranda gave her cousin a blank social smile in reply and knew she could expect to be the butt of every bout of irritation in Lady Clarissa's life from now until the blessed day she could return to Nightingale House. Oddly enough, Celia's nasty little act signalled she wasn't as sure of herself as she appeared. Miranda wished she could tell her how foolish she was being and save them both a deal of trouble, for his lordship would marry his elderly housekeeper before he shackled himself to Mrs Miranda Braxton for life.

As she made her own way upstairs, Miranda supposed Christopher Martin Thurrold Alstone probably deserved Cecilia Georgiana Ennersley-Grant, who at least knew how to go on in the highest circles. Yet if Celia thought he would be as easily manipulated as most of the men in her life had been, Miranda suspected she was in for a shock. The iron-willed man under that sophisticated exterior would never make a complacent husband to be led about the salons of Mayfair by a wife he had only wed for convenience. No, the earl would be demanding; he would insist on children to spoil Celia's exquisite figure. The thought of them made Miranda feel sick and shaken and glad to reach the sanctuary of her room at last.

Her one regret was those children, she told herself firmly, and she would be a fool to deny how much she longed for them. It was a battle she had fought with herself five years ago when marriage to Nevin Braxton exiled her from home and family in more ways than one. She ignored the familiar pain and reminded herself there were plenty of waifs in the world in need of love and affection. More than enough to fill the emptiest arms, in truth, and, now she had money of her own, she could help more of them to have a future.

Within the hour Wychwood was buzzing with rumours of all sorts of odd clauses to the late lord's will and Miranda felt bound to correct Leah's misapprehensions at least.

'So I am bound to stay for a month,' she concluded, 'although I might wish to be almost anywhere else, but there is to be no matchmaking by you or any of the rest of the staff, if you please. For one thing it won't work, and for another it's embarrassing for both the Earl and myself, and rather insulting to Cousin Celia, who will make a far better countess than I ever could.'

'No, she won't, half the servants would give notice before she even got back from her bride journey,' Leah told her disgustedly.

'We have rarely seen her better side,' Miranda heard herself say lamely, nearly as surprised to hear herself defending her childhood enemy as that lady would be herself. 'Celia is beautiful and has the dignity and presence of a great lady, as well as a true sense of propriety.'

'And a heart of stone to go with it. Can you really forget how spiteful she was towards you and Master Jack when we were young?' Leah asked as if that would be a betrayal of the past.

'She was jealous, and it's not her fault Aunt Clarissa passed on her resentment at not being the heiress to Celia.'

'Well, you watch out. They hated you then and they still do now.'

'Maybe, but they will soon see how the land

lies and leave me alone,' Miranda assured her confidently.

'Aye, but you remember that if they could get away with it they'd put hemlock in your soup rather than see you wed his lordship.'

'Oh, I'm sure they would stop short of that,' Miranda insisted lightly, 'but promise to say nothing of what I've told you outside this room? As countess, Celia will be in the position to make your and Reuben's lives intolerable, and I'll be too far away to help you.'

'If she marries his lordship, we'll be leaving Wychwood, don't you fret, Miss Miranda,' Leah assured her militantly, then sternly ordered her mistress to take a rest before dinner. 'Because you'll be needing all your wits about you from now on, with those two cats watching you like you're their last meal,' she warned theatrically, and left in high dudgeon when Miranda laughed at such a ridiculous idea.

Left alone, she couldn't help but brood over the conundrum her grandfather had left behind. He must have known what a rackety countess he was offering his heir in her, and that the choice was really no choice at all. She had endured five years of exile because of that very unsuitability and a bitter smile lifted her generous mouth. No,

Grandfather could not have seriously intended her to be the next Lady Carnwood, so what had he been up to? Was it a clever way of saying sorry? If so, she wished he had just said it while he was still alive and let her come home, instead.

She supposed Christopher Alstone could always forfeit the bulk of the Alstone fortune and a precious part of his own company. Strangely enough, she found that she felt no satisfaction at his dilemma. Even more surprising was the odd jag of pain that seemed ready to crush her at the thought of him wedding Celia. All that misplaced passion, and his vital warmth and power chained to an ice block for the remainder of their natural lives seemed an appalling waste somehow.

Maybe he would put his comfort before his company and refuse to dance to Grandfather's tune. She considered that idea for a moment and realised how hard he must have fought for what he had. In his shoes, would she have done half so well? she wondered. Probably not as a woman growing up in poverty. She would very likely have ended up on the streets long since, and didn't that prove her point? Somehow the new earl had kept his sisters from that appalling fate and set them on the path to happiness against all the odds. She had to admire such unswerving purpose and loyalty.

She shook her now aching head to clear it of misplaced compassion. Christopher Alstone, Earl of Carnwood, would never insult all that he was now and all that he had made himself, by allying his name with that of a notorious woman. Exasperated with herself for even thinking about such an unlikely outcome, she pulled the pins from her hair and felt it tumble down round her shoulders with a sigh of relief. Deciding she could be excused a short interlude of peace and quiet while she had the headache, she lay down on the daybed, trying to crush a sly whisper of disappointment that she didn't live in a fairy story after all.

It was just as well that she had snatched that fitful sleep, Miranda thought later when the evening was blighted by that strange will. Although they ate in the more comfortable parlour and had no need to shout at each other across yards of mahogany, the tension in the room was palpable.

'Excellent fowl,' Mr Poulson finally commented, almost as if he was thinking aloud.

'And a very fine wine, thank you, Coppice,' Kit added with the smile that had already endeared him to the servants at Wychwood, if not all those above stairs. 'If you would have the port brought through to the Countess's Sitting Room, I am sure we gentlemen will undertake to behave circumspectly,' Kit said smoothly, and it was so before Lady Clarissa could argue.

'Wychwood is more comfortable than ever now,' the lawyer observed, looking as if he would very soon be asleep now the tension of carrying out his delicate mission had been released.

'Yes, it's a fine house in a rare setting,' Kit agreed with a distracted frown.

He was too busy covertly watching a fine woman in that rare setting to take much notice of desultory conversation. There was no doubt that the old man's will had landed him a facer. He could ignore it, of course, especially as he felt no need of further wealth. Wychwood and the biggest of the subsidiary estates were his outright, so he had enough rents coming in to keep them in good order. The trouble was that stake in Stone and Shaw, and it baffled him how the old man had managed to get hold of such a large one without either himself or Ben realising what was going on.

He had to respect the old fox, however harshly he would like to curse his ingenuity. His predecessor had known exactly how to bait his hook, realising how such a loss of power could affect the company. They could start up another and bleed

the old one of resources and custom until it was
worth very little, but Kit's pride was bound up in
the company he had started from nothing. Losing
it would cost him dearer than the interfering old
curmudgeon had probably known.

He and Ben had proved to themselves and
everyone else that a man could be born in the most
squalid streets in London and still claw his way out
of the gutter. Stone and Shaw had dowered his
sisters and taken him and Ben wherever they
wanted to go, and he would bitterly regret the loss
of it if it failed. Well, it would not fail, he resolved,
watching Mrs Miranda Braxton face her stony-
faced relatives with effortless poise, for there was
his means to an end.

Even if she was the antithesis of the convenient
wife he had planned for himself, she was the only
Alstone female he had the least intention of
marrying. He contemplated what he had managed
to find out about the clinging Mrs Grant so far and
shuddered at the idea of wedding such an iron tur-
tledove. Meanwhile he covertly watched his true
quarry with a relief that nevertheless made him
frown. As Miranda Alstone, the untried young
beauty who last set foot inside Wychwood Court
five long years ago, she must have been breathtaking: an unfledged innocent with the fabulous

promise of her maturity still to come. Regret threatened to shipwreck him at the thought of her so frighteningly vulnerable and so completely betrayed.

He would accustom himself to her stunning loveliness, he supposed, and somehow he would arm himself against the heedless, passionate nature hidden under it. Once seen and never forgotten, true, but the glory of what might have been couldn't hurt either of them now. He hadn't managed to forget her in five years of trying, so he might as well make her his countess and set about the delightful task of slaking his passion for a woman he should never have let himself want with almost every waking thought in the first place.

Then he wondered if he could actually bring himself to do it, cynic as he was. Did he want control of the company back so badly that he was willing to wed a wife all other men would envy him, and probably try to seduce away? Yet it was true that his desire for the lovely dockside goddess he had thought Miranda Braxton must be had never quite gone away, so he might as well wed and bed her, if only to put paid to five years of bitter frustration. He would just have to make sure that the bored rakes of the *ton* realised he was a very possessive husband indeed, and a very dangerous man to cross.

Then there was the fact that as his countess she would be unable to so much as breathe on another man without him knowing about it. He hoped his instincts and observations were true and she had indeed learnt some sense. As his wife she would stand in need of it, if she was to grace his bed and board. Then the very thought of seeing his naked wife grace the former location rendered him completely unfit for polite company between one breath and the next. Averting his hot gaze from the delicious, and quite oblivious, Mrs Braxton, he found the little lawyer's shrewd gaze on him and almost let his own drop.

Maybe the Alstones had been right about him all along—perhaps he wasn't fit for good society. Miranda had been raised a lady and he shouldn't be sitting here lusting so hotly after a woman ostensibly under his protection. Of course, she would not have married him five years ago, even if he had possessed the gall to turn up here and court the belle of the county. Then he had still been little more than a promising sea captain with a finger in too many pies. What would she have made of a man with only a foot on the ladder that would take him to today's dizzy heights? That he was still a gamble, the son and grandson of men who had wasted their substance with reckless abandon?

It was better this way, better for her to know him as a tried and tested man of the world, not a wild rover led by carnal desires. Thinking of which, it was high time he brought this painful interlude to an end. Getting to his feet, he managed to angle his body so only he and the shrewd little man of law knew of his ridiculous state, and left the room to blow another cloud in the fitful moonlight. He hated to depend on anything, even tobacco, but he was quite aware that it was Miranda's spell he was determinedly fighting, not that of a slender roll of leaves.

Miranda managed not to watch his lordship go, and tried to pretend it was a matter of indifference to her if the infuriating man was present or not, even as she contemplated the idea of four weeks of nights like this one with something close to despair. She had no intention of letting greedy, heedless emotions rule her life once more, she assured herself, and she would stick it out for the sake of her precious independence. Never again, she had sworn to herself and meant it so fervently would she even think of letting passion rule her. Yet an insidious, wanton voice still whispered that she had never before been subject to Christopher Alstone's own peculiar brand of temptation.

Attending to the tea board with apparent zeal, at least she could let her mind wander while her hands nimbly carried out the familiar task without much thought. The trouble was that my Lord Carnwood could too easily be fitted into that ridiculous fantasy she had dreamed up so many years ago, and gloated over so foolishly ever since. So all in all it was hardly surprising the new earl made her pulses race, considering he could easily have walked straight out of her dreams, but to allow fantasy to fog reality was ridiculous, and dangerous. So she decided to forget her imaginary hero as she sipped her tea and longed for this day to be over so she could go to bed and strike at least one day off her tally.

Once in her room, she subsided into a chair by the fire to brood on that day. She finally allowed tears to burn as she considered the idea that Grandfather had still loved her after all. In all likelihood she could have come home years ago and he would probably have received her with gruff relief, and an exhortation to show better taste in future. Except by then she couldn't face him. Exile had seemed a just punishment for being such a fool, and at least it had made her appreciate her new home, even if it was too late to go back to her old one. Security, she decided with a relieved sigh. That was what she had now, and in three weeks and six days' time she could go wherever she pleased and do whatever she wanted.

She went over to the little rosewood desk Grandfather had given her for her sixteenth birthday, and pulled out a sheet of paper on which she could write to Lady Rhys. She would not sleep easily tonight, and anyway she must tell her godmother what a ridiculous situation Grandfather's will had pitchforked her into before anyone else did so.

For almost two weeks Miranda managed to restrict contact between herself and the new earl to the most superficial of levels by avoiding him whenever possible. In the daytime it was easy enough, as the housekeeper was eager to discuss the linen and china cupboards with one of the family, at the same time as updating Miranda on the sayings and doings of nearly everyone on the estate. Her willingness to consult even such an unimportant person as herself told Miranda how Lady Clarissa had neglected such matters over the years. Swallowing her exasperation with her aunt, who publicly martyred herself to duty while privately doing little or nothing, Miranda helped the housekeeper tackle a great many decisions beyond her remit.

What his lordship thought of her interference she had no idea, but he said nothing as small repairs were made and new china and linen began to arrive. Miranda concluded cynically that if any of her innovations made him uncomfortable, she would very soon hear about it. Yet she refused to let herself settle too easily into such a role so, as the day-to-day running of the house improved, she deliberately spent more of her time visiting her old friends on the estate with Leah for company and propriety.

Yet even Miranda couldn't come up with a plausible excuse to avoid being thrown together with Lady Clarissa, Celia and the Earl when they were all invited to the vicarage for dinner. Luckily Celia made sure that she sat next to his lordship on the way there, so Miranda was spared all but the most superficial contact with him. Even that was enough to render her extremely wary of touching him as he waited for her to be the last lady to exit the coach, and she silently cursed the good manners that forbade him to ignore her and carry on as her aunt and cousin did.

'Running scared, my dear?' he murmured as she hesitated to put her gloved hand in his.

'Why, should I be?' she returned crossly and risked the contact rather than be thought a coward.

'A faint stirring of common sense might perhaps warn you to be,' he returned softly.

Lady Clarissa was glaring at the sight of them hand in hand, straining to hear every word they said and failing, to her obvious disgust, so was it to be wondered at if his words made her shiver? Miranda made herself ignore the ridiculous tingles of awareness running through her at even so casual a touch, and pulled her hand free the instant her feet were on the ground. This wasn't the time or place for a confrontation with him or her aunt, so stalking off as fast as her legs would carry her had nothing to do with his absurd warning.

Chapter Eight

Throughout the hours that followed, Miranda tried to second Julia Draycott's attempts at lightening the atmosphere in her elegantly decorated home, but it was an uphill struggle. As the ladies awaited the gentlemen after dinner, Miranda wondered if the Earl's tardiness at declaring himself was grating on Celia's nerves as much as it was on her own. Surely once he was engaged to her cousin Miranda need not fear any more of those disturbing encounters with him? Yet tonight he seemed oddly angry with her for some reason. Could it be he was expecting her to jockey for attention with Celia? If so, he didn't know either of them very well.

Instinct told her he wouldn't attempt the seduction of his fiancée's cousin under his own roof, but was that the very reason he was delaying? She truly hoped not but, as with that absurd exchange when she left the carriage just now, she often felt he was stalking her with far more skill and attention than she knew how to avoid. Christopher Alstone was like no other man she had ever encountered, and there was something in his dark eyes that warned her he would be very hard to deny if he once made up his mind on a course he intended taking.

No, he couldn't wish to marry her, not with all the strikes she had against her name, but if he didn't, why wasn't he plaguing Celia with his watchful gaze and implacable patience instead of her? It felt as if he was waiting for her to be subtly goaded into going the way he wanted, then she would fall straight into some trap he had ready for her and she would not even see until it was well and truly sprung. The whole situation was grating on her nerves, she assured herself uneasily, as she unclenched her jaw and did her best to take in what was being said.

'A little music would be pleasant, Mrs Draycott,' Aunt Clarissa announced, once she had finished criticising all the changes made to the vicarage by its new occupants and informing her hostess how much better they could have been achieved if she had been consulted. 'I do not consider it incorrect for Celia to play the pianoforte now we are only in black gloves.'

Evidently she had not heard her darling play for a while, or she might have spared them.

'I am very rusty, I fear,' Celia wisely acknowledged as she brought the ordeal to an early end and stood up with a rueful smile that almost won Miranda over. 'Your turn, Cousin Miranda,' she declared, managing to alienate her again immediately.

'I have no music,' she protested, but it did her no good.

'Use mine, Mrs Braxton, there is a stack of it on the small table yonder,' Julia Draycott insisted with a desperation that could only win Miranda's sympathy, even if she was about to be fed to the lions herself.

Bracing herself to fumble under her aunt's scrutiny as she always had in the past, Miranda was surprised to find her fingers flying over the keyboard as she managed to lose herself in a favourite piece, then softly merge it into another. After all, playing what pleased her beat being the butt of her aunt's bad temper now she had run out of things to criticise about her hostess's taste and housekeeping abilities. Unfortunately she lost track of everything else as well, and came back to reality only to find Lord Carnwood at her shoulder and herself the centre of attention.

'That was excellent indeed!' Mrs Draycott exclaimed and, as Aunt Clarissa was looking more sour than usual, perhaps it had been.

'You have been hiding your light.' Celia was outwardly generous, even if the icy glitter in her eyes belied her words.

'Not at all,' Miranda said, all too conscious of the man watching her so intently now the music had stopped. 'Sometimes I play for the children,' she admitted unguardedly.

'Children?' he asked quietly.

Why did he have to latch on to such a trivial comment? He really was the most exasperating man she had come across, and now Celia and Aunt Clarissa were looking too interested for comfort as well. Perhaps all three of them believed she had a couple of little bastards concealed at Nightingale House, in defiance of her godmother's virtuous reputation, if not her own.

'Sometimes the orphans Lady Rhys interests herself in give a concert and I play for them,' she finally said.

'And you interest yourself in them too?' his lordship asked softly and she feared he might be in danger of thinking her better than she was from the hint of approval in his dark eyes.

'Naturally,' she said lightly, 'I should have to be

a hardened recluse to live at Nightingale House and not take an interest in those around me.'

'There is more to it than that, isn't there?' he demanded, undercover of Mrs Draycott's servants bringing in the tea-tray.

'More to what?' Miranda replied cautiously, having fallen into too many bear traps to rush into another.

'The occasional evening of proving how noble you are, sparing time for nasty rough little creatures more accustomed to running wild on the streets? Oh, I think not, Cousin Miranda. From the contacts I retain in the East End, I know very well Lady Rhys gives those children far more than cold charity, and how fervently I wish a few others would follow her example.'

'Oh, so do I!' she agreed impulsively, for she found one or two of the philanthropists she had met in her godmother's company very chilly indeed. 'She claims to be stingy, because she takes a few abandoned waifs into her home and has no interest in founding an institution. We all beg to differ, because those she does take in find they are home in every sense of the word.'

'Then you class yourself as one of her desperate cases?'

'Yes, and the rest of the world agrees with me.'

'Only those with nothing better to do than shred the reputations of others out of boredom or viciousness,' he argued and left her abruptly to hand out teacups at his hostess's playful request.

Miranda puzzled over that comment all the way back to Wychwood, in a carriage that suddenly seemed uncomfortably cramped for all its luxury. At least her preoccupation helped to blot out Aunt Clarissa's regal pronouncements about everything her hostess for the evening had done wrong, and all she would have done right in her place.

If Christopher Alstone had really softened his disapproval of her to that extent, she had better be prepared to run long and hard if she was to avoid being ruthlessly cornered into an arranged marriage. She felt both too much and too little to contemplate such an idea, even if she hadn't sworn off marriage five years ago. Then there was the fact that she was all too deeply attracted to him already to risk falling for his particular variety of dangerous charm. Yes, it behoved her to watch out for whatever moves he intended making next in this odd game he was playing. As long as she kept aloof, he could not say the words that would make the rest of the time she must spend here bitterly uncomfortable. In time he would accept the inevitable, which was either marry Celia or lose a fortune.

Something told her it would the former and pain lanced through her with such force that she did not have to lie about the headache she claimed to avoid his lordship when they got home. And that was another thing, she decided, as she climbed into her blessedly warmed bed and reviewed the last few hours—she had to stop dreaming about him in this ridiculous fashion. In her dreams her silly mind had replaced her pirate with the Earl of Carnwood's brooding good looks, and her waking self could only deplore the switch from unattainable fantasy to all too present reality.

Miranda woke up in the middle of the night when something, or someone, interrupted her ridiculous dreams of Kit Alstone and wondered exactly when had she come to think of him as 'Kit'? One night he had told them his sisters always called him so, but that was no reason for her to even consider such an intimacy. Silently cursing her wayward imagination, she sat up in bed and let her eyes grow accustomed to the vague details she could pick out in the shadows, trying to dismiss the superstitious shudder that ran through her.

Deciding she must have imagined the idea that some small noise had awoken her, she groped for the tinderbox to light her candle and read herself to sleep again, but instead dislodged her book so it landed on the floor with a thud. Immediately there was a scurry of movement from the direction of the desk then, before she could spring out of bed and challenge the intruder, she felt a draught as her door opened swiftly and whoever it was sped through it.

For a moment she sat shocked and not quite certain if she was awake, until her faith in her senses returned and she felt for the tinderbox again and managed to light her candle at last with hands that stubbornly refused not to shake. When she held it aloft, she gasped at the mischief someone had wrought on her papers. Temper promptly overcame caution and she was out of the door before she had time to wonder if a pretty china candlestick was really the best protection against an intruder. Bolting across the wide landing, she wasn't sure what she intended to do, but her instinct to give chase had come to the fore so strongly that she failed to see Kit before she ran full tilt into his muscular form.

'And what the devil are you doing up at this time of night?' he muttered grumpily as he took the precariously held candle from her and set it on the nearest side table.

'I might ask you the same question,' she whispered back.

'You might, but I asked mine first.'

'Oh, get out of the way, you infuriating man, you're helping him get away,' she raged at him as furiously as anyone could who was trying not to rouse the household.

'What are you talking about, woman?'

'Someone was in my room,' she muttered, wondering why she had ever believed him to be a man of action.

That reluctant admission seemed to galvanise him enough. Grabbing her candle again, he marched into her chamber, then returned just as swiftly with a cloak he must have hastily taken from her dressing room, looking downright fierce in the flickering light as he did so.

'Keep still,' he ordered brusquely before wrapping her in the dark folds and beckoning her to follow with a look that told her he didn't trust her out of his sight. 'He'll be gone by now, but at least we can find out if they came from inside or outside the house.'

'Within, of course,' she whispered impatiently, 'burglars come to steal, not to risk their necks playing spiteful tricks.'

'Shush!' was all the reply she received.

Shaking her head in infuriated denial, she followed him downstairs where they could at least argue more freely.

Kit ordered her to stay behind as he examined the footman sleeping soundly in the hall, before beckoning her on and ruthlessly seizing her hand to conduct her on a search of the downstairs.

'Stop wriggling,' he admonished as she fought an urge to stump off upstairs in high dudgeon, and an even stronger one to stay and find out if he really could be the lover of her heated fantasies.

The longer she spent in his company, the worse that feral curiosity became; how she wished she had slept on while someone took liberties with her possessions after all. In the flickering light of one mere candle, the Court seemed too deserted and intimate for her feverish imagination.

'No sign,' she whispered when they had circled the staterooms and were back in the hall.

'No, but someone drugged Simmons, and that doesn't argue for Wychwood being invaded by fairies,' he informed her in an impatient undertone that told her a great deal about his opinion of her determination not to take this seriously.

'Nor to it being invaded at all,' she admitted ruefully as she watched the happily oblivious footman and could not help a shiver.

'Indeed,' he acknowledged savagely, and held the light up to the great oak front with its bolts and locks firmly shot home. 'I don't think we even need to inspect the kitchen door—even if it's unlocked and the scullery maid in the same state as yon lad, I refuse to believe this was a stranger's work.'

'Should we try to wake him?' she said as she peered at the snoring footman with concern.

'No, he's breathing well enough, we might as well leave him to sleep it out.' With that, Kit turned his attention from Simmons to herself and Miranda blinked in the sudden light.

'What?' she asked, trying to look cool and un-affected by her adventure.

The last thing she wanted was for him to realise how hard she was having to fight the need to cling to his warm strength like a limpet. It was just shock, she told herself, as she somehow met his gaze without giving herself away. He looked back at her for a few long moments, then shrugged his broad shoulders, looking as if he despaired of her wits.

'Whoever it is, the mess they made argues spite, if not hatred,' he informed her, just as if it was her fault someone disliked her so fervently.

Her gaze slewed back to his, certainty of just who hated her enough to take that risk suddenly clear in her mind. She hesitated, then held her tongue. What good would it do if she told him? He might think she was out to claim the advantage in a race she hadn't the least intention of entering.

'Maybe,' she admitted and stepped a little further away from the security of his large figure. 'Or perhaps it was just plain mischief.'

'Try telling that to Simmons in the morning,' he argued with an impatient frown as he once more manacled her wrist as she attempted to sidle even further away. 'Keep still for a moment, woman,' he chided impatiently and then seemed to rue her very presence as he considered what to do with her. 'You can't sleep in your room tonight,' he finally concluded.

'Well, I have no intention of spending the night anywhere else,' she snapped back, trying to keep a grip on her own decided temper as it butted up against his implacable will.

'It wasn't a proposition, you silly female,' he barked back disagreeably, then moderated his tone in deference to the sleeping house. 'I suggest you either lock yourself into another room or sleep with your maid for the remainder of the night, that's all.'

Blushing furiously at his brusque dismissal of

an almost mechanical defence of her honour, she shifted her cold feet on the marble and looked up to see what looked perilously like tenderness soften his fierce expression.

'You'll catch your death standing here arguing black's white with me,' he said with a wry smile and tugged her toward the stairs.

She hung back until he turned so impatiently that he spilt hot candle wax on his hand and swore briefly.

'I apologise,' he murmured, and flicked off the cooling wax.

'You should put your hand in cold water,' she chided.

'It's not even a proper burn,' he protested, showing her where the smooth tanned skin was hardly even reddened.

'I dare say not,' she returned with apparent indifference.

'So let's get you to bed before one of us is carried off with a chill.'

He sounded brusque, but his strong fingers were once again caressing hers as if they had an independent will. Feeling that gentle stroke with a sudden excess of sensitivity, she cursed her knees for threatening not to hold her up much longer. Somehow she doubted that had anything to do with the cold.

'I am quite capable of looking after myself,' she argued robustly, but she didn't wrench her wrist out of his loose hold all the same.

An unholy grin greeted that perfectly sensible declaration and she was tempted to prove it to him by insisting he lit another candle for himself and returned hers before they parted very swiftly. Unfortunately he didn't look in the least amenable to such a suggestion and she bit her tongue and stared back at him in sullen silence.

'Where does your maid sleep?' he asked, as if restraining some infuriating masculine joke of his own and she blushed rosily once more. 'Ah, I see,' he said as that flush warned him of Leah's probable unavailability.

'Reuben intends to marry her,' she defended hastily.

'Just as well,' he replied dourly and she cast him a sceptical look. Surely he wasn't setting himself up as arbiter of the morals of his household? Not after the way he had behaved on her first day under his roof.

'It's their business what they do,' she told him shortly.

'I agree, but anyone can see that you and your maid are more like sisters than lady and servant. If he hurts her, he will answer to me.'

'I'm more than capable of looking after Leah's interests without your help, my lord,' she informed him snippily.

'You might think so,' he said with condescension. 'Just try interfering between them and you'll soon find out how unwelcome you are.'

'Aye, well, that's how it should be between a man and his love,' he admitted contrarily and watched her with amused anticipation of an argument.

Instead she veered away from the subject. 'I intend to go back to bed now. We came down here to see if there was a thief ransacking the place and patently there is not, so it's high time we parted,' she said stiffly, giving their joined hands a pointed glare. She wanted no false declarations of affection, but why had her avoidance of his deliberately trailed statement infuriated him so? Suddenly he looked very intent on something about her, and how had she played this so very badly? For a while she had almost let herself feel comfortable with him, and now that edge of tension she seemed to have been perennially teetering on since she met him was plaguing her once more.

'So it is,' he said in a dangerous undertone, and the glint in his eyes warned her of trouble. 'But now we are alone, except for a nigh-comatose youth, it's high time we got round to the kissing part of being cousins again, don't you think? I should hate to disappoint your low expectations.'

'I thought the boot was on the other foot,' she protested lamely.

'Just be quiet, Miranda,' he ordered and pulled her close.

'Let me go,' she whispered, even as she felt her heart beat like a blacksmith's hammer against his broad chest in a mix of fear of what she might let him do, and anticipation of how wonderful it might be if she did. Too wonderful, she thought bleakly, when he was about to marry her cousin. 'Let me be, you barbarian,' she reiterated, and tried hard to be furious with him after all.

'Say it and mean it, Venus,' he promised cunningly, 'and I might.'

'Let me—'

There was time for no more, for his lips took hers in the most sensual, challenging, longed-for kiss she had ever even dreamt of. As calamity hit her full on, she admitted to herself how deeply she had wanted it to engulf her and leave her with no choice but to succumb to a force of nature. She struggled to free her arms, so she could wind exploring hands round his strong neck and urge him even closer. It was far too forward and revealing, but, oh, it felt so good.

'I have waited so long for you,' he murmured, raising his head to gasp in a harsh breath at last.

Again that snag of something half-remembered, half-dreaded, made her falter, but he lowered his head again and scouted every thought but him from her dazed mind. His new kiss was both magical and indescribably sensuous. He was gifting her with everything she had expected when Nevin first kissed her, and found only a man incapable of such generosity. How could she have settled for second-best? she wondered, then drowned in fiery sensation and forgot Nevin Braxton had ever been.

Raging desire took her under in a flash of fire and such warmth it reached all of her, from her toes to her fingertips. Kit Alstone was some sort of wizard. She felt her bemused senses come alive everywhere he touched her, so hot and brilliant as she felt against the fact of him. He moved his mouth on hers in a sensual slide, then angled it so she opened to him as if that was what their mouths were made for. Now they were matched in the timeless equality of lovers, she could seduce as mercilessly as he did and exult in doing so. She let her tongue explore his with such finesse she only realised what a curb he had put on himself when he let go and tangled with hers to take over the dance.

Rather a fine dance it was as well, if not one likely to be permitted in any lady's drawing room. The thrust of his tongue was too explicit, the answering hunger that seemed liable to burn her alive if it wasn't appeased far too unrestrained to be anything but private. Desire pooled and burnt at the very heart of her as her heartbeat sang and her breath came short. Soon their bodies would go beyond reason and sensual passion would destroy the emptiness she had known for so long, and, oh, what sweet promises would be fulfilled once they merged their striving bodies into one glorious whole…

'No! I won't,' she managed to gasp out, as much at herself as at him when the inevitable end to all this screamed in her head and an even greater chasm of isolation loomed afterwards.

'Sorry, my sweet, but you already are,' he murmured.

He went to capture her mouth again and she flinched away. If she once let him do that again, she would be lost, she would yield everything. It couldn't stop there, wouldn't stop there when neither of them would let it. However much she longed for children, she knew the sins of the parents were always visited on the innocents such fleeting unions produced. Part of her still argued that nothing so fiercely tender could be a sin, but unfortunately the world would still name it so.

'I won't be your mistress, my lord,' she told him rather desperately.

'I should wait until you are asked if I were you,' he informed her austerely and yet she saw something almost like pain in his eyes.

She could read him, she discovered without triumph. This mighty conundrum of a man had laid himself open to her and now she must refuse to see, turn her back on his need and desire and the exquisite intimacy.

'Let me go,' she said and really meant it, so he did.

Shivering in the chilly marble hall, she hugged her arms about her body, trying to still its shaking and avoid his scrutiny.

'A simple no earlier would have been better,' he finally observed as if they were discussing the weather.

'I didn't know,' she admitted and let some of her confusion show.

'I can see that now,' he allowed and she shivered again. 'Oh, let's get you up to bed, woman. I never yet forced myself on a female yet and I'm not going to start with you, however much you insist on provoking me.'

'*I* insist on provoking *you*?' she echoed incredulously. 'That's rich, considering you did nothing but antagonise me when I arrived.'

'It was that or try to seduce you on my carriage sweep, in front of half the household.'

'You don't strike me as the type of man to fall victim to love at first sight, my lord, but it's not love you're referring to, is it? Just lust.'

'Never underestimate the power of such simple passions, Cousin.'

He looked as distant as the most stern chaperon could desire, so long as she had not seen their disgraceful conduct just now.

'Heaven forbid,' she returned with a hostile glare. 'Goodnight, my lord.'

'I always escort a lady back to her door, Venus,' he murmured with an intent in his dark eyes she told herself she had no intention of reading.

But why did his misnaming make her feel as if she was about to recall an unlikely world peopled by heroes and monsters, and stark with both terror and delight? She gave him one of the downing looks she had perfected over the years, but even she knew her heart wasn't quite in it. Her frosty glare only made him smile and release her with a courtly bow. Now thoroughly cross, she snatched the only light still burning and swept up the stairs as fast as the wavering light of the candle would allow.

'I shall lock my door,' she informed him regally as he followed, despite her attempt at a magnificent exit.

'Good, but first I will check your bedchamber.'

'I am quite capable of doing that myself, thank you very much.'

'Not to my satisfaction,' he dismissed and thrust past her to inspect her former sanctuary again. 'Very well,' he admitted with a nod to where she stood just inside the door with her arms folded and a militant expression on her face. 'Sit on the bed and I'll rub your feet warm.'

'You will do no such thing!'

'Don't be ridiculous, my sisters used to suffer with chilblains when we were children and I often rubbed cold toes to prevent them,' he ordered and somehow managed to sound so reasonable that she very nearly did.

'I am quite capable of attending to my own feet, thank you,' she informed him coolly.

He grinned and she felt her heart flip, then race, as she wondered if it was as obvious to him that she dare not let him touch the smallest part of her. If he did, she might beg him to stay, and that would do neither of them any good when they woke up to what they had done.

'I should have thought you would enjoy the spectacle of seeing me on my knees before you,' he joked inexcusably, since the image sent all sorts of unsuitable images flashing through her wayward mind. Luckily he then stood back and looked stern once more. 'Lock the door after me,' he urged after he had silently and efficiently made up the fire, so her toes would not be frozen after all.

Following him to the door at last, she hurried him on his way, before she lost all chance of sleep and self-respect and begged him to stay.

'Goodnight, sweet Miranda,' he murmured before ghosting out of the room and waiting for her to shoot the bolt home.

Chapter Nine

At last Miranda sensed he had gone and allowed herself to lean against the oak panels and sigh gustily. It had been a close-run thing, forcing the inner siren only he seemed capable of rousing back into her prison cell, but she had done it, with a little help from the gentlemanly instincts he claimed not to have.

'Venus?' she murmured thoughtfully as she plumped down on the rug by the now-glowing fire. 'Why on earth must he call me that?' she asked herself and felt that other world momentarily gape at her feet again.

Rejecting it as a chimera, she decided her feet were quite warm enough to make sleep possible once more and made herself return to her bed. Once there, she carefully forced out the idea of her intruder forcing a way back in with more evil intent than just spoiling a few papers. The last thing she wanted was to offer whoever it had been a sign of weakness by staying in bed late tomorrow, or wilting about looking wan and worn. Lying back on soft down pillows, she forced all thoughts of mystery invaders and tall, handsome and dark-haired rescuers from her mind and ruthlessly composed herself to sleep.

Next day the last thing Miranda felt the urge to do after an eventful night was wilt. She was too angry with the top-lofty lord of Wychwood to feel the least fatigue, she told herself, once she realised he had ordered her to be watched every moment of the day. Having water spoil one of her precious letters from her godmother and ink spilt on her lovely rosewood desk was definitely not enough to warrant the watch-dogs she encountered at every turn. First she tried to go for a walk in the gardens and was trailed by two footmen and a maid. Knowing it was not their fault, she contained her fury until she had walked off some of it. Then she marched upstairs to find the estate carpenters installing locks on her windows and Leah supervising the installation of a truckle bed in the tiny dressing room next to her spacious chamber.

'No,' she burst out, no longer caring who heard

her, 'I'm not having that. If you intend to guard me, you can dratted well share my bed, Leah Smith. It's big enough in all conscience and I won't inflict that broom cupboard on my best friend.'

Leah flushed with pleasure, but didn't let such a public declaration of friendship from her mistress divert her for long.

'His lordship wants Sukey to sleep in the dressing room and you won't want her disturbing you with her silly prattle, ma'am,' she corrected.

So he was considerate enough to tiptoe round Leah and Reuben's shocking conduct, was he? Miranda suspected Leah would probably insist on staying close to her whether she wanted her to or not, but it warmed her heart that he was capable of such consideration. Not that she intended to let it cool her righteous anger when he was being so absurdly over-protective. The deserted seventeen-year-old she had once been might have revelled in such manly determination to safeguard her, but Miranda Alstone was a very different creature now. Staying angry with him prevented consideration of any other emotion she risk feeling for him as well of course.

It seemed to work well enough for the next few days, except for her nagging suspicion that Kit was only waiting for the right moment to prove her wrong. Meanwhile, she watched carefully for any sign that he was courting Celia in earnest, and failed to see anything in his dark eyes when they dwelt upon her cousin other than cool assessment and even downright scepticism. Still, she reassured herself, many a marriage of convenience began with mere tolerance, so that didn't forbid the union her grandfather had wanted so badly.

Another uneasy week ticked by, and the remaining one began to look like eternity. Yet if she broke the terms of the will, the whole would be under question. The very idea of leaving her sisters to endure genteel poverty instead of plenty and the approval of society, made her square her shoulders and determine to go on as nothing else could have done. Kate and Isabella would have all she had been denied, even if she had to forbid them any direct contact with their errant elder sister to achieve it. Even so, Miranda began to suspect the strain of this ridiculous situation was showing in her shadowed eyes and lack of appetite when Leah embarked on a relentless campaign to do her good.

'Here we are, Miss Miranda,' Leah informed her mistress as she swung into Miranda's bedchamber in her own inimitable style one fine April morning. 'Good as new and I dare say it'll fit you better than ever, now we've taken half an ell out of it,' she went on as she waved a familiar dark green habit Miranda had left behind when she fled to Nevin's dubious protection.

They had not expected to stay at Wychwood and Miranda had brought no riding attire, but Godmama had promised to send more of her gowns with her last letter and Miranda had been quite content to wait for them.

'I dare say it would do very well if I actually wanted to ride. Exactly what time is it?' she asked irritably, feeling distinctly weary in the face of so much energy.

'High time you was up, unless you're thinking of becoming as big a slug-a-bed as Miss Celia,' her old friend replied, handing her the tray Coppice had obviously insisted she must be given, despite Leah's determination to get her lady up and doing on such a fine morning.

'Luckily I'm not, or you would probably bully the household into waking me at some unearthly hour every morning just for the good of my soul.'

'Well, it's nine o'clock, and time you were out of bed,' Leah returned with an expression of such conscious virtue on her pretty face that Miranda threw a cushion at her. 'You always was a heathen, Miss Miranda,' she informed her sternly. 'And Reuben says he'll have the Moonchaser ready in half an hour.'

'Is she ready to be ridden, then?'

She had avoided the stables since her return, knowing she would find it harder to leave her old friends there, human and equine, if she allowed herself to haunt them as she had once done. Then, of course, there was the fact that Kit spent most of the time there, when he wasn't busy with estate matters or his complex business affairs.

'You need to gather your wits, Miss Miranda,' Leah chided. 'She's a six-year-old now with a yearling of her own out in the paddocks, and she's in sore need of a good run, what's more, and Miss Celia would ruin her if she got near her. Reuben says his old lordship refused to let her ride any horse but the Witch these last few years. Said they were well suited apparently, and quite right he was, too, if you ask me.'

'Luckily I wouldn't be so rash.'

Hiding a smile behind her abundant hair as Leah untangled the bright mass and confined it to a net, Miranda could just imagine how well that embargo had gone down with Celia. Her cousin prided herself on her horsemanship, which con-

sisted of imposing her will with liberal applica-
tions of the whip on the most placid of animals.
Grandfather had taken it off her, on pain of her
being sent back to her half-brother to ruin his
stable instead if she acquired another. If Celia had
tried such tactics on the Witch, she would have
been bucked off before they left the stable-yard,
Miranda concluded with considerable satisfaction,
and almost wished she had been there to witness
it.

'Good morning Reuben, Leah has decreed that
I am to ride this morning,' she greeted the head
groom half an hour later.

Reuben flushed and looked a good ten years
younger than he was entitled to. 'She took it into
her head it'd do you good, Miss Miranda.'

'And I dare say she's right,' she admitted and he
smiled his relief.

'Then come and meet the Moonchaser again,' he
replied, enthusiasm scouting his concern that his
Leah might have finally overstepped a line that
didn't exist between Miranda and her best friend.

'Oh, Reuben, she's grown into such a beauty,'
Miranda breathed as she made friends with the
mare all over again. 'Do you remember me, you
lovely creature, or are you just expecting treats?'

she asked as the grey nuzzled her with seeming affection.

'Here you are, Miss Miranda.' Reuben handed her a carrot and stood back to admire the pretty picture they made, nearly backing into the formidable form of his new employer as he did so.

'Good morning, Cousin,' Miranda greeted him happily enough, too pleased with the beautiful mare to remember she had every cause to be wary. 'She was only a yearling last time I saw her, and I well remember the night she was born. Grandfather and I thought we would never save both her and her dam, but we did it with Reuben's help, didn't we, Reuben?'

'Aye, Miss Miranda, that we did. His old lordship never put the mare to stud again, though, so it's a good job the Moonchaser breeds better or we'd have lost her line.'

'Which would be a great shame, don't you agree, my lord?' Miranda asked earnestly.

'She's a fine animal,' he admitted, 'although I suspect she's a bit light in her upper storey. Still, I'm glad you intend to ride at long last and I dare say you can manage her or Reuben wouldn't have brought her in for you.'

'Indeed, she and I can be brainless together,' she said rather sourly.

'Unlikely, but you must admit that she's skittish and silly. I had best accompany you this first time at least.'

'Reuben will vouch for my ability to deal with both,' she said stiffly, finding that her pride was still alive and well after all.

She refused to let him take the thrill of riding a fine animal from her with his insistence on protecting her even outdoors. The threat was negligible, and he was making a five-act tragedy out of a silly farce.

'Miss Miranda can ride any horse in the stable, my lord,' Reuben agreed.

'I could five years ago, but I suppose I might have grown rusty or hamfisted. We must let his lordship judge for himself,' she conceded when she saw Kit's mouth tighten and realised it wasn't in Reuben's interests to alienate his new master.

She wondered if Kit was one of those gentlemen who was always taciturn in the mornings. In future she must avoid him even more assiduously before noon, but for now she would endure his disturbing company if it made him concede she could ride with a groom in future.

'I'll saddle the mare, but I'm not sure your stallion will let me near him, my lord,' Reuben admitted and they both went into the stables to attend to the horses.

Miranda was relieved to be given a few minutes in the yard to accustom herself to the idea of Kit's unadulterated company after a week of meticulous avoidance. She could hear him chiding the mysterious animal gently and by the time she heard hooves on the cobbles she was intrigued.

'Wherever did you find such an exceptional creature, my lord?' she enthused as she took in the power and strength of the stallion, allied as it was to the refined features and brilliant eyes that showed there was more than a dash of Arabian in his breeding.

'It's a long story, Mrs Braxton,' he replied and swung into the saddle with annoying ease as she settled herself in her own saddle with Reuben's assistance.

It really was most unfair that ladies had to be confined to the side-saddle, she decided, as she recalled long-ago days when she, Reuben and Leah had stolen away for a day on the moors, all three riding astride and none the worse for it. 'Then one day you must entertain us with it,' she returned calmly and indicated that she was now ready to move off.

No doubt he would insist on her going first, so that he could watch her every move like some fierce-eyed eagle.

'Which direction would you suggest?' he asked
her and confounded at least one of her expectations.

'The Tops?' she asked, with a quirk of her
eyebrows at the head groom to confirm that the
way was clear.

'Good notion, Miss Miranda, they'm both
itching for a gallop.'

Kit thanked Reuben politely, but his frown
returned as soon as they were alone.

'We'll have to see about that gallop,' his infuriating lordship put in, obviously still dubious about
the quality of her horsemanship.

'Yes, you might not be able to keep up.'

'And you might not find it as easy as you think
to get back in the saddle after so many years,
Cousin Miranda,' he told her rather austerely.

'I have ridden quite recently, thank you,' she
replied, even as she wondered if ambling around
on one of Lady Rhys's well-trained Welsh greys
had prepared her for this.

'Have you, indeed?' he replied with a frown and
gently urged his stallion into a trot as they turned
into the ride leading up to the Tops.

'Yes, my lord, and you won't get rid of me quite
so easily,' she muttered at his disappearing back
and let the Moonchaser accelerate in his wake.

Even so, she could feel muscles she had not used in a while pull as they finally came out at the top of the bridle-way and stopped to survey the scene before them.

'Isn't this wonderful?' she gasped impulsively, looking to him for confirmation that this was indeed one of the most ruggedly beautiful sights in a fine land.

'Magnificent,' he returned, with a peculiarly husky undertone to his baritone voice.

Confused by the suspicion that he was not looking at the landscape when he agreed with her, she refused to meet his eyes and returned to contemplation of her beloved peaks.

'Even after the grandeur of Snowdonia this takes my breath away,' she said, and couldn't understand why she was letting him see how moved she was to be home, even if it was for a matter of weeks. She let her eyes wander over the tors, and those strangely formed outcrops seemed timeless. The whole panorama was matchless to her eyes, and she fancifully felt her heart settle at the sight of her native hills and peaks laid out before them. 'Have you ever seen anything like it?' she asked, wanting to share her pleasure.

'Never. I can tell it's very dear to you,' he said in an odd tone of voice that made her look at him and hastily look away when she saw his eyes were on her.

'Yes, it is,' she admitted at last, 'inestimably dear.'

'The place suits you somehow.'

Miranda took a long look around the windswept outcrops and close-grazed hollows, the distant blue of the high peaks and wondered if that was a compliment or no.

'At least we can safely let them gallop here,' she challenged him, pointing to the gallop the grooms used to exercise the most fiery of their charges. 'If we hurry, we might even get home before the rain comes,' she added with an assessing gaze at the serene-looking horizon.

'Pessimist,' he accused, smiling at last as he waited for her to precede him.

'You'll see,' Miranda replied with an answering smile, eager for the wild thrill of speed as she and the Moonchaser raced against a worthy opponent. Sensible Mrs Braxton could take over again when they returned to the house, she decided, giving her mare the office to gallop.

Kit followed the lithe figure with his eyes and wondered why he put himself through such bodily discomfort, just to watch Mrs Miranda Braxton ride like the wind. He had felt no need to torture himself before he met her, and his head groom could have followed her without suffering in like fashion. He was quite certain Leah Smith was woman enough for a far more restless rogue than Reuben would ever be, so why couldn't he bring himself to trust anyone else with Miranda Braxton's safety?

Because he was an over-anxious idiot, he assured himself stoutly, and it took little urging to send the Maharajah in the mare's dancing footsteps. Lord, but the woman could ride! She adapted her body to every nuance of the grey's stride and controlled her playful high spirits without apparent effort. Miranda had been more aloof than ever of late, and some hunter's instinct had warned him to allow her a respite. The question was when to put the pressure back on and make her see that she was fated to become his wife? Something told him he would need every ounce of guile he possessed to win her, but win her he would somehow. He had known since that kiss in the freezing hall that she must be his countess.

Until then he had been inclined to let the late earl's ridiculous scheme die with him, but suddenly everything was possible. It made no odds that he was on fire for her whenever she so much as walked into a room. Abiding passion was not love, he reassured himself, and neither was his determination that nobody would ever hurt her again. No, they would run in harness together as if they were born to do so, but their marriage would be built on passion and mutual affection. Love would spoil everything. Yet it was only by concentrating on his own fiery mount that he managed to divert himself from the tortuous burn of desire that shot through him at the very thought of Miranda sharing his marriage bed. Letting her know it just now would probably drive her away again, and he wasn't the stuff martyrs were made of.

'Are you conceding the race, my lord?' Miranda turned and taunted him from her hundred-yard advantage. 'Moonchaser certainly thinks she has you two slow-tops well and truly beat!'

'Then she is mistaken.'

He let the great stallion have his head at last, and they leapt across the gallop at a pace rarely seen outside the racetrack. Of course he was too big to allow the stallion to reach his true speed, but even so they were too much for the smaller mare, even with such a fine rider on her back.

'Oh, that was wonderful. I can't tell you how much I have longed to do that again,' Miranda told him impulsively, as they slowed their respective mounts to a walk before the flat land began to curve up again.

'I can imagine—you certainly weren't made for cramping propriety.'

Somehow Kit knew he had hurt her with those careless words. Her sparkling eyes lost some of their joy and suddenly her smile was a sham, not the glorious truth it had been just seconds ago.

'It's high time we turned back,' she told him in a flat, polite voice and turned the grey's head towards another ride that would lead them to the great Tudor mansion he still couldn't call home.

Idiot, he chided himself. Somehow or another he had to persuade her that marriage to him would be nothing like being wed to a drunken sot, and that some off-colour gossip about her first marriage meant nothing to him whatsoever. Hurting her would get him nowhere, and he had a very real need to protect her, over and above that self-serving consideration. He eyed her supple figure as she rode far enough away from him to render conversation impossible without shouting above the noise of the horses' hooves. With a supreme effort, he enforced his usual iron control over his errant desires and got himself under control, urging Maharajah to canter in

Miranda's wake and wondering how to settle her ruffled feelings.

Once she was his wife, nobody would be allowed to speak scandal about her, or even hint that she was tainted with her late husband's sins. After all, what use was there in fighting your way up from poverty to power if you didn't use it to protect you and yours when you finally attained it?

'You ride like Diana herself,' he told her when they drew level again.

'Thank you, my lord. So can I ride out without your august company from now on after all?'

'Cousin Kit,' he corrected with a patience he didn't quite feel, 'and of course you can, if you will occasionally agree to ride out with it.'

'Since I will be riding your horses, I can hardly refuse the company of their owner,' she returned with a social smile that made him grit his teeth in frustration.

Miranda controlled the restless mare and decided horseback was no place to indulge in even the most polite of arguments.

'Consider them your own for the duration of your stay, Cousin Miranda,' Kit replied, and there was such gentle mockery in his eyes that she had to cling fiercely to her determination to resist him.

'Thank you,' she said, and told herself to be pleased that lowering clouds and a strengthening breeze meant they must now hurry home.

Despite the exhilaration of their gallop, she was acutely uncomfortable whenever his dark brown eyes rested thoughtfully on her, as if considering a conundrum he had nearly worked out. Was he really tempted to balk at the prospect of a lifetime of Celia's chilly loveliness? If so, she somehow had to stop him proposing an alliance that would fly in the face of everything she believed in, and hurt them both when she had to turn it down.

He was no callow young man raised to think himself a little too important, too entitled to the good things of this earth. Kit Alstone was tried and tested; a man who had forced his will on an often uncooperative world, and risen from the depths his father had reduced his family to at an age when his peers were only just out of school. She admired his strength and iron determination; she was even honest enough to admit that she revelled in his hungry kisses and sensual touch, but she wouldn't marry him if he begged her to on bended knee.

Chapter Ten

Miranda encouraged the Moonchaser into a trot and was glad Kit chose to check his mount and follow them rather than catch up. She was tired of pretending to be indifferent to a man who might have mapped her world for her, if she had only met him instead of Nevin Braxton all those years ago. At the end of next week she could leave here with what she wanted—her independence. She had no intention of accepting the Earl of Carnwood's hand, even in the unlikely event that it came accompanied by his heart.

Suddenly a mighty crack sounded loud in the sunken path that long use had made of the ancient bridle way she had chosen as the quickest way home. Miranda felt a blow as if a branch had fallen across her upper arm and tried to shrug it off. Even as she was doing so the Moonchaser reared up in terror, then kicked back, ridding herself of her rider and escaping such outrages becoming her one obsession.

'Curse you, you damn fool creature!' Miranda heard his lordship shout above the thunder of the grey's hooves, even as she suddenly had to let go of the reins after all.

All her early training deserted her as she allowed this odd weakness to overtake her and released her grip, and hitting the hard ground with such a thump should have terrified her more than it seemed to be doing. She vaguely listened to some far more inventive curses from his lordship, as he leapt from his own horse and came to kneel beside her with very little thought for what the stallion might do without him.

'Can't think why I let go. Grandfather would have been furious,' she managed in a soft, breathless tone even Celia would have been proud of.

Kit's face was anguished, his eyes dark as night and his mouth set hard. He looked as if he was holding back an impulse to howl his outraged feelings to the indifferent heavens as he bent over her with what looked like acute anxiety in his stormy gaze.

'Never mind that accursed mare, I'll have her shot for making bad worse,' he gritted and she tried to shout her nay at such a preposterous idea, even as he seized the sleeve of her habit and ripped it out of the bodice.

'Stop!' she protested, puzzled by the weakness of her voice and the buzzing noise in her ears. 'You'll ruin it,' she chided as if that was all that mattered in the midst of a calamity she was fast losing the will to understand.

'Just as you will surely ruin me, my darling,' he responded with anger and steel at war with what looked oddly like fear in his dark eyes.

'Mistaken,' she told him earnestly, unable to curb her tongue from telling all her thoughts all of a sudden, 'you despise me.'

'If only I could, Venus,' he replied tersely, but with a hint of that devilish grin she had secretly come to look for twitching at his firm mouth as he uncovered her wound.

She watched his absorbed expression while the odd sense of detachment that had descended on her increased rather than going away. At least it was an alternative to the pain she was at last conscious of, and she wondered hazily if it might be worth this to see such concern in his dark eyes, and feel the infinite gentleness in his touch as he examined the bloody wound on her arm.

'You'll live, Miranda,' he assured her after a

long consideration of the agony it was now becoming, 'although not through any fault of your own, I dare say.'

'And just why is everything always my fault?' she joked feebly even as she disgusted herself by letting the darkness that had been beckoning close in and suck her into the most peculiar whirling darkness.

Grimly ignoring an impulse to fall at her feet in an unmanly faint from remembered terror and sheer relief, Kit padded the wound with the large and surprisingly sensible linen handkerchief he found in her pocket, then tied the makeshift dressing in place with his cravat.

When he heard the unmistakable crack of gunfire and saw that sudden flowering of blood on her arm, he had felt as if the world might end without her in it, except that would require her to be in his world to start with. No, Miranda Alstone could have his passion, his consideration and even his name, but his heart was still his own. Anyway, everyone knew Kit Stone had no heart, so he could be in no danger of parting with it to the woman he intended to marry.

He watched her pale, still face and felt the organ he had just denied himself turn over, before settling with a thump. Which only went to show how inadequate the language was to describe a man's more complex emotions, he told himself crossly. He loosened her tightly buttoned habit and stock and took off his coat to roll it up and provide some cushioning for her head, beside that great mass of vibrant hair doing its best to escape the net it had been wound into in a vain effort to control it.

His lips lifted in a wry, tender smile as he studied the wayward locks of this equally wayward woman. Still softened, his mouth kissed her snowy brow as if it had a will beyond his. He savoured the feel of her silky skin under his sensitive touch and gently repeated the caress. As she was no fashionable lady to feign a faint and trust masculine impulsiveness to force them into a compromising situation, she would never know. He saw her frown as if she was coming back to consciousness and sat back with brooding eyes to watch her fight her ills. His eyes dwelt on her white face and the tension about her mouth and eyes that had not left her even in unconsciousness. Protectiveness swept over him in such a rush that his fist clenched and he sprang to his feet, looking for a dragon to slay on her behalf.

Coming to *his* right senses for the first time

since he heard that shot, he cursed himself for an idiot. Someone had just fired at her and could be out there yet, waiting for a chance to try again. He started towards the thicket-like hedge that lined the bridle path, then paused to try and recover some of the famous cool self-command that had suddenly deserted him. If she was the target, he could not leave her unconscious and vulnerable while he combed the place for a hidden assassin to kill with his bare hands.

Tempted to stand braced over her prone body and primitively shout 'Mine!' to whoever might be listening, he sat beside her. At least no blood had stained the dressing he had wound around her arm yet, but it was cold now and the fine drizzle would soon soak her. Deciding that untamed impulses were sometimes right, he crouched over Miranda to shield her, and waited impatiently for rescue.

Miranda finally came to her full senses when her rescuers lifted her up to place her in his lordship's waiting arms. Fluttering a quick glance up at him in the approved fashion for young ladies of far more sensibility, she hastily closed her eyes again and tried to make sense of the impossible. Kit looked tender and concerned, as if his formidable attention was solely on his need to keep her safe. Surely she must be dreaming? Trying to summon her usual common sense, she found it flown as her heart beat fast and light with the heady thought that this might be real. Surely she wasn't going to fall headlong into the arms of the first man who looked at her as if she mattered?

'Ouch!' she muttered darkly, as an unwary movement jarred her arm and provoked a pain that jarred right through her.

'Keep still, then,' he ordered her sharply and she decided she must have been mistaken about the concern in his hawk-like gaze after all.

'What happened?'

'You fell off your horse,' he informed her tersely, as if she might have done it just to annoy him.

'Did I?' she asked dubiously, as another wave of pain assaulted her reeling senses. 'Feels like an elephant rolled on me,' she joked weakly.

'You did come a cropper,' he informed her coolly.

'How ham-fisted of me.'

'Yes, wasn't it?' he asked with mock-politeness and she risked opening her eyes again, to see his jaw clenched and his eyes hard on the path ahead of them, as he concentrated on making their ride as smooth as possible for her.

'Did your horse stay with us, then?' she persisted, to distract herself from the burning pain in her arm as much as to know the answer.

'Not he—both those wretched nags will be back in their stables luxuriating by now. I should have brought this brave steady fellow out to start with.'

Miranda forced her eyes away from the Earl of Carnwood for a moment and glanced at the chestnut head in front of her. 'Rowan,' she said sagely and nodded. 'Grandfather always said he had an old head on young shoulders, although by now he must have caught up with himself.'

'He has, but I should have favoured his good sense over Maharajah's spirit when riding out with you, Mrs Braxton.'

'He couldn't keep up.'

'My thoughts exactly,' he agreed.

'Gracious, we seem to be in accord for once.'

'Maybe,' he replied gruffly and she watched his intent face for a few moments, before deciding even such terse conversation distracted her from the pain in her arm and the bruises making themselves felt all over her body.

'How did he get here?' she asked.

'Reuben brought him. Now keep still and behave yourself!' he barked as she tried to slew round and see exactly who was behind them.

'That sounds more like the lordly Lord

Carnwood we all know,' she told him mockingly, even as she fought the faintness that was threatening again.

'I beg your pardon,' he said stiffly, frowning at the path ahead as if he wished it would magically land them back at the stables between one breath and the next.

'Must have fallen on my head,' she assured herself.

She both heard and felt a rich chuckle vibrate through his mighty torso as he shifted her in his grasp. He even spared a quick look at her pale face before once more fixing his gaze on the way ahead.

'Maybe that would have knocked some sense in,' he observed laconically.

'I doubt it,' she replied ruefully and contrarily wished him a little less all-powerful, because then it might not feel so comforting to be held in his arms.

'Then don't do it again, I don't think you could manage on any less than you have now,' he chided gently, for all the world as if he was concerned.

'I will endeavour not to, for it hurts like the devil,' she heard herself say with a detached sense of horror.

Miranda Braxton managed alone; she certainly didn't repine that there was no strong and manly shoulder for her to cry on when the world became a little too hard or lonely for her.

'How much further?' he called back to the men following so carefully in their wake that she had hardly registered the fact that they were there.

'Half a mile to the highway, my lord,' Reuben's voice called back and Miranda tried to see over Kit's shoulder just how many men were with them.

She caught a glimpse of three grim-faced men, sharp eyed and angry as they watched the countryside around them with deep suspicion.

'Someone shot me!' she finally concluded and shock made her try to sit upright, before weakness and Kit's determined opposition changed her mind.

'Hell's teeth, woman, are you trying to finish the job for them?' he barked as he tightened his hold about her waist and still managed to urge Rowan into a smooth trot.

Kit knew they were too tempting a target for a sniper, if one was bold enough to have stayed around after his first shot. Instinct told him the man was long gone, but not so far away he couldn't try again another day. At least for once he was too preoccupied to react in his usual fashion to the warm and delightfully curved female in his arms, he thought gloomily. So every cloud had a silver lining, even if he would far rather take that bullet himself than watch her suffer.

Because he had been lagging a little behind her when she was shot, he knew that shot had been meant for her. While he had enemies enough to fill a stagecoach, inside and out, what had she ever done to deserve such a deed? Of course, a terrified poacher might be bolting for home at this very moment, thinking up an alibi as he went, but intuition and experience told him the shot had been deliberate.

It was a huge relief to finally reach the road, where Kit's coachman was waiting with the most luxurious carriage in the coach house. He should have known the ever-faithful Leah would be waiting with it. Today Miranda's enemies had proved themselves very real indeed and he had failed to protect her. No wonder Leah didn't trust him to bring her mistress home in one piece. Of course, he had thought the only danger was from someone trying to frighten her off, but that shot had missed her heart only by a chance jolt in the path.

'What have they done this time?' Leah asked, anxiously watching Miranda's pale face as Reuben and another groom lifted her down as gently as they could.

Once he could jump down and pass steady

Rowan's reins to the third groom, Kit sprang into the carriage to take Miranda in his arms. It was his duty as a gentleman to shield her from an uncomfortable journey, he assured himself, and eyed his minions coldly, daring them to protest. Yet something told him his staff wouldn't speak scandal about Miranda if she rode naked down the village street!

'Drive carefully rather than fast,' he cautioned the coachman and set himself to take as many of the bumps out of their journey for her as he could as he leant her unhurt side into his and braced his legs to keep her steady.

He wondered fleetingly if Lady Clarissa would actually kill her niece. It was obvious that she disliked her, but surely her refusal to hide the fact was an argument in her defence? And, of course, murder was *shockingly* bad *ton*. He shifted impatiently and concluded he was hunting in the dark until he had more information. Then he saw Miranda bite down on her full bottom lip and immediately regretted his restless movement. He whispered an apology to her with such tenderness that Leah watched them thoughtfully, then nodded for some reason he couldn't spare the effort to question just at the moment.

* * *

'Soon be home now,' Miranda murmured, comforting Kit for her hurt as she relaxed into his embrace once more and wished she need never leave it.

She knew perfectly well that she would have to, so she lay quietly and tried to rise above the haze of pain now burning her mistreated arm. It was almost worth being shot to ride in my lord Carnwood's arms like a damsel of old with her knight, she decided with a sigh. Even the pain in her arm subsided every now and again and it seemed a very long time since she had felt so secure and protected. It was all a lovely illusion, of course, but one she was not yet inclined to dispel for reality. As soon as they were back at the Court that would intrude. Until then, Miranda closed her eyes and allowed herself to dream for once.

Kit was her loving husband, her fantasy went, and they were riding home from a ball, tired and content with each other as only lovers could be. She was cherished and understood and fiercely desired by her lord, and under their contentment was an urgent need to experience the joys of the marriage bed once more. At that point her own imagination scandalised her so thoroughly she opened her eyes, to see Leah watching her with far too much understanding in her eyes.

'Almost there,' she warned, telling Miranda the world was about to encroach even if that meant the doctor and a comfortable bed were at hand.

'Yes,' she agreed fatalistically as the carriage turned into the northern avenue. 'The tower looks even more derelict from this angle,' she observed absently as they passed through the gates of the east lodge.

'You leave me so little time for trivial tasks like repairing the ruins on my estate, Cousin Miranda,' Kit said with ironic apology. 'I'm just too busy rescuing you from assassins to take care of it at the moment.'

'It needs putting right though, my lord, and never mind what Miss Celia says,' Leah cautioned. 'Her majesty isn't like to have half of it tumble on her, considering she hardly ever goes outdoors.'

Miranda was faintly surprised Celia hadn't joined them on their ride. It wasn't like her to miss a chance to fascinate her quarry and she had a good seat on a horse, if one could be found who was not terrified of her. It was just as well Celia had let them evade her, though; Miranda didn't feel like coping with Celia's fussing and fainting when she wasn't in command of her own senses. Nor could she have rested content in Kit's strong arms if she had to endure Celia's amateur theatricals and steely glances while she did so. With that in mind, Miranda insisted on climbing out of the coach with only the support of his lordship's strong arm when they reached Wychwood.

'Otherwise the whole neighbourhood will think I'm on my deathbed,' she joked, but felt the loss of his strength so acutely her knees wobbled.

He even let her take a few unsteady steps before he swept her up in his arms again. Telling herself she was breathless because of the speed of it, Miranda gave in and allowed herself to be carried into the morning room. There he laid her on the *chaise-longue* and barked a succession of orders at the servants who had come crowding into the hall.

Her pain wasn't altogether physical now, Miranda decided. Bidding farewell to the illusions she had allowed herself while she lay in Kit's arms hurt nearly as much as her arm. He was not for her and one day soon he would wed Celia. If only she could leave and save herself any more pain, but she must endure almost another week before she could do that.

'Send another man after that doctor,' Kit barked at poor Coppice when he was rash enough to appear to see what he could do to help.

'Done, my lord. We knew when the mare came

back with blood on her saddle as he would be needed.'

'Then bring brandy and hot water.'

'Doctor Gross doesn't approve of strong spirits for invalids, my lord,' Coppice argued stalwartly.

'Then bring me the brandy and Mrs Braxton will have hot water and spotlessly clean linen torn into strips, and kindly stop Lady Clarissa or Mrs Grant from disturbing us.'

'I can hardly prevent such an outcome in my position, my lord.'

'Tell them I told you to,' Kit urged with a smile—a smile that Miranda would have seen off every one of the famously tyrannical Patronesses of Almack's to gain, she decided wistfully.

'Very well, my lord,' the stalwart butler replied with a martyred sigh, 'I shall endeavour to convey your wishes to those concerned.'

'Thank you, Coppice,' Miranda managed, but still in the die-away tone that annoyed her so much, 'I am dreading a scold for getting myself shot.'

'Don't worry, Miss Miranda, I shall see they leave you alone,' the butler assured her stalwartly.

Kit quite expected him to seize some of the ancient pikes arranged artistically in the great hall and arm a couple of his footmen with them. He wondered what magic his own particular witch practised on all those around her, with a few notable exceptions, that even impassive Coppice looked ready to expend his last breath protecting her.

'Why do they dislike you so?' he asked once the man had left to take up guard duty.

'Aunt Clarissa resented the fact that her father remarried and produced an heir,' Miranda said, knowing perfectly well to whom he referred.

'Would she have inherited had none of you existed?'

'No, the estate has always gone with the title.'

'Then why hate you and not me?' he asked reasonably enough.

'Because my father was the heir and my brother Jack the next in line? I don't know, I never could understand how Aunt Clarissa's mind works.'

'It's hardly your fault you were an Alstone and not an Ennersley.'

'But poor Celia wasn't even born an honourable,' she imitated Lady Clarissa's haughty voice and won a smile.

'Well, neither was I,' he argued.

'You didn't let the lack of a meaningless form of address define you.'

'Maybe not,' he admitted, clearly puzzled that

anyone would. 'Anyway, your aunt could always leave,' he added abruptly.

'Then she would hate me all the more and feel free to spread gossip with no check on her tongue,' she told him, and shifted unwarily to argue her point. Raw pain shot through her, letting her know the agony only abated when she was still.

'You can trust me to deal with her when the time comes,' Kit informed her impatiently and she hadn't realised how tense he was until his shoulders relaxed when he heard the sound of a horse's hooves on the drive. 'Let the doctor tend you without an argument, and in return I won't ask any more questions.'

'They distracted me from the pain, my lord.'

'You must be feeling bad to comfort me for my sins, my dear, and my name is Kit,' he corrected with a wry smile and an unreadable look.

Chapter Eleven

Kit strode off to meet the physician, and no doubt rattle off another series of orders any sensible man would probably ignore. Miranda then endured stoically as the physician picked out every fragment of cloth from her wound and cleaned it before redressing it. All in all, she was mightily relieved when it was over and the Earl was re-admitted. Kit took one look at her ashen face and shadowed eyes and a formidable frown knitted his brows, so she promptly changed her mind and wished he had stayed away.

'It's high time you were in bed,' he informed her abruptly, 'and no argument, if you please.'

'I hate lying a-bed in the daytime,' she argued on principle.

'I take it you would rather be running a high fever by the end of the day and put the good doctor to a great deal of inconvenience because you're too silly to do as you're bid?' he countered abruptly.

'If my presence is so irksome, then I will certainly relieve you of it, my lord,' she replied, staring steadily back at him.

'Not under your own sail you won't, Mrs Braxton.'

'I most certainly will, my lord,' she replied with a decided nod. 'Respectable widows always retire to their bedchambers unaccompanied by gentlemen, day or night.'

'Once we reach it, you may do so with my blessing,' he said impatiently.

'Do you intend to lend me your arm, then?' she asked in the voice of sweet reason. Raging at him would probably make her mistreated head thump and she certainly wasn't going to admit it sounded a wonderful idea.

'I do not,' he informed her abruptly and, ignoring her indignant squeak of protest, effortlessly lifted her into his arms once more.

'You can't carry me upstairs,' she gasped, aghast to discover that not even the pain in her arm could blank out the fire that re-ignited whenever he touched her. If she wasn't careful, she might forget to be respectable when they both arrived breathless at their destination after all.

'A challenge, Cousin Miranda? You really should know better by now,' he said with a little too much understanding of her state of mind in his eyes.

'No, good sense.'

'Oh, that,' he dismissed with a wicked grin.

'Yes, that. Put me down and kindly remember the proprieties, my lord.'

'The proprieties be damned.'

'Never, my lord, for you don't know when they might damn you back,' she replied with a wistful droop to lips that strove hard not to wobble at the thought of what she had given up by doing so.

'With half the household hovering about the place, I'm more likely to be berated for neglecting you if I let you make your own way upstairs than condemned for carrying you,' he told her.

To make the idea even more irresistible there was a gentling in his dark gaze as he shifted her and gave her a smile of such understanding it silenced her until he reached the half-landing.

'If ever I met a more awkward, opinionated female, I'm relieved to say I cannot recall her,' he told her ruefully when he stopped for a brief rest.

Miranda knew she was in deep trouble when she had to fight not to smile adoringly at him like some witless acolyte. Instead she stalwartly tried to convince herself that nestling into his arms wasn't exactly what she most wanted to do, even with the pain in her arm and a swimming head.

'Are you going to try your strength and my patience by insisting on trying to walk up the next flight, Cousin Miranda, or will you finally admit you need me?'

'How can I?' she whispered.

'Easily,' he murmured, 'all you have to do is trust me.'

'I would, if only I could,' she whispered back and even that humbling admission only won her a furious look.

She reflected bitterly on the past as he shouldered her bedchamber door open and carried her over to the bed. If only she had stayed here, quiet and unwed with her family. Then she could have met his enigmatic stare with trust, and all the promises she would never give another man. Despite the anger she felt in him, he placed her gently in the chair by the hastily kindled fire and stood back to survey her pallid face and shaken blue eyes.

'I suppose it would be too much to ask that you tell me everything, but I must warn you that I will probably find out anyway,' he warned.

There was infinite assurance in his deep voice, and he met her gaze so steadily it seemed more like a promise than a threat.

'Please don't,' she gasped out involuntarily, flinching away from the thought of the grim face he would show her if he found out the truth about her past.

'Won't it set you free then, Cousin Miranda?' he asked, cynicism back in his eyes.

'No,' she admitted on a defeated sigh, and leaned wearily against the pretty silk cushions her late mama had selected for this room with loving care.

Maybe if she tried really hard she could will her memory back to those happy times, and ignore the hollow feeling in the pit of her stomach that had nothing to do with her weakened state and everything to do with him. Seeming to recognise that she was in no state for an inquisition, he stood back and her well-wishers surged forward to fuss over her. All the time they did so, she was conscious of him watching as the bed was warmed and the fire fanned, before a few hard looks from Leah and the housekeeper finally scouted him.

'I must go,' he said, giving Miranda a last unreadable look before he did so.

'Thank you,' she said and he stopped and looked back with raised eyebrows. 'For staying with me,' she added softly.

'And I was so tempted to leave you lying there and go about my day-to-day business,' he informed her sardonically, before finally marching out of the room as stiff-backed as a tin soldier.

'I think you just offended his lordship,' Leah observed unnecessarily.

Miranda sighed. 'Yes, I seem to be good at it,' she agreed.

'It's easy to hurt someone as cares for you,' Leah said sagely.

'Nonsense, he can't wait to be rid of this particular unwanted guest,' Miranda tried to assure her lightly, and failed.

'He can't keep his eyes off you,' her maid insisted.

'And you must need spectacles, Leah.'

'I can see through a millstone well enough, although it's plain to tell that you can't, Miss Miranda.'

'I thought you had brothers to visit today,' Miranda said tartly.

'They have waited five years to see me—a few hours either way won't hurt us now.'

'Had an argument already, have we?'

'No, an agreement,' Leah told her with a self-satisfied nod.

'That's the first time I ever heard it called so.'

'Yes, an agreement that you still need me more than they do,' her old friend went on just as if she hadn't spoken.

'That's ridiculous,' Miranda protested, genuinely upset that Leah could neglect her family for her sake. 'It's only a flesh wound,' she went on, appalled at the weakness of her own voice.

'From a gunshot.'

'A poacher mis-shot,' Miranda argued.

'Poachers round here shoot better than that—it was no poacher.'

Considering that Leah's brothers were reputed to be the finest and most stealthy of that breed working in the area, Miranda took her word for it. 'An accident, then,' she offered gamely.

'And if it wasn't?'

If it wasn't, that meant someone was trying to kill her and Miranda couldn't think why they would bother. 'What else could it have been?' she asked uneasily.

'An enemy.'

'I have none bitter enough to risk hanging to shoot me,' Miranda was stung into protesting, even as she dwelt uneasily on the odd feeling she had of being stealthily watched by hostile eyes lately.

'What about that worthless varmint you married?'

'He's dead, and I had more cause to shoot him than he had to put a bullet in me, even if he wasn't. No, it was an accident and some poor soul is no doubt shaking in his boots in case fanciful creatures like you decide it was deliberate and track him down,' Miranda insisted.

'Leave her be now, Leah,' rebuked the housekeeper with a sidelong look at Miranda's pale face and shadowed eyes. 'His lordship will find out just what's afoot.'

'Yes, an accident,' Miranda murmured rebelliously, but she accepted the posset Leah handed her all the same, then let herself be gently undressed and put to bed by her well-wishers.

It was dark when Miranda woke from nightmares she was thankful not to remember and, as her senses came back to her, some instinct warned her to keep still. There was someone in her room again, but surely that was nothing to worry about? She had been vaguely conscious of people coming and going all day and Sukey was probably snoring away in the dressing room as usual. She frowned as she recalled his lordship's deep voice and tried to recall what he had wanted. Ah, yes, he had come to ask how she did, and been shooed out by the women who had stayed with her all day. A weak part of her wished they had let him stop with her, especially now when his strong presence would have scared away any intruder.

The best thing to do was feign sleep until she found out what was going on, and what a fool she would feel when it turned out to be one of the maids trying not to wake her. Unable to discern one shadow from another, she strained her other senses as the hairs on the back of her neck rose and she fought an irrational need to leap out of bed and run. Luckily the pain in her arm had subsided to a dull ache and she forced herself to breathe deeply and evenly, as if she were asleep and oblivious to whatever was going on.

It was probably the housekeeper, she reassured herself, checking she was not feverish, or maybe Leah had decided to sit up with her after all. Yet still she lay listening, and at last heard the door being stealthily closed, having been left open in case she called out in the night, she assumed. Anyone intending to check on her welfare would have brought a candle with them, so the pitch darkness argued that her instincts had been right. Her thoughts racing frantically now, Miranda tried to plan her escape from whoever was now moving stealthily toward her. Fear shivered down her spine and stole her breath as she slitted her eyes open far enough to search darkness so complete she almost despaired of her own senses.

Then she felt the intruder ghost past her and she

heard the window open and something being thrown out. Nobody but a lunatic would break into an occupied room to throw things out of the window, so which occupant of Wychwood Court had run mad? Then those stealthy footsteps turned back toward her as if their owner was confident of the way, even in the pitch dark. Suddenly the chill breeze from the open window seemed almost warm as something far colder menaced her. Giving up on surprise or dignity, she shot out of bed and ran for the door. The dark figure sprang after her with a feral snarl and she felt a clutching hand rip at her nightgown, aiming for her throat and latching on to mere cloth as the delicate lawn ripped and Miranda snatched herself free at the last moment.

Now that she couldn't spare the breath to scream, she cursed herself for not doing so on waking with every nerve prickling a warning. Better to be thought a hysterical female than become a dead one after all. At a disadvantage in her stark white gown, she tried to remember where the brass nightstick was at the same time as trying to track her attacker through the gloom. At last her clutching fingers grasped whatever they could find like a talisman. A full carafe of water might not be the ideal weapon, but being defenceless was infinitely worse.

It occurred to her that the dark figure was circling her, intimidating her with a set purpose in mind, and she felt the chill of the night air on her back and suddenly realised what it was. If her attacker got his way, Mrs Miranda Braxton was going to have an accident of the most tragic kind tonight. A fall from her window when feverish from her wound and perhaps out of her senses, and one more Alstone would lie tidily in the family vault. How inconvenient if the unlucky widow was found with scratches or suspicious blows on her body—not that a fall onto the flagstones below would leave much of her to be examined, she supposed.

She had nothing to lose by making as much noise as possible, so Miranda threw her weapon at the stealthy figure and heard it hit target with such satisfaction that she almost forgot to run. When a startled grunt of pain was succeeded by the sound of glass crunching under soft-soled shoes and a muttered curse, she remembered to flee at last. The villain now had cut feet as well as a sore head, but a sibilant hiss of fury sped her flight. Sheer hatred seemed to reach out to her like an extra weapon as the rasp of steel being pulled from a short scabbard told her that her enemy had an even more brutal plan if the first one failed.

At last her voice came to full and vigorous life again and Miranda screamed her terror to the world. She ran even as she shouted for help, amazed by what volume desperation could produce. Fumbling open the catch of her door, she felt a relentless, murderous hand slash at her from the darkness even as she ran into the corridor still screaming for help. Why didn't Kit come? She almost shouted the question she had been asking herself ever since she awoke and knew something was wrong. How could he be asleep when she was in such dire need of him? Almost tipping over the edge of hysteria was a novel experience and not one she cared for, but, after all, she had endured a hard day.

'What the hell's going on?' the deep, dark voice she had been waiting for bellowed out of the semi-darkness as Kit ran up the stairs towards her, lit by a branch of wildly flickering candles he must have grabbed as he ran.

'Rouse the household, you idiot!' she yelled back at him, desperately afraid her attacker would aim the knife at him when he made himself such an easy target.

'No need when you've done it for me,' he told her as he came closer, but he clasped her shoulders with hands she was almost certain were shaking. 'What is it?' he demanded breathlessly and she noticed at last that he was fully dressed, even if he looked less immaculate than usual.

'Someone just tried to kill me,' she informed him in a chilly little voice even she couldn't quite fathom, 'and now he's getting away.'

'Where?' he demanded roughly and his eyes were coldly furious.

She pointed shakily toward her room and, despite her terror, shadowed his steps as he flashed the light of his candles round the room. The pretty muslin curtains were splashed with water and her attacker's blood, and a trail of equally gory footprints marked a course toward the window, after crossing those that had chased her so ruthlessly through the darkness. She turned the key she suddenly noticed was on her side of Sukey's little room and saw the unfortunate girl lying there terrified as well as roughly bound and gagged.

'Gone,' Kit exclaimed in disgust as he examined the rope that had been wound round the central pillar of her mullioned window.

'No—' Miranda saw the rope tension and wobble '—he's still there!'

Even she was shocked by the speed with which he bent and grasped the rope, hauling on it furiously as it tensed under its load. Then he grunted and let it snap out of his hands.

'He jumped,' he snarled as if it was her fault. 'Stay here and for heaven's sake mind all that glass.'

Using her embroidery scissors to cut through Sukey's bonds, Miranda helped the girl stand up. They eyed each other and considered that order dubiously after their ordeal.

'Be damned if we will,' Miranda rapped out.

'And be damned if I'll let you run round the house like that and add an ague to everything else,' he growled back and hurriedly shrugged out of his coat, throwing it to her before he ran downstairs again.

Of course she scrambled into its precious warmth, then ran after him with Sukey in tow as fast as their shaky legs would allow. Leaving the maid to exclaim and sob to the startled watchman, Miranda arrived at the French doors leading out of Kit's precious library and into the garden just as he stepped back through them.

'Gone,' he informed her succinctly and scanned the hastily assembling household with an appraising eye.

Surely he didn't think one of them was responsible, but Miranda could read nothing but impatience on his face as he greeted them laconically. 'Nice to know that if Bonaparte and his Imperial

Guard ever turn up, you'll all be up in good time for their victory celebrations.'

'Now there's no need for that, your lordship,' Coppice scolded rather bravely, considering a frown was almost drawing Kit's dark brows together.

'You're right,' Kit admitted, 'Stay here and guard the women while I take the footmen to search the grounds, although I dare swear the rogue's got clean away by now. He's dangerous, mind.' Kit turned to Miranda, who was now chalk pale and visibly shaken as shock took over from the desperate necessity to survive. 'Did he have a weapon?' he barked abruptly.

'A knife.'

He cursed fluently as he took in her battered state and looked as if he might heave the heavy library table over just to relieve his much-tried feelings.

'He's armed, then, and is obviously dangerous, but at least Mrs Braxton wounded him so we might find some blood to tell us which way he went. You stay here and don't leave this room alone for any reason,' he ordered the housekeeper and her maids as they ventured into the room at last, poor Sukey cautiously bringing up the rear.

'You too,' he bellowed at Miranda as she moved toward him.

'You'll need your coat,' she informed him in a

chill voice as she gave it to him, and wrapped herself in the large cashmere shawl draped over the chair where she had read so often as a girl.

'My thanks, but I am well able to manage without it,' he replied ungraciously as he shrugged into it, then turned on his heel and strode off to join the search.

'And good riddance to you too,' she muttered darkly as she eyed his retreating back with such a mix of exasperation and longing that Coppice hastily ordered fires to be stoked and water boiled for tea to give everyone else something to do.

'And Miss Miranda ought to put on something decent. In fact, she should be in bed by rights,' the housekeeper observed with a shocked glance at Miranda's sadly dishevelled appearance.

Stifling a laugh she dare not let out lest it wobble and betray her, she looked down at herself and shuddered. 'I really don't think I could,' she said.

When Leah and two of the braver maids insisted on venturing upstairs for a change of night rail and her lovely warm dressing robe, Miranda meekly adjourned to the Countess's Sitting Room and submitted to being fussed over and inspected for further damage.

'I knew I should have stayed with you tonight,' Leah scolded either herself or her mistress. 'I swear you could find trouble alone on a deserted island, Miss Miranda.'

'No need to look for it, it always seems to find me,' she joked.

'Then take a little more care of yourself, do,' Leah demanded and Miranda saw the housekeeper nod her agreement.

'I would promise to sleep with a loaded pistol under my pillow from now on, but I might shoot you one fine morning by mistake,' Miranda replied in a voice that fought hard to be light-hearted.

As Coppice knocked and informed them that tea was about to be served in the library, just as if it was the middle of a normal day, they adjourned there and the maids once more swarmed round the housekeeper in an agitated huddle. Sukey had evidently been waxing eloquent in their absence.

'Now sit yourself down, Miss Miranda, and try to be quiet for five seconds at a stretch,' Leah chided, regally ignoring the flutterings of lesser maids.

'A little *ennui* would be rather nice.'

And it was ridiculous to long for Kit to come back and lock her in his strong arms until the rest of the world faded away. Yet Miranda wanted him to hold her close with a fervency that shocked her.

'Tea, ladies,' Coppice announced from the doorway.

The familiar ritual was soothing, even if taking tea in the middle of the night would have seemed quite bizarre to an outsider.

'Excellent,' Miranda announced bracingly, 'we will take it together, lest his lordship roar at us for disobeying orders.'

So they scattered round the room with their cups and the housekeeper dispensed tea with Coppice's dignified assistance. Miranda was ordered to keep still and rest her arm whenever she offered to help, and it became ever more of an effort to sit straight-backed as she sipped the fragrant China tea.

What if the searchers actually found that deadly assassin and he lashed out at them? He would have the advantage of only striking enemies wherever he thrust out in desperation. Fervently hoping they would fail, she tried not to envision Kit being mortally injured while she sat sipping tea. Then a few quick steps on the terrace outside and he was back, bringing cool night air and a whisper of the fresh moors with him. As if his abundant vitality braced them, the occupants of the room stood or sat a little straighter.

'Good,' he observed as he took in the unconventional tea drinking.' I will take a cup myself, if you please,' he said, with an encouraging smile for Leah and a frown at Miranda, whom he obviously expected to be meekly reclining on the sofa as if she was about to go into a ladylike decline.

'Was there no sign of him?' she asked, furtively examining him for any sign of hurt. Seeing none, the worst of her tension drained away and suddenly wilting didn't seem such a bad idea after all.

'Only a few bloody footsteps on the terrace, then it's just as if he vanished to nothing.' He sounded cool and even slightly disappointed, but Miranda knew there was more he was leaving unsaid. 'The men are going through the house to find out where he got in, so when everything is secure again we can all go to bed and sort out the rest in the morning.'

Which might satisfy everyone else, but it did nothing to quiet the questions buzzing determinedly in Miranda's head.

'Where am I to sleep?' was the only one she asked, knowing he would not speak of the rest with the staff eagerly on the listen.

'With your maid in the room next to mine, with the windows shuttered and the doors locked and bolted. Tomorrow we shall contrive something more suitable, but at least you will have help in the unlikely event he tries again.'

Celia's superior dresser sniffed from her

position as upright as a suit of armour just inside the door, where she had haughtily disapproved of everything that had occurred so far in curl papers and a very buttoned-up dressing gown, which Miranda privately considered quite an achievement.

'Has anyone enquired after Lady Clarissa and Celia?' Miranda asked.

'They are safe a-bed like proper ladies, of course,' the dresser informed Kit regally, as if Miranda was too unimportant to deserve an answer. Obviously in her opinion proper ladies should stay in those chambers even if the house were on fire, or under attack from vicious murderers.

'Then no doubt you will wish to see if they require anything,' Kit returned blandly, and what else could the wretched woman do but go?

Miranda watched with awe as Kit ordered the rest of his household about to his satisfaction, and they seemed to go about their appointed tasks cheerfully enough. Then somehow she found herself alone with the master of the house in his brightly lit library, with the curtains closed against any malicious eyes and a fire bright in the hearth. At least there was nobody left to protest such impropriety.

'I will see her safely to your new room myself,' Kit had reassured Leah, as her steadfast defender went meekly upstairs with the rest.

Chapter Twelve

'You might have asked me what I wanted,' Miranda protested half-heartedly once they were alone and Kit was eyeing her sternly again.

'I'm a damned fool, but I'm not a lunatic,' he informed her in a driven voice and, ignoring her token squeak of protest, took her in his arms so as to avoid her injured arm and sat down with her on the sofa that suddenly seemed extremely appealing after all. 'Be quiet,' he ordered as she gave a token murmur of protest, then settled her into the warm embrace she had been secretly longing for ever since she woke up.

There was little of the fizz and fire that had arced between them from the moment they met this time. For a few terrifying minutes tonight it had seemed to Miranda that she was going to die; that they would never have a chance to sit like this, to inhabit this lovely stillness and warmth that suddenly seemed infinitely precious. The loss of all she hadn't let herself know she craved until now was unthinkable, so she relaxed against him with a heartfelt sigh and refused to think.

'I needed you,' she whispered, as her muscles gave up their tension and contentment stole through her in its wake.

'And I could have lost you,' he murmured softly as she burrowed her head into his shoulder as if he was her strength and refuge.

There was deep and potent emotion in his voice as he made that admission. Heart singing, despite her aching body and tired mind, she made herself look up from the security of his muscular shoulder and meet his gaze.

'Then you would have minded?' she asked.

He took in a deep breath and seemed to bite down on the passions she saw raw in his eyes for long moments as the library clock ticked the seconds and the fire hissed and glowed in the hearth. At last he seemed to trust himself to speak and his voice was crisp and a little impatient of such silly questions as he informed her, 'Indeed I would, Mrs Braxton.'

'Family is always important,' she informed him with a hesitant smile.

'You really are a beautiful idiot,' he said with a wry grin as he tucked her weary head back into the hollow between his shoulder and chin as if she had been born to fit there.

Nuzzling into security such as she never remembered knowing before, she turned a little to allow herself to breathe and gave a contented little sigh. 'D'you really think I'm beautiful?' she murmured sleepily.

'I always say what I mean, especially to you.'

'Then you must really consider me a harlot?' she asked, those awful accusations coming back to haunt her as she struggled rather half-heartedly against his compelling embrace.

'I never called you that, and whatever I thought before I knew you properly was wrong,' he informed her gruffly and met her indignant, tired eyes with frustration and banked desire in his own. 'But be assured that I want you with every breath I take, Miranda, and I have done since I first laid eyes on you all those years ago. So you will have to put any roughness of speech down to my appalling upbringing—it is a poor indicator of my feelings.'

That sounded perilously close to an apology and she rewarded him with a dazzling, slightly muzzy smile.

'That's nice, then,' she announced, and laid her head back on its favourite resting place as fatigue surged through her like some unstoppable tide. 'All those years ago?' she muttered in protest, even as sleep took her like a long-lost lover and she sank into its embrace as if she had been drugged.

'Nice?' Kit said indignantly and then gave her sleeping form a rueful smile.

How his goddess could call the need ripping through him as her soft curves fitted so perfectly against his hard body 'nice' was beyond him. Only Miranda could have come up with such a ridiculous, revealing word as that and then gone to sleep on him, so he couldn't show her exactly how 'nice' the surging desire, the hot wanting that burned between them, could be. Not that he could make love to a woman who had been through what she had endured today and meet his own eyes in the mirror in the morning when he shaved. He had some shreds of honour left, despite his enemies' opinion to the contrary.

She shifted in her sleep, making a soft sound of satisfaction as she insinuated herself even deeper into his arms. Never had he felt such a sense of rightness as holding her gave him. Even such a chaste embrace with her held more appeal than a hundred nights in any other woman's bed, and he knew at that moment that he was a lost cause. She was the only woman he wanted, *the* woman, and she had been for five long and frustrating years.

It was Kit's turn to sigh as he told himself they couldn't stay like this all night. She needed to rest for one thing, and he was human for another. The feel of her in his arms was a seduction in itself and one he had to resist until he had her agreement to their marriage. A wicked light softened his eagle-eyed gaze as he considered his ultimate reward for such patience. Soon he would have her in his bed for good, and then she had better forget about such mundane needs as sleeping for a while. Five years of need would not soon be sated, and he would think of another excuse to keep her awake and dizzy with their mutual desire when that one ran out.

First he must find out who was plotting against her, before they wed and became so absorbed in each other that neither could think straight. Kit felt the restlessness he had known so often as a boy and young man calm, along with the need to prove himself better than his peers, and knew his priorities were different now. For long minutes he sat and savoured the fact of her, curled neatly across his lap as if born to fit there. His strong hand was infinitely gentle as it stroked her caramel-coloured hair, while the other held her close as if he never intended to let her go.

Finally he made himself move, and even then rose with her still cradled across his chest, wondering how he would make himself release her to anyone's care but his own tonight. For her sake he must; she had suffered enough for the sins of others, he decided, and deserved his most careful protection from now on. With a frown he fervently hoped his enquiries would soon yield fruit, before her enemies could hurt her further.

He would hunt them to the ends of the earth if they so much as touched her again, but he been unable to prevent the appalling danger she had been in twice today. It took all his strength to fight the urge to carry her to his lair and keep her safe, and to the devil with the conventions. Miranda deserved more from those who cared for her than she had received in the past, and he would see she got it now even if it killed him.

'All those years ago?' Miranda awoke with the question on her lips and a hollow opening out in her heart.

He was gone; she might have known he would be she informed herself sharply, trying to pretend it was for the best. Yet as she tried to put the calm and sensible Miranda of the last few years back together, the wretched creature seemed remote as the Russian steppes.

'What did you say, Miss Miranda?' Leah asked drowsily, and gave a mighty yawn before stretching luxuriously and shaking a stray curl out of sleepy eyes.

'What time is it?' Miranda asked as she emerged from her reverie and tried to pretend she hadn't been dreaming of Kit.

'Long past time we were up, I expect, and I'm more than ready for my breakfast. Shall I send for a tray so you can eat it in bed for once?'

Since Miranda had no wish to meet the earl's acute gaze over ham and eggs this morning, she eagerly agreed, then regretted it when Leah subjected her to one of her homilies over them instead.

'So when are you going to marry his lordship, Miss Miranda? He's obviously in love with you, and if you wed him at least he can protect you and the rest of us can sleep of a night again.'

'Well…' Finding she could not think of anything sensible to say, Miranda floundered around for some nonsensical social reply and found even that had deserted her. 'That is…no, I mean... Oh, dear my tongue has tied itself in knots. You know I can't remarry.'

'You'll have to, Miss Miranda, you can't let Miss Celia ruin his life.'

'He could forfeit the money and not marry either of us,' Miranda heard herself suggest diffidently, and wondered where the wonderfully resolute creature she had thought herself had wandered off to. The very thought of becoming Christopher Alstone's wife made her knees go weak, but that didn't mean she was fool enough to accept him.

'You never reneged on a challenge in the old days.'

'That was then, and we should not suit,' Miranda insisted stubbornly.

Leah snorted so expressively there was no need to say what she thought of that lie. If things had been different, even Miranda thought she and Kit could have been happy, but unfortunately they were not.

'There are reasons why I can't marry him even you don't know, Leah.'

'Then tell him. I swear you can trust him, for he's that sort of man.'

Miranda felt such yearning, such a dizzying longing at the very idea of marrying Kit that she was very glad to be sitting down. 'No. How could I watch him being set at less than he is for having wed me?' Miranda burst out, goaded into telling the truth.

'You set too much store by the spiteful tongues of a few nasty-tempered tabbies, Miss Miranda. It's high time you stopped letting them rule your life.'

'Well I certainly refuse to be badgered into marrying a man who hasn't even asked me to, even to persuade you to leave me be.'

Leah sniffed loudly, but set about her business as gently as she could. Miranda's trunk had arrived at last and there was no need to wear one of the three muslins she had brought with her yet again. Leah chose a prettily figured round gown with a long sleeve that would accommodate the dressing on Miranda's arm and set herself to the serious business of outflanking Celia's maid once again.

Kit's mouth tightened as he watched Miranda come downstairs some time later with Leah determinedly at her side, despite her protests that she would be quite safe in broad daylight. Miranda saw him nod faintly in Leah's direction, and her answering smile as she obligingly took herself off. With allies like that, she hardly needed enemies, so somehow she must convince Leah that her plan to throw her at the new earl would not work.

'Why aren't you wearing a sling?' Kit demanded as he shut the library doors behind them.

She was so busy thinking it unfair of him to choose a battleground that reminded her so potently of last night that she forgot to protest such impropriety. Avoiding looking at the sofa where he had held her so securely that she must have gone to sleep in his arms, she confronted him over the desk he had made his own, the stack of ledgers and paperwork on it attesting to his many obligations.

'Because I don't care to ape the invalid,' she replied coolly.

'You prefer to risk permanent damage rather than spoil the line of your gown, I suppose? I had not thought you so vain.'

'I am not in the least bit vain,' she protested, before she even thought about the words that came so hastily out of her mouth and blushed.

Once upon a time she had spent hours on end planning her *toilettes* and scheming how to draw her beaux ever deeper into infatuation with her. Maybe Nevin's attraction for her had been that he refused to worship at her silly little feet, she thought now, and squirmed.

'Prove it then and wear this,' he replied smoothly and offered her the knotted silk square Leah had tried to persuade her to wear earlier.

'I seem to be surrounded by conspirators,' she muttered darkly as she slipped the offending material round her neck and defied him to come any closer while she fitted it round her aching arm.

She would not let him see what a relief it was to have it supported, or explain it had not been vanity that made her refuse it, but a desire not to remind herself and everyone else she had been shot at yesterday and attacked last night. She suppressed a shudder and tried to assume the air of calm composure that had stood her in such good stead of late years, only to find he could shatter it with ridiculous ease.

'No,' he told her softly, 'you are beset by well-wishers and should be glad of it. My staff seem to adore you for some strange reason.'

'Odd in them, is it not?' she asked shakily.

'Not in the least, they show remarkably good taste,' he assured her with a smile she couldn't read, and rang the bell before she could think of anything else to say.

'Tea for Miss Miranda,' he told Coppice when he appeared in reply, 'and I will take more coffee, if you please, along with anything more substantial you can charm out of Cook.'

'Certainly, my lord.' The butler bowed and left with a faint smile that was almost avuncular.

'Did you miss breakfast?' she asked, wondering

why he was hungry so soon after it, and thought she saw him shudder at her question.

'On the contrary, both Lady Clarissa and Mrs Grant joined me at the breakfast table this morning,' he admitted woodenly.

'Oh dear, it's hardly surprising you're hungry now, then,' she replied incautiously. Realising how rude that sounded, she corrected herself hastily, 'That is, I'm sure they were anxious to discover all they could about last night's uproar.'

'They had ample opportunity to do so at the time,' he said impatiently.

'Aunt Clarissa and Celia never appear once they have retired for the night. They would consider it most improper to be seen in their night rail.'

'Let's hope the house never burns down, then. I refuse to risk my life rescuing them because they are too refined to appear less than perfectly turned out for the occasion.'

'I dare say they would yield to necessity in that case,' she informed him solemnly, but an image of them, all offended dignity and mortified pride among the smoke and ashes, proved irresistible and she chuckled.

'I devoutly hope we never have to put them to the test,' he said with a smile that made her wonder if she had been weakened by yesterday's ordeal after all, for her fine resolutions were in danger of melting away.

Reminding herself of the realities, she stiffened her backbone to sit very correctly in her upright chair and contemplate her folded hands.

'I wish to…' she began just as Coppice entered with one stalwart footman carrying a groaning tray.

No question but his lordship was a firm favourite with Cook, and, as he thanked them and took a bite of toasted muffin with obvious enjoyment, Miranda could see at least one reason why. Cook loved to see people enjoy her food, so, after feeding an invalid and two finicky ladies for the past few years, she must be in her element with her new master.

'Excuse me, I was sharp set and quite forgot my manners.'

'There is nothing to forgive, my lord, and I breakfasted quite heartily so I should not be tempted to eat any more.'

'Why not?' he said with a frown of impatience for the convention that said gently bred females should only pick at their food. 'Good food is a gift, and you will hardly grow fat in one day. You have lost a deal of weight these last five years, my dear, and could do with eating a few more of Cook's delicious pastries rather than worrying about seeming greedy. I heartily dislike females who starve themselves to appear interesting—it seems an insult to those who lack the chance to refuse anything they are given.'

'I can quite see how it would,' she replied rather hollowly.

Noting his reference to her much plumper build of five years before with a sinking heart, she wondered if she really wanted to know the worst after all. While she considered one problem among a sea of them, she sipped her tea and gazed absently at a thrush hammering a snail on the flags in order to feed her nearby babies.

Miranda was glad last night's intruder had not destroyed the nest as he scrambled past the honeysuckle under her bedroom window. Somehow it seemed a hopeful sign. Even when she was gone from here, she wanted Wychwood to be a happy place, for her sisters' sake, she assured herself edgily. Kit Alstone was too big a man in every way to resent the fact that her sisters would inherit a large slice of what should have been his if he failed to carry out Grandfather's wishes.

Celia and her mother would lose more than mere money if Kit didn't marry her cousin, because the new earl would never tolerate not being master in his own house. Knowing them, she thought they would prefer to lose the money rather than their social position as the pre-eminent ladies in the area if he ordered them to leave. Kate and Izzie would be much happier here without Lady Clarissa and Celia criticising and carping all the time, of course, but would they be safe from their poisonous tongues when they one day joined the wider world? From a purely practical point of view it might have been better if Kit married Celia, but every instinct Miranda possessed screamed an emphatic negative.

Now Kit had finished the muffins and drunk his coffee, and was sitting back in his chair watching her with a mix of emotions in his dark eyes. She had been right last night and she could read some of them, but she was too preoccupied with a cowardly urge to turn and run back upstairs and declare herself too fragile for this interview to take advantage of it. Running would just put it off, she told herself, and next time would be worse when she had to face his steady scrutiny knowing she had retreated from it before.

Just as well to get the truth out in the open and finally cross herself off Grandfather's race card. In a week she could go back to Snowdonia and help Lady Rhys with her good causes instead of being an additional charge on her. Odd how hollow that scheme sounded as she met Kit's level gaze and felt her heart lurch with need to tell him happy little lies instead of the truth. He looked born to sit there, easy and assured of his natural dominance. Born to privilege instead of misery, he would still have possessed that bone-deep confidence in his own ability, and an equally ingrained truth to himself and those he loved.

He was a good man and she was not his equal. There could be nothing between them, and yet the possibility ran strong and deep below the serene surface of this elegant room and their polite rituals among the teacups. Possibilities she had to shatter and walk away from, if she wanted him to keep his self-respect untouched by her sins and she fervently did.

'Marry me,' he urged abruptly, his smile both a promise and a demand.

'Certainly not,' she snapped back, shaken by how very much she wanted to reach out her hand and lay it in the one he was holding out to her, establishing a connection between them that she instinctively knew he would never break.

She could do it; take what he offered and turn her back on her own honour. The pull of it was dark and potent under her abrupt refusal, and part of her badly wanted him to ignore it and push at her no.

'You are so poor at the art of a gentle refusal, I could almost think you unpractised in it,' he observed as if he was remarking on the sayings and doings of a chance-met acquaintance, not the woman he had just asked to marry him, however little choice he had of Alstone brides.

'On the contrary, I am so experienced in the way of it that I know very well a polite "no, thank you" will get me nowhere. Gentlemen are importunate when they have convinced themselves that they crave a certain possession, and you, my lord, are sorely in need of a wife.'

'Gentlemen may be so, but I do not see women as possessions,' he disagreed shortly.

'I apologise, then; I fear I have insulted your pride.'

'No, you may have tried to, but I'm not so easily put off. Remember my origins and stop fending me off with genteel platitudes, Miranda.'

'I refused you, my lord, and I meant it. I can see nothing equivocal in my words,' she forced herself to say calmly.

'Nor can I, but I still intend to have the truth out in the open between us, refuse as you might to believe that we were made for each other,' he replied as if they were discussing the weather and she felt a contrary urge to slap him. 'Have you noticed that Coppice had the effrontery to shut the door behind him, by the way? I have one more well-wisher in my campaign to win you for my bride than I thought and, as he is invariably right, I shall take comfort in his support.'

'You have too many supporters already,' she muttered unwarily and he looked a question at her. 'You seem to me to be surrounded with them,' she explained.

'How fortunate for me. You are not convinced by such a flattering show of solidarity?'

'No, I'm not. It's a ridiculous idea.'

'If I were a sensitive man, I might be hurt by such a brusque dismissal of my pretensions,' he replied smoothly.

'Are you telling me that you're not such a man?' she challenged right back.

'I'm telling you that I intend to marry you, Miranda. You were born to be my countess and I won't let you refuse me for the sake of misplaced pride. For one thing, you would graciously cover my own inadequacies as an earl,' he added ruefully.

'What nonsense, I was born a fool and grew into the role,' she insisted brusquely, because she might cry if she softened even slightly.

'Rubbish.'

'It's true, and it's not at all polite to argue with a lady.'

'There you are, you see? How am I to go on without you to put my deplorable manners right?' he asked with apparent innocence. 'And it's not kind to palm me off with social chit-chat and lame excuses, my dear. Are you in love with someone else?'

'No, of course I'm not,' she spluttered unwarily, then instantly regretted letting such an ideal opportunity to escape this painful scene pass.

He sat back and watched her with sleepy satisfaction in his eyes and, despite a strong urge to throw something at him, a furtive shiver ran through her disobedient body. He wanted her; it was there in his half-closed gaze and sensually curved mouth. She wanted him right back and he knew it just as surely. Well, he couldn't have her, and they would both be doomed to disappointment if she was fool enough to throw herself at him.

'Love is an illusion,' she assured him earnestly, devoutly hoping it might turn out to be so. She had no desire to find herself in love with the devastatingly handsome wretch in addition to longing for his sensuous kisses and the gentled power in his bone-melting caresses.

'Since you believe so, there is nothing to stand in the way of our contracting a marriage of convenience,' he said in such a reasonable tone that she knew she had just tripped on her own defences.

'Except common sense, and the fact that you disliked me on sight,' she snapped back, infuriated to find herself growing more agitated as he became calmer and more apparently reasonable.

Instead of making him suitably furious in return, she saw with a kick in her silly heartbeat that her words had made his eyelids grow heavier and even the certainty in his smile became seductive.

'Now there you are very much mistaken, Mrs Braxton,' he assured her, and there was no chance of error in reading his response to her this time. Desire and determination were twin compulsions in eyes that were velvet soft and yet utterly resolute all at the same time. 'I liked you all too well.'

'Then you hid it admirably,' she told him, trying hard to sound sure of herself and her self-control, as a familiar dread stalked her every breath.

Chapter Thirteen

Would she never be rid of it? This insidious sense that something fevered and impossible was in fact real, and all too possible? It had stalked her since that terrible time when Nevin had caught her trying to run again, and drugged her to keep her passive to his sadistic commands. The reality of it had been bad enough, without her mind refusing to make some sense of the tangled twists of dread and fantasy that had knotted themselves together in her poor head at the time.

'Tell me,' she said at last, stiffening her spine to meet whatever secrets he knew about her with composure.

'Tell you what?' he asked and his eyes were sharper, more defended somehow.

'The truth,' she insisted bravely. 'You said something last night about meeting me before. Tell me about it now, please, for I don't recall all that happened at a certain time in my life. It seems unfair of you to withhold illumination from me, however painful it might prove to be.'

Her chin raised defiantly, Miranda dared Kit to condemn her for whatever she had done. All she needed was just enough dignity to get her upstairs before her pride gave out and she disgraced herself with tears and pleas for understanding. From somewhere she found enough to remain stiff-backed and steady as she watched him search for the right words.

'Five years ago I saw a fallen goddess across a crowded room,' he told her at last, in a voice he might have used to pass the time of day with an acquaintance.

Miranda began to shake, despite his smooth tone and shuttered gaze and his strong fingers flexed as if to reach toward hers, before he stilled them again and carried calmly on as if he was trying to make the telling as gentle on her as he could.

'She was a being of such beauty and corrupted innocence that I would have sold my soul to the devil in order to possess her, even for one night in her arms. I didn't know then that Olympians can't be possessed without their consent, but she has haunted me ever since she evaded me.'

Her hand went to her shocked mouth and numbly explored the curves of lips that felt as if they had felt the touch and sureness of his mouth against hers just as she had in her dreams all these years. Then the fact of him now, separated from her by a few feet of mirror-polished mahogany instead of a hundred frantic dreams, finally embedded itself in her reeling brain.

'You were real?' she whispered at last, wondering that she still had the power of speech after such an extreme shift in the running of her world.

'As genuine then as I am now,' he acknowledged with a wry smile, both caution and hot memory in his gaze.

'I thought I imagined you to…to…' She heard her own voice tail off and searched for words to explain her own confusion and compulsion at the time. 'To lighten the darkness, I suppose,' she finished and felt an ignoble leap of her pulses as her words caused a flash of something hot to enter his intent expression.

'You were tragically alone,' he prompted gently and she gaped at him, hungry for understanding and yet defensive, in case it opened her to the tears begging to fall and weaken her in her own eyes as well as his. 'At least you were until your stalwart maid tore you away from such an ungallant rescuer,' he amended with the same devilish grin she remembered from that night.

'I made a stupid mistake, my lord. I wouldn't listen to any of the people who truly cared about me and tried so hard to open my silly eyes,' she told him with a determined steadiness that, if she did but know it, made Kit's very gut wrench with pity, and searing fury nearly overmaster him against her sewer-rat of a husband. 'If I was alone I brought it on myself, I was such a idiot,' she finished in a flat voice that accepted just how deluded she had been, and how shockingly she had woken up to that folly once it was too late.

'You were seventeen years old, sheltered and cosseted and knocked off balance by your brother's illness and your parents' deaths. Easy prey indeed for such a charlatan as Braxton, and if he isn't rotting in hell for taking advantage of you, then there is no divine justice.'

'Can you see Leah ever being taken in by such a straw man?' she asked him fiercely. 'No, of course you can't. She saw through him the instant he stepped down from the coach at Jack's side; outwardly so concerned for his charge and inwardly plotting how to turn his temporary inclusion in a nobleman's household to his own advantage.'

'Ah, but I doubt he wasted much of his charm on her when he already had you in his sights,' he said in an attempt to mitigate her self-condemnation.

'Maybe not,' she conceded.

'Certainly not; indeed, I hardly noted what a pretty girl your maid is myself once I had set eyes on you, Venus.'

'Please don't joke about it,' she begged him. Although he wouldn't condemn her sins, she knew there was worse to come.

'I have to,' he told her, letting a hint of the passionate emotions he was rigidly controlling show in his eyes at last, 'it's that or rage at a dead man I wish I could follow into hell and damn more than he already is.'

'Lucky you cannot then, Nevin did enough damage while he was alive without adding your immortal soul to the list.'

'Yet I am on that list,' he insisted, stubbornly fighting every attempt she made to exclude him from the dark past. 'That animal made me see you through his own rotten and distorted eyes that night. Although I longed for you, I hated you for turning me into a brute beast, Miranda. So don't try to turn me into some princely rescuer out of a fairy tale, I was very much less the night I first met you, and several times since.'

'You still rescued me and I fall well short of the ideal myself. A very poor heroine I was that night if my memory is at all to be trusted, standing there like a wanton and silently begging for your dishonourable attentions. It seems to me now that must be what I did if you really were there after all.'

'Oh, I really was and you were truly glorious,' he argued a little unsteadily, as if he were back in that squalid tavern setting eyes on a wonder, 'a goddess in eclipse, or partial eclipse at least.'

Sometime over the last few minutes they had both stood up and now she made herself stay on her feet, blushing furiously and staring at the floor as the truth of that night finally separated itself from the haze of laudanum and shame that had blurred it ever since. Finally she raised her eyes to his and admitted what she saw as the truth.

'I was shameless,' she whispered, and wished pride would let her flee so she could hide from his steady gaze.

'You were beautiful, and I haven't properly got you out of my head in five long years. If not for your scum of a husband, I would have seen you for the jewel you are and carried you off forthwith. The question is, would you have come with me willingly when you were in your right senses again, Miranda?'

'I might well have done, but it would have been wrong.'

'How so?'

At last she let her eyes drop and even did her best to avoid his too-perceptive gaze this time, for how could she tell him the truth?

'I was married,' she procrastinated, still hoping against hope she could avoid telling her last, shaming truth.

'To a man who beat and drugged you before trying to sell you to the highest bidder? The law that binds a wife to such a man is more of an ass than even I thought it,' he condemned harshly.

'Yet still it does.'

'I would have cared for you, looked after you and kept him away. Anything to have you in my bed and my heart, Miranda, then and now.'

It was too much of a declaration for her, too much altogether, and she flinched from the idea of inflicting pain on him, but she still had to do it.

'And you would have shamed yourself in doing so,' she said quietly.

'Never! How can you call what is between us shameful?'

Hearing the rawness in his beloved voice, the pain of believing her less divine and more human than he had thought, she felt as if anything that hurt him would pierce her too. Even so, nothing less than the full truth would deflect him now, and that would hurt them both unbearably.

'Easily—you are an honourable man, for that is what you were then and are now. I am not a fit companion for such a man.'

'Rubbish, it is I who am something made out of nothing. Do you think my path to riches was paved with saintly deeds and quixotic good will toward my fellow men, Miranda? If so, you will be bitterly disappointed when you find out who, and what, I really am.'

'I am quite sure that you trampled on orphans and ground poor widows into the dust on your path to glory, my lord,' she said with a wobbly smile that told him she believed the exact opposite.

'Not quite, but fighting to get out of the pit so many fall into, I trod on a few of their faces to reach the light,' he admitted as if he expected her to reel back from him in horror.

'I have occasionally been to the East End of London with my godmama, you know?' she replied more steadily. 'I know what abject poverty can do to people, and also what the people there sometimes do for one another when they have nothing themselves. You and your sisters must have had it harder than most, being outsiders, being different.'

'We tried very hard to be the same, but you're right, we were different. They thought we believed ourselves better, although my mother often had to pawn everything she could lay her hands on so we could eat.'

'Pray stop trying to convince me you robbed graves and sold children, my lord, for I won't believe you if we stand here arguing until next Christmas.'

'It wasn't quite that bad,' he conceded, 'but my sisters and I have come a long way since then; indeed, there was a very long way to come.'

'Then all credit to you for not sitting and waiting for someone like my godmama to come along. You would have had a long wait as she only began in earnest when her husband died.'

'But it would have been worth it if you came with her,' he told her softly. 'So you'll just have to marry me, d'you see, Miranda? If only to make up for being too young to rescue me from squalor and my devil of a father.'

The humour in his gaze, the conviction in his words, despite her efforts to dissuade him from thinking her better than she was, severely weakened her resolve. She felt herself wavering, and that would never do.

'Celia and I are not the only marriageable women in the area,' she told him earnestly, even as she knew her heart might break if he wed one of them.

Kit was tempted to shake her for thinking any of them even existed by her side. How could she stand there, indigo eyes serious as she cast about the neighbourhood to find him a suitable wife? The only woman he had the least intention of marrying was here, and more temptation than a man should rightly be subject to. It took all his will-power to listen to such arrant rubbish as if he was perfectly civilised, and he told himself severely that she needed time and a more leisurely courtship. With Braxton all she had got was lies that should have stopped his black heart in mid-beat, and with him he wanted everything to be different. Yet time was the last thing he could give her.

Married to him, she could be properly protected night and day, and if the idea was very much to his taste, his rampant and more-or-less continual need to make her his wife in every sense of the word was as nothing beside her safety. The appalling thought that he should offer her a white marriage had occurred to him fleetingly, only to be rejected with vehement loathing. Anyway, such gallant notions would become nonsense as soon as he was shut up in a room alone with her and he made a liar of himself.

His Miranda was an honest woman, and he should have found a way to follow her and win her five long years ago, irrespective of the worm she was married to. Braxton had done nothing to deserve her loyalty and look what a life of it she had lived since in his unappealing shadow, relentlessly pursued by spiteful gossip and innuendo. When the rogue died they could have married and by now would have begun the brood of brats he suddenly discovered he wanted very badly, just so long as she was their mother and his gallant wife.

Well, he might have been fool enough to waste all those years, he decided, but he refused to throw away any more. It had taken far too long for him to admit to his fate, but now he sensed he was within an ace of finally attaining it. His body clenched in familiar, driven craving for her and her alone, but this time he used it to sharpen his determination to tread carefully with her, instead of dismissing her ridiculous notion she wasn't good enough for him with the impatience it deserved.

'A young lady of impeccable breeding and spotless reputation would not do for me at all,' he told her with apparent frankness.

'Why not? You're as good as any man who might ask them, and a great deal better than most,' she fired up in his defence, and coming very close to being kissed until she agreed to anything he asked of her if she did but know it.

'I'm touched by your confidence.'

'That didn't come out quite as I meant it to,' she admitted.

'All the same, I will not trouble the local belles, it wouldn't be fair to raise their hopes of a peeress's coronet when I fully intend to marry you, Miranda. No bread-and-butter miss would do for a man who has once settled on a goddess to fulfil his every fantasy.'

She blushed furiously, and once again he had to exert all his will-power to keep him sitting across from her, looking to a casual observer as if they were having a reasonable discussion about matters that didn't greatly concern them.

'I'm certainly not a goddess and I seem to recall a good many who were did not behave particularly well, and I still won't marry you,' she said.

'And I have no intention of ruining any of those well-brought-up and polite young ladies' happiness by insisting one of them wed me, and even less of spoiling my own by asking Mrs Grant to be miserable with me for the rest of our natural lives. Given the conditions of your grandfather's will, I think you *will* marry me, Miranda, if only to see that I get my company back and come fully into my own.'

She shot him a dubious look that put her in great danger of being very thoroughly compromised. Kit fought the temptation to set about such a delightful plan immediately and waited politely for the next piece of nonsense to fall from her otherwise delightful lips.

'I truly can't marry you,' she informed him stiffly and stood up. 'I am deeply sorry that you will lose complete control of your company by my refusal if you won't reconsider and wed Celia, but I cannot accept your proposal. I'm very sorry, your lordship.'

She sounded so sincere that Kit's heart jarred as he momentarily faced failure. No, he had not permitted the idea to enter his head with any seriousness since the day he decided he would not endure another blow or curse from his drunkard of a father when he was all of eight years old. Miranda meant far too much to him to give her up so easily. He didn't love her, of course, but she filled some dark corner of his soul with light and need. He couldn't love Miranda with the easy passion of her own kind, born of security and privilege and the knowledge that, yes, they really were rather a good catch and not too obnoxious with it.

But he needed her. Her compassion would make up for the hard place inside him where he had shut the little boy who might have been too open and vulnerable if he had let himself feel. Then he recalled her spitting fire at him the day she came here and hid a smile—she was no perfect, lifeless débutante, secretly intent on catching herself the finest husband on the market at whatever cost to either of them. She was also the one woman he could contemplate making love to for the rest of his life with a leap of joy in his heart that told him he would never feel the least desire to stray.

'Only consider how disappointed Coppice will be,' he teased, then flinched as he saw something close to agony flash into her deeply blue eyes.

'I dare say he will forgive me,' she quipped with apparent lightness.

'He might, but I never will,' he said, refusing to play her game any longer, however valiant it looked from where he stood, burning for her body and mind. 'I need you, Miranda,' he went on truthfully. 'At the very least you know this place inside and out, and could teach me to manage it properly for the benefit of all those who now depend on me.'

'You do so already, Cousin. The estate workers and servants are very ready to love you, especially when you are providing them with new roofs on their cottages and schools for their children.'

'Basic human needs,' he assured her gruffly and Miranda was tempted to damn them both and marry him after all.

He was so resistant to praise she sensed the damage his father had inflicted during his woeful boyhood went deeper than he would ever admit; yet his first consideration on inheriting had been the welfare of others. What a fine husband he would make some lucky creature, she thought wistfully, but unfortunately that woman could not be her.

'Needs that are not met on too many estates,' she insisted in an attempt to divert him from such a painful subject, 'to the shame of many of their owners, if they only would sober up long enough to feel it.'

'I'm no saint, so don't try and paint me as one, and I'm afraid I can't offer up false shame for my sins.'

'I wouldn't have you do so,' she told him with a smile that threatened to wobble precariously. 'If I wed any man it would be you, my lord, and I do thank you for the honour, even though I can't accept it.'

'I may only be a rough businessman, but I will not treat you as a chattel like Braxton did, for all he claimed to be a gentleman. As my wife you will hold a secure position in the world as well as being respected and cherished, and wanted, Miranda. Very much wanted.'

She found herself confronting him, deep-blue eyes to fathomless brown, despite her determination to make a dignified exit on some gracious refusal he would take as final. His long-fingered hands reached toward her and her heart leapt and sang in response to the very idea of being in his arms again, then faltered and sank as stern reality bit harshly into such wonderful daydreams.

'I must go now, my lord, we have been alone too long,' she told him as formally as she could manage when her heart felt as if it might break at any moment.

'That you must not,' he said, refusing to play the game of meekly rejected suitor and let her escape with the lie between them that it didn't much matter.

'Please?' She hated to beg any man after humiliating herself in front of Nevin on one occasion she strove hard to forget.

If begging was what it took to get her out of this room without ripping her heart out and baring it to his cool scrutiny, then she would do it without a pause. Anything rather than finally say the words that would have him avoiding her as assiduously as she ought to be avoiding him.

'No, you are my equal and ideally suited to be my wife. Marry me, Miranda,' he insisted and she could read need in his tense mouth, desire in his intense gaze and something else that threatened to take her breath away.

'I can't, please don't make me tell you why.'

'I must, for we need each other, Miranda. Nothing short of bigamy should stop us marrying each other.'

A hollow laugh escaped her as the irony of him hitting upon such a disbarment sank in. 'That would work; in fact, it would do very well for me, my lord,' she said very deliberately, but it took all her courage to face him with the truth in her eyes.

His own suddenly looked flat, as if he had received a great blow and did not quite know how to defend himself. 'You're already married? I thought that devil's spawn was dead.'

'He is.'

'Then you must have secretly wed another!'

Anger flashed into his eyes and how she hoped it was because she was thwarting his plans, and not because he felt the same pain that was threatening to fell her. Recklessly she decided to tell him the whole truth. It seemed unlikely that anything else would stop him, and he deserved that much from her anyway.

'No, but he did,' she whispered. 'I *am* a Jezebel, you see, my lord. The gossips were more right than they ever knew when they called me so.'

'Your marriage was invalid? He cheated you even of that?' he demanded, fury plain in his eyes at her latest revelation, but it must have killed any other passion he felt for her.

'I cannot see how much more plainly you wish to hear it. Nevin Braxton was already married when he wed me,' she admitted painfully. 'The name I bear is not mine, but I am such a coward that I kept it to hide what I am from the world. Nevin was a young girl's fantasy, and later her nightmare. I don't exist, you see, my lord, and you should have attended more closely to the exact wording of my grandfather's will. If you remember, he called me Miranda Alstone *known* as Braxton, in order to make sure that my inheritance would be legal.'

'Then he knew?' he asked incredulously.

'Blackmail was Nevin's stock in trade,' she confirmed.

'In his place I would have killed the bastard and roasted his black heart over a bonfire,' he averred furiously, and she believed him.

'Imagine Grandpapa's fury and frustration when he was not strong enough to do so, the blow to his pride.'

'And your humiliation, what of that?' he protested her order of pain and she couldn't let him see how his doing so warmed her cold heart. 'Braxton deserved to die by inches for what he did to you,' Kit went on, 'and he would have done if I had only known.'

'I don't think he ever intended to wed me,' she excused the inexcusable for some odd reason. 'The threat to run off with the daughter of the house usually netted him a tidy sum, which he took as his right, needless to say, and then changed his name and moved to another part of the country. Idiots such as myself are never keen to publish our folly, you see. Yet I insisted that we elope to Gretna, and would not listen to his idea that we should lie low until I was so compromised we would be allowed to marry. So we were wed over the anvil, and that could not be written off as some silly schoolgirl infatuation.'

'Married, yet not married, if what you say is true?'

'Why would I lie about such things?' she asked indignantly. 'You see, now you believe me every bit as bad as I am painted, and that's bright scarlet without a doubt.'

'You wrong both me and yourself,' he assured her gruffly and this time she was drawn inexorably into his strong arms, as if their coming together was inevitable as a force of nature and he intended to give her no chance to resist it. 'You're no less to me, but far, far more, you little fool,' he chided as he held her close, just as if it was what they had been created for.

'Don't pity me, Kit,' she murmured, holding his gaze when she would far rather have nestled into his strong arms and pretended the world and all the painful realities it contained had gone away.

'I should never be so unwise,' he assured her softly, and lifted a slightly unsteady hand to soothe back one of her errant curls.

Chapter Fourteen

Miranda took strength from his nearness, just as she had last night, but this time she knew more was offered and accepted than mere comfort. He had not reeled away in horror, or looked at her with withering contempt, but he would not ask her to marry him again. If the truth ever came out, her shame would drag them both down and she could never permit that to happen.

She let herself relax into his powerful embrace and savoured this never-to-be forgotten reality, the very precious now. Soon he would have to let her go. He would offer her words of empty comfort and try to absolve her of blame before he walked away, for he was a good man, whatever he tried to pretend to the contrary. But he would still let her go, and probably be mighty relieved when she went as well, even if he pretended otherwise to soothe her pride.

At least this time she would have memories to eclipse the ones that had been stillborn that first night, when she had thought him the creation of the opium Nevin had poured down her, struggle as she might. He was real, and an irrepressible remnant of the headlong girl she had once been exulted in that reality. Her fantasy lover; her raffish devil-may-care pirate with his sensual, knowing gaze so deep with possibilities that a woman could lose herself in it was here, no fantasy, but wonderful reality.

Even when she had thought him the product of her imagination, he had eclipsed all other men and forced her to realise what a fool she had been to fall for Nevin's surface charm and golden beauty. Yet Kit was rich by his own efforts, and Earl of Carnwood by birth. She knew how to pick a hero after all, she decided with bitter humour, as she contemplated the dull future she must now endure without him.

'So when shall we be wed?' he said as if all she had done was try his patience a little with a silly story.

'Are you mad? Of course I won't marry you.'

'Why not?' He sounded only mildly interested, and she tried to move out of his embrace so she could stare up at him in puzzled wonderment from a suitable distance, but the stubborn idiot wouldn't let her go.

'I should have thought that was perfectly obvious,' she told him snippily, needing to assure herself she was not moving through some sort of dream world where the normal laws of nature did not apply.

'Not to me.'

'Then it should be,' she informed him acerbically, feeling faintly aggrieved that he was forcing her to spell out what they both knew. 'I am a fallen woman. No self-respecting gentleman would marry such a one as I became the day I ran off with my sick brother's tutor.'

'Ah, but I never said I was respectable, now did I?' he told her reasonably, as if that disclaimer changed everything and made the world outside this room unimportant.

'You are an earl and a gentleman, and I have no intention of causing you to be considered anything less than you are. I have my pride after all.'

'Yet you refuse to allow me any?'

Now he sounded altogether less reasonable, and she saw with something close to despair that his mouth had set in a stubborn line and his dark eyes were brilliant with purpose.

She could not let him make her into a crusade he insisted on winning. A part of her might desperately long for the protection he was offering so rashly; she even conceded to herself that the temptation of no longer standing alone against the world was nigh irresistible, but it would not overwhelm her. Could not, she decided regretfully, and firmed her own mouth as she fought the urge to yield him anything he wanted, whatever the cost. It wasn't love that made him ask again, it was stubbornness and a hatred of being bested.

'Yes, for it's misplaced if it urges you to do this,' she told him, wishing he would let her go.

The feel of his warmth against her chilled body was making her weak and now of all times she had to be strong.

'Do you think I have anything less than respect for you, Miranda? You face the world with dignity and honour, and refuse to allow the petty-minded bullies who spread lies about you to bring you down. How could I have anything other than pride in what you are, what you have made of yourself? I cannot do other than honour you, even if your stubbornness makes me want to carry you off to my lair and keep you there until you see reason.'

'You didn't think so when you kissed me the day I arrived.'

'You must make allowances for five years of

bitter frustration poisoning my tongue,' he informed her gruffly.

Temptation and desire shot through her; a tangled thread she tried desperately to ignore as it tightened and gnawed at her almost like pain, and, oh, it was forbidden! He sounded so driven, so reluctantly sincere that she believed him, longed for him, and struggled even harder to be free of him.

'I won't marry you,' she insisted.

She felt torn between the idea that she was saying goodbye to all that mattered in life, and a building frustration of her own that he would not concede she was right, before she broke and took whatever she could have. A night in his arms sounded like heaven just now, but the next day she would have to walk away and that would be agony. Better not to know such heady delights than have to live without them for the rest of her life.

'Nothing stands between us but your stubbornness and fear of scandal. There is no reason we should not wed,' he told her reasonably.

'Well, there is for me,' she countered and as she heard her own argument it sounded childish, as if she might stick her tongue out at any moment like a defiant schoolboy.

'Then you are not the woman I thought you.'

'No,' she insisted furiously, 'I'm not! I'm not the woman anyone thinks me, except the few who laugh up their sleeve every time I make some small bid for respectability. I am an unmarried woman who has lived with a man as his wife; don't you see that puts me beyond the pale in every way?'

'No, and nobody has called me small for a very long time. It's you who insist I'm respectable, which I never will be, so you're caught by your own argument this time, madam.'

'No!' she very nearly shouted at him. 'I'm not, nor do I intend to be. I won't marry you and spend every day waiting for the truth to come out. I refuse to subject either of us to such public humiliation.'

'Very well, I'll just have to see to it you're unmasked from the off.'

'But you can't do that,' she faltered.

The sheer horror of even contemplating what such a revelation would do to her sent her hands to cover her cheeks, in dread of facing the outraged stares of society and the prospect of watching him grow furious on her behalf every time her disgrace was slyly referred to.

'You care about what everyone thinks of you

that deeply?' he asked with apparently genuine in-credulity.

'Of course I do, how could I not?'

'Sticks and stones,' he remarked matter of factly and Miranda finally realised something of what life must have been like for him growing up with Bevis Alstone for a father. Did that give her the right to subject this strong man to derision for marrying a woman his peers would only consider taking as a mistress?

'They would break my bones, though,' she admitted sadly, thinking every blow he took on her behalf would hurt unbearably. 'You wouldn't let the insults pass you by. Whatever you think now, you would fight duels with some and find yourself black-balled by the rest.'

'Good, for a damned nuisance it all is. I have far too much to do to dress myself up like a peacock and caper the night away at Almack's or Carlton House. So don't lump me in with the idiots you grew up with, my dear. I would give this title up tomorrow if I could, aye, and this old barn with it, if it wasn't for the fact that you obviously love it.'

'A nuisance?' she asked hollowly, every idea she had been raised with suddenly under attack.

'Yes, all this protocol and expectation gets confoundedly in the way of real life. My neighbours consider me obliged to entertain them, my tenants suffer the delusion I know what I'm doing and then there's the entire Alstone tribe. They once regarded me as a liability, but now I am head of the family they are intent on becoming my pensioners or for ever handing out unwelcome advice about how I should run my life at every turn.

'I have spent most of my existence being disapproved of and sniffed at by so-called good society, my lovely, and would heartily welcome a return to that happy state. It's probably even your duty to rescue me from such dreary respectability,' he told her with a smile that made her forget everything but the fact that she desperately wanted him to be quiet and kiss her.

'Your sisters could not agree with you,' she objected half-heartedly.

'They grew up on the same streets as I did, and their husbands are proud of them, probably more so than if they had lived exemplary lives in the nurseries upstairs, if the truth be known. Don't think to find support from that quarter, my dear. They will love you for taming my wild ways, let alone civilising me and showing me how this new life I seem fated to live should go.'

'I have told you before that I am not your dear,'

she informed him absently, and the odd notion that he might need her was very appealing.

'You know nothing of such things, my sweet idiot,' he replied softly and she couldn't even summon a spark of temper in response as he lowered his head and kissed her at long last.

He was quite right, she discovered dazedly, not even his previous kisses had prepared her for this. Unable to tell him so, she uttered a soft moan and fell headlong into pleasure and intimacy with a breathtaking sense that she was about to walk off a precipice and find out whether or not she could fly. So far it felt wonderful, she decided, as he pulled her closer into his already overwhelming embrace. She struggled rather feebly for enough room to watch him with whatever it was she felt for him naked in her eyes. He loosened his hold just enough for her to remove her hands from between their eager bodies at last and put them to good use.

'Know this at least,' he murmured, and fitted her even more emphatically to his mighty form, hard muscle smoothing and gentling against slender curves as his wondering, knowing hands slid up her back and she felt every whisper of movement, every inch of herself, cry out to him and receive the answer she wanted.

'I do,' she gasped in appreciation, wound ever

tighter into the coils of loving and wanting him that bound her to him.

Loving? She spared a half-horrified mental protest at that thought. She let out a small moan as his mouth again found hers, as if only by learning every soft curve and whisper of it could he begin to satisfy himself that she was his. She rose on tiptoe and insinuated herself even closer to his tightly muscled torso as her legs wobbled and she leaned into him for rather more than support.

'Not here and not now, Venus,' he chided with a laugh that ended in a moan as she refused to relinquish the sensual world they had made between them and arched across the space he thought to create between them.

'Tonight,' she invited wantonly between lips that felt gloriously imprinted with his taste and touch, the very breath that rasped between his own wondrous mouth taken down into her, becoming part of her.

'Not unless you promise to make an honest earl out of me afterwards,' he joked a little unsteadily.

She leant back against the arc of his strong arms to look up at him and saw very serious intent in his velvet-dark eyes, and a potent mix of sensuality and stony determination that she discovered to her annoyance only made her love him more.

'I told you why I can never do that,' she protested, familiar loneliness creeping back, even as they stood only inches apart and took stock of each other.

'But I fully intend to make you change your mind.'

'Nobody can change the fact that I'm disgraced. I refuse to let you be mired with my shame and folly.'

'You're no such thing,' he insisted impatiently.

Now his dark brows were all but a line, and his beloved face a mask of resolute purpose as he stared down at her as if looking for the weak spot in her armour that would give him an opening to defeat her. In business he must be formidable and no wonder he had gained a fortune, as well as the respect of his fellow businessmen and the finicky *ton*.

'Your refusal to acknowledge the truth doesn't make it less true.'

'Stubborn, pig-headed woman,' he chided, 'you always have to be right, don't you? Well, in this case you couldn't be more wrong, and I don't care how long it takes to convince you of it. Somehow I'll do it in the end if I have to walk to Snowdonia and camp out on your doorstep when I get there until you concede I mean what I say.'

'You won't you know,' she informed him with a distinct sniff and a fierce frown of her own.

'Want to lay me odds?' he asked provocatively, a rather predatory gleam breaking through the storm in his dark eyes.

'Ladies don't wager,' she said primly.

His eyebrows rose at that and he held her at arm's length then, as if examining a rare curiosity. 'What a whopper,' he teased, 'even ignorant merchants like me know perfectly well that some of them wager a great deal too often. What will you risk against my dead certainty, my dear one? A kiss, or a favour perhaps? Or maybe that precious honour you claim not to have?'

'You would take my honour in return for being acknowledged to be supremely and unmistakably right?' she asked indignantly.

'Only so that I can give it back to you,' he told her softly, and the wicked smile in his dark eyes should have warned her of his nefarious purpose, as he snapped her back into his arms and kissed her breathless.

This time it was a deliberate assault on her reeling senses, not some gentle, almost reverent wooing of a precious lover. Miranda felt the blood sing in her veins and had never felt more alive in her life. She met his insistent mouth with fiery hunger, all the possibilities of loving and letting him love freed as she found a new force of nature.

Heat turned her limbs to an unsteady means of getting closer to such delight.

She clung shamelessly closer, gave him back heat for heat and welcomed the flash of stubbornness in his stormy gaze, as he kept his eyes on her all the time their lips hungrily moved in a dance as old as Adam and Eve. In that moment all the possibilities between them were emphatic and acknowledged. With him everything would be right, where between Nevin and herself it had been so wrong.

Dismissing Nevin to outer darkness where he belonged, she smiled against her lover's mouth, for he would be her lover, whatever he believed to the contrary. With heat and sweetness like this between them there could be no other outcome. Now his wicked hands were playing over her until her very skin seemed charged with lightning wherever they lingered, and she felt her breasts growing heavy and shifted her stance so one of his strong legs thrust between hers and the truth of his rampant arousal was explicit.

Boldly she moved closer, pressing her aching breasts against his powerful chest. She felt breath heave into his lungs and deliciously accentuate the sensation of soft curves brushing tense muscles over strong bone. His heart stuttered, then raced, and she felt like the goddess he had named her. She could not doubt he wanted her very badly as his strong, long-fingered hand trembled ever so slightly before it cupped the weight of her breast in awed appreciation.

'Please?' she gasped.

Miranda let her head sink back in sensual satisfaction to watch him move his strong hands from their magnet just long enough to lift her by the soft cheeks of her bottom on to his broad desk. He impatiently pulled aside the soft muslin of her gown to suckle on a proud amber nipple as she begged him to and hot pleasure shot to the very core of her.

The small part of her mind still working told her it was just as well he had sat her here like the wanton she was, for she could not have stood on her own two feet if all the secrets of the gods had been on offer at that moment. Never had she even guessed a man could offer a woman such frenzied, melting delight. So much about the act of love that had been closed to her opened like an opulent June flower, and beckoned her to drown in the colour and scent and velvet feel of it.

She moaned her pleasure as his sensitive mouth whispered against her sensitised skin, teasing and tormenting her in a place that had until now been something of a mystery to her. He was releasing so much of her that had been captive to suspicion and even downright fear, and in his arms, as they opened untold depths to each other, she gloried in it. Then his sorcerer's hand loosed the muslin from her other breast and joined in the feast as she let out a long groan of extreme satisfaction.

He raised his mouth for long enough to kiss a trail to her other, neglected nipple, just as his hands deserted it to smooth over her slender thighs and found them as malleable to his touch as the rest of her. She felt him part her legs and impatiently push up the soft muslin out of his way, and only longed to have him sate the need that demanded and at the same time pleaded for him, and all he was, at the very core of her. Involuntarily her legs wrapped about him and she felt her world shift to encompass such incredible intimacy, and sensed the infinite promise of what was surely now inevitable.

His breath warmed the sensitised skin, damp and cooling in the air now his mouth was poised to leave her breasts and mesh with her shamelessly pouting lips again. She discovered that his hands were callused from working with his precious thoroughbreds, and all the more arousing for it, as they swept up the exposed length of her

creamy thighs. Again she gasped her infinite satisfaction with such a scandalous state of affairs,
and his mouth took hers with promise and fire
and demand all mixed up with tenderness and
need. He wouldn't be able to stop now, she
decided with extreme satisfaction, she would have
her wonderland for however short a time, and then
afterwards he could still find an impeccable
society virgin to become his countess.

Almost as if he could read her mind, he raised
his tousled dark head, 'Marry me,' he demanded,
and suddenly his implacable will was as apparent
as the unmistakable need his body had to drive
them both to passionate, desperate satisfaction.

'No,' she murmured, halfway between protest
and disbelief.

'Then I'm sorry to disappoint a lady, but I can't
possibly compromise my principles,' he assured
her with an air of conscious virtue, then stepped
back as far as their clinging bodies would allow.

'You can't stop now,' she protested hotly, every
inch of her passion-ravaged body crying out for
fulfilment.

'Whoever told you that was a self-serving
bastard, or perhaps he was a lying, conniving,
apology for a man with no principles to uphold. I
have nothing in common with Braxton, and it's

high time you realised it,' he said, with fury leashed in his deep voice.

She gazed at him with frustrated disbelief, 'If you had, then at least I wouldn't be in this ridiculous position now,' she informed him crossly.

'Excellent, I would hate to think my future wife was the kind of woman who made the same mistake twice.'

'Would you? As I have yet to meet your prospective countess, I'm hardly qualified to give an opinion of her.'

'No, I know,' he said with a significant look at her disgracefully dishevelled person. 'You're not the woman you think you are, my dear,' he assured her, and she couldn't bring herself to snap back a clever answer when she saw such tenderness and promise in his softened gaze. How unfair of the man not to give her the argument that would have got them both out of this situation with at least some of her defences still intact.

'I won't marry you, but I could be your mistress,' she offered, holding his gaze steadily as his eyes blazed with frustration and fury, as well as something far more dangerous to her peace of mind she dare not name even to herself.

'No, you couldn't, it would flay you,' he rasped out, and in direct contradiction of the temper in his dark eyes, he gently set about undoing as much of the damage he had caused to her once respectable appearance as possible.

'I should be the judge of that. I admit that I want you, but it seems I could wait for ever for satisfaction, so scrupulous and pernickety as you are in your requirements of your women, my lord.'

'I have but one requirement of you, Miranda,' he insisted implacably, 'and that is for you to become my wife as soon as the law and the church allow it.'

'Which is the one step I will not take, even for you.'

'Then we can only ever be distant relatives,' he told her, as he lifted her gown up over her shoulders and teased the buttons back into place that he had so precipitately undone such a short time earlier.

'I will come to your bed,' she threatened.

He grinned at her. 'My virtue is unassailable, you vile seductress.'

She could not but laugh, even as he used the strong hands that had just driven her to the edge of sanity to lift her off his desk and set her back on her feet. Her soft gown showed signs of its recent misuse and he brushed a hand over it to smooth her down, and even that fleeting contact caused a warm shiver to shoot through her as her legs threatened to give way again.

'At least you're not trying to marry my fortune,' she quipped back, 'your own being infinitely the greater.'

'True, I'm only after your beauty and grace—oh, and your misplaced pride and stubborn lioness's heart. I fully intend to win by fair means or foul, Miranda. I refuse to let you use me and then cast me aside like a worn-out glove,' he insisted with a wicked grin.

'How very noble.'

'So at least I own that quality in more than mere fact, after all—my detractors would be shocked,' he said.

'Then they are not worth a snap of your fingers and you obviously have a very poor sort of enemy, my lord, ones who know you not at all.'

'Being that they are my enemies, that's just the way I like them. That way they do me and mine less damage,' he insisted arrogantly; if she didn't love him so much, she might have thrown something at him for being so supremely sure of himself.

'And do you really think they would scruple to use my past against you if I were ever fool enough to marry you?' she asked crossly.

'Only the once,' he said and there was such smooth and deadly danger in his quiet voice that she shuddered, before the idea of having such a single-minded protector warmed her to the very soles of her feet.

'I'm glad I'm not your foe, then.'

'So am I, particularly as you're going to be my wife.'

'No, Kit,' she insisted bleakly, torn between pride that he should ask again after what she had told him and agony that she could never accept.

'Then there can be no passionate nights for us, Cousin Miranda,' he warned lightly, yet there was a relentless purpose about him as he did so.

'That seems harsh,' she admitted with a sad attempt at humour.

'It is,' he replied starkly, apparently impatient with her game of 'let's pretend this doesn't hurt'. 'You have a right to martyr yourself, I suppose, but I don't see why you should put me on the rack as well.'

'Better than being pilloried when my story comes out.'

'When will you finally believe that whatever the so-called polite world thinks of either of us is just so much straw in the wind to me?' he asked in bitter frustration and began to pace the room to vent his pent-up feelings.

'Never,' she replied with a sigh for his stubbornness.

'For heaven's sake, why not?'

'Because in a few months, or perhaps even a few years, you will hear yet another snide giggle or a half-hidden sneer at your wife behind your back and wish you hadn't let your passions rule your head. No, don't try and silence me, Kit. Even if you never felt such slights or cared about their petty-minded rules, what of our daughters? I suppose a boy might weather being the offspring of a notorious woman, maybe even gain a little cachet out of it at school, but not girls.'

'If you think they will be so poor spirited as to take such nonsense to heart, then we had better disown them before their mama and papa can decently get into their marriage bed and make them. Can you really think our children would be so lacking in backbone as to condemn you for being taken in by a plausible rogue, when you were too young to be let out of the schoolroom yourself? You underestimate them, my dear, and I dare say they will be far too busy with their own lives to worry about ours.'

'I wish I could believe that,' she said with a half-smile. 'I should have liked children,' she admitted and fought hard not to sound wistful.

'Then have them with me, Miranda. The very thought of another man getting you with child makes me feel murderous, so if you think to wed some poor obscure man without this ridiculous title nature has burdened me with, be warned that I will be dangerous indeed if you try it. Ironic, is it not, that if I had stayed a ruffian, you would probably be more inclined to accept my offer than you are now I have succeeded to the family honours? Shall I renounce the title to convince you it means nothing to me?'

'Don't be ridiculous—anyway, I don't think you can,' she protested, shaken by the very thought that he would consider such a thing for her.

'So I am condemned to wear it round my neck for the rest of my life like Coleridge's Ancient Mariner did his albatross? Such an undeserved sentence seems a little unjust, don't you think? I might even call it lunacy, if I were not such a polite and mannerly gentleman nowadays.'

This last was said with such bitterness that she could not doubt the passionate feelings behind his words and a faint sliver of doubt began to break in on her certainty. No, she couldn't let him do it. He might as well hate her for a few months now as a whole lifetime later, when he came to realise how right she had been to turn him down.

'No, there are many good women in the world, most of them better than I am by a very long distance.'

'Yet it is not your virtues that attracted me to you in the first place,' he bit out.

She flinched from the heat and fury in his eyes, as well as her own acute sense of shame. He had witnessed that terrible scene when Nevin had auctioned her off like a prime heifer at Smithfield Market, one she now remembered in full and cringed away from even after five years, and he was the one man on earth she would have think her better than she actually was.

Chapter Fifteen

'I apologise,' he added stiffly. 'That outburst only proves I'm no gentleman, something that might help my case if I hadn't just insulted you.'

'I'm sorry too,' she whispered, unable to find words to explain properly.

'Sorry that you were deceived and mistreated by a brute who should have been beaten within an inch of his life for so much as laying a finger on you, let alone for beating and humiliating you before he sold you to whoever had the fattest purse? How was that your fault, Miranda? How did you lay yourself open to such a terrible betrayal? And why the devil didn't your grandfather punish him for his sins by banishment to the ends of the earth at the very least, instead of exiling his own innocent flesh and blood?'

'Wales is not the ends of the earth, you know. In

fact, it is in many ways much more civilised than England, if the truth be known, and has been since long before we even knew what poetry was.'

'I dare say, but why did he make you stay there for so long, Miranda?'

'I should have thought that was obvious,' she replied rather sharply, for she had loved her bad-tempered grandsire, despite that painful edict.

'Not to me.'

'Because of the girls, of course,' she admitted painfully, angry with him for making her say out loud that she had been, and still was, a danger to their good names.

'And in what way have they benefited from your absence?'

What was wrong with the man? 'They were not nigh pitch,' she told him in a hard, bitter voice and at last tears rose up in a huge wave that refused to be blinked back.

He covered the space between them in two strides and pulled her back into his arms. She went like iron filings to a magnet; too helpless in the grip of emotions she had locked away for years to resist him. Hard sobs seemed to rip out of her throat of their own accord and she wept into his broad shoulder as he carried her across to the sofa they seemed fated to end up on after all, and there he sat down with her cradled in his arms and let her cry. Nothing would stop the tempest at first, not the thought of his probable embarrassment or even plain vanity at the idea of him seeing her red eyed and dishevelled.

Her disgrace and gullibility, banishment from her home and even the shock of finding out that her dream lover was no dream, added to the mishaps of the last few hours and broke some barrier within her that had held too much back for too long. In future, the voice of returning common sense informed her, she would do better to give in to her feelings more often, so they didn't splurge out all over the first person to tell her it wasn't all her fault. Then, at last, the flood ebbed and she was left wondering what could follow such a cataclysm but a lot of mopping up and a dismayed survey of the wreckage.

'I'm sorry,' she whispered out of a throat that felt scraped raw with all that crying, and a hiccuping sob silenced any further apologies as she tried again to regain some self-control.

'Don't you dare apologise,' he warned with an ominous growl.

'Sorry,' she repeated helplessly and shrugged at her own foolishness, before subsiding against him and breathing as deeply and evenly as she could, until the dry sobs subsided to an occasional sigh and then a moan of attempted protest as he gently kissed her.

Feeling very afraid that it was as much of a promise as the one he had made her to keep asking until she gave in, she turned her back on nobility and good sense and kissed him right back. The whole thing was in danger of becoming very heated indeed when he raised his head and sucked in a gasp of his own.

'Tell me again how meek and cold-blooded those daughters of ours are sure to be,' he teased, even as he ran his hands through her hair as if he could not help caressing the shining mane that had tumbled down round her shoulders during that last heady storm of emotions.

From somewhere she found the energy to shake her head at him reproachfully. 'It's not considered fair to kick your opponent when she's down,' she reproached him with a watery smile.

'Just a gentle tap to remind you that we're on the same side, Venus,' he informed her, and for all the softness of his voice and the gentle mockery in his eyes, she knew he was deadly serious.

'It's been so lonely,' she finally admitted, and felt the hard tension in his body, even as she knew he was only angry on her behalf.

'Your sisters missed far more by living without you than they would have if only your grandfather had brazened things out,' he informed her after a while.

'I can't see how he could have,' she protested absently, trying very hard not to let her hands explore the intriguing plains of his beloved face.

'Then you obviously have no idea how much they miss you, you little fool. They talk of seeing you again every time I visit them in Bath, and of when they can come home again, of course,' he said and she wriggled so she could stare up at him.

Somehow being called a fool didn't make her as furious as it should do, when the concerned frown pleating his brows made her long to run a soothing finger over them, and invite him to think of something less vexing, like kissing her. She was really far gone if she couldn't even work up a small spurt of temper, she decided distractedly, and clasped her hands together to stop them doing something wilful while her thoughts were elsewhere.

'Pay attention, madam,' he chided, and she wondered if he was a mind reader or, even more dangerous, if her love for him made her easy to read. 'You would go to the stake for anyone you love, and your sisters know it. They needed your love and warmth and loyalty, not a hostile aunt and an indifferent cousin in your stead, which is why I refused to let them come back until I have worked out a far better arrangement for their comfort.'

'Grandfather would not let me near the girls with such a scandal nipping at my heels. Lady Clarissa would never have allowed it.'

'He ought to have told her to accept his decision and stand with you, or leave his house and do her worst. No sensible man would have kept that stony-hearted old besom and not you, my hot-headed, warm-hearted Miranda.'

'I don't think it was a question of preference, but of comfort,' she defended her grandfather rather half-heartedly.

'Yes, I dare say he didn't fancy the battle royal it would have cost him to get rid of her. He should have had more courage.'

A small voice she tried to ignore whispered that he was right, but Miranda was too loyal to openly admit it. 'She was his daughter and I think he had always felt guilty about her,' she excused him instead. 'His first marriage was arranged and not happy, and apparently my aunt is very like her mother.'

'Then maybe he has my sympathy after all. The

painter who took his first countess's portrait couldn't conceal her likeness to the Basilisk,' he said irreverently.

'Do you wish to hear this tale or not, my lord?' she asked sternly.

'Behold me silenced.'

'For as long as it suits you. But Grandfather doted on his second wife and their son, so Aunt Clarissa must have felt like an outsider until she left for Ennersley.'

'And what a pity she didn't stay there, instead of returning here to play the martyred widow,' he said caustically.

'She does seem to take delight in repulsing the affection of her family, other than Celia, of course,' she reflected aloud.

'Your aunt was a mature woman when you ran away and quite capable of looking after her own interests. You were no more than seventeen at the time and should have been in the schoolroom, not facing the world alone.'

'I had Godmama, and Grandfather was still grieving for my father and was worried about my brother,' she protested weakly, finally letting go of the myth of a wise and mighty grandparent she had believed in for so long.

'All the more reason to hold his family close,

and children should come before embittered and over-indulged adults.'

'True, and he should have stepped in and forced your father to part with you and your sisters as well,' she admitted. 'When my parents died I must have put my faith in them on to him, but I see now that he was a man and not a hero. I had to wait for one of those,' she added slyly, with a sidelong look at her grandparent's successor.

'Hussy. I wonder if there is not more to this than you have ever considered. How much does your aunt hate you, Miranda?'

Shock took the easy answer from her lips as she realised just where that question was leading. 'No, she wouldn't,' she gasped. She nearly sprang to her feet at the outlandishness of the ideas buzzing through her head, except her shaking legs probably wouldn't hold her, and she was very much more comfortable where she was. 'She couldn't,' she asserted with relief as the methods chosen by her attacker hit home.

'Not even to ensure that her darling could become a countess as she herself could not by right of inheritance?' he argued implacably, obviously not sharing her habit of seeing the world in brighter colours than warranted. 'She was his eldest child and most suited to the role, in her own eyes at least.'

'It would be most improper to get rid of me just to give Celia a clear field, and propriety is her god.'

'Only so long as her impropriety is not discovered. Isn't that the rule she and her kind live by?' he said cynically. 'Sin as you please, but don't get found out?'

'I dare say, but she still can't be behind the attacks on me.'

'Then tell me how your sorry tale came to be known outside the family. Have you ever wondered why Braxton persisted with his dishonourable intentions, long after it must have been clear he wouldn't get anything from your grandfather?'

Struck by the logic of his argument, she still couldn't accept her aunt's complicity in Nevin's savagery. 'She can't have conspired against me so cruelly while pretending it was all so shocking. Anyway, she's not that good an actress.'

'I think you underestimate her. A mother with overpowering ambition for her only child would clear you out of her path whatever it took, my darling. You're far too lovely not to put her ewe lamb in the shade.'

'But Celia is beautiful,' she protested, feeling under siege by shock after shock as he revealed to her how much of a mirage her early life under this roof had been.

'As a marble sculpture is beautiful, perhaps, but not as a living, feeling creature. Why do you think she has not remarried in all these years?'

Miranda found herself excusing her cousin, despite the appalling suspicions of her that had already taken such strong root in her mind during yesterday's misadventures. 'I suppose she is wary of it after making such a disastrous first marriage.'

'I asked a few questions in the right places at Horse Guards, and found her husband was heir to a baronetcy and a tidy estate in Northamptonshire. Not such a bad marriage, on her part at least,' he told her, and the expression of distaste on his handsome face told Miranda at least that Celia might as well pack her bags and go, for all the good staying here for the next few weeks would do her.

'Then why not talk his prospects up instead of down?' she asked in genuine bewilderment.

'Odd, isn't it? And once I began to ask questions, a great deal I found out mystified me. People seemed distinctly weary of answering them for one thing, which made me wonder if your grandfather asked those questions before me.'

'But his will,' she protested, angry on Kit's behalf that Grandfather had merely demanded he marry one of his granddaughters. If he had known

Celia was a liar, and perhaps worse, he could have condemned Kit to a lifetime of disillusionment.

'He had me investigated as well, I believe, so perhaps he had more faith in my judgement than you do,' Kit said laconically, just as if he had read her mind and dismissed the possibility as ridiculous.

'You don't mind such an intrusion on your privacy?' she asked incredulously.

'No, I would have done the same thing myself in the circumstances. Anyway, your cousin undervaluing her husband's prospects wasn't a crime, for that was all they were unless his father predeceased him.'

'Poor Celia.'

'Yes, and that's another thing,' he insisted relentlessly. 'How come she is "poor Celia" instead of rich Celia? Her forty thousand pounds seems to have all but disappeared.'

'She has expensive tastes?'

He laughed. 'Yet she has enjoyed free board and lodgings ever since she and her mother came here. How many years ago was that, by the way?'

Wondering why it mattered, Miranda searched her memory and vaguely remembered Celia spoiling her eleventh birthday party with her icy contempt.

'About eleven years ago, I think—she must have been about seventeen,' she told him.

'A fortune untouched in such a way should have accumulated, so the next question is—where did it all go?'

'I have no idea, nor the least inkling how to find out.'

'No, but luckily I have both.'

'Why go into the past?' she protested, thinking of all the uncomfortable facts she would have liked to conceal about her own.

'Because everything out of kilter is a potential clue to who might be attacking you, and that is very important to me indeed.'

'It should not be, we can never be more to each other than distant cousins,' she reiterated, but even she heard the note of doubt in her voice as she said it.

'You can't wish my feelings away just because they don't suit you.'

'They honour me,' she retorted, goaded into declaring the truth.

'Then at least try to look a little more flattered by them.'

'I can't, you would do better to ask Celia, she may be poorer than everyone thinks, but at least she hasn't got a blasted reputation that will drag your name down with it if you marry her.'

'Strange though it may be, I prefer warm, bad-tempered women to cold, calculating witches,' he told her. What would it take to convince him she would not wed him?

'And I prefer not to cause more harm than good to those I love,' she told him crossly, then realised just where her unruly tongue had led her this time. As an argument against them marrying, something told her that was not her finest moment.

'So you do love me?' he asked mildly, as if discussing the weather at one of Aunt Clarissa's interminable 'at homes'.

Trust him to latch on to her indiscretion, and his expression was so intense, so absorbed in her answer that she could not lie, even though she wanted to quite badly. 'Of course I do, you stupid man.'

'Then you could at least try to be a little more encouraging.'

'No, I couldn't.'

'Vixen,' he told her, not in the least put out by such stern discouragement. Why should he be when she had given him such excellent ammunition to shoot her down with?

'I still won't marry you,' she insisted stubbornly.

'You will, my dear, like it or no.'

'Then I don't, and I won't.'

'And why I should be so eager to put my head in the noose, when you will be such a contrary, naggy-tempered excuse for a wife, I shall never know,' he goaded her, evidently believing that provocation had worked so well last time it was well worth trying again.

'You don't need Grandfather's money,' she defended herself stoutly.

'No, but I do need you and I'm not above using his will as an excuse to get you up the aisle some time before the Last Trump.'

'Blackmail never did sit well with me, my lord.'

'Maybe not, but what about an appeal to that tender heart of yours? That will prove a steadfast ally to me, I think, despite your bull-headed de-termination to make us both deeply unhappy for the sake of some unimportant detail.'

'It's not a detail, it's a scandal at the very least,' she said crossly, wondering how much longer she could hold out against his iron will. For ever, if need be, she told herself wistfully and refused to waver.

'Only if we let it be. But for now we really will be hopelessly compromised if we don't part soon, you brazen creature. I have no wish to have it whis-pered that you tricked me into marriage by spending a scandalously long time closeted in my library with me,' he said with such an air of pompous rec-titude she wanted to throw something again. 'So I suggest you put your hair back up and let me leave you to the solitude you have been enjoying for some time now, if anyone should be unmannerly enough to ask,' he went on as if she wasn't glaring at him in a distinctly unloving fashion.

'No doubt we quarrelled so spectacularly that you stormed out into the garden mere moments after Coppice inadvertently latched the door,' she agreed sarcastically.

Even so, she felt distinctly flustered by the time she had battled with her rebellious curls under his amused gaze for long enough to get them under some semblance of control. A pity, then, that she could not say the same for her thoughts. They were all over the place as the intimacy of the moment punched through her resolution to resist him. Suddenly she could envisage years of becoming scandalously ruffled by his husbandly attentions, and her heart yearned for such un-thinkable luxury.

'Don't look at me like that,' he rasped at her, heat and promise in his fierce, tender expression once more.

'Then please go, my lord,' she appealed, turning her back on the seductive notion of caving in and going out of the double doors side by side to face the world together from now on.

'This time,' he managed tersely and she was left watching his beloved form retreat into the gardens as she wondered if that had been more of a threat than a promise.

Even as he walked away Kit knew Miranda was his, and had to restrain an urge to punch the air in triumph. She was brave and beautiful and as contradictory as the four winds, but she was still his, every stubborn inch of her. It was there in every soft murmur and yearning sigh she had made as he kissed her and adored her as he now knew no man ever had before. As he walked out into the sunlit spring gardens, he contemplated her feelings and his own with more joy than he had known in years.

What a fool he had been, thinking he could wed her and bed her and seduce her inch by delicious inch, until she wanted him as desperately as he did her, and all the time keep his heart aloof while he did so. The less-than-wonderful revelations of the last half-hour punched through his euphoria as his mind went back to that first meeting so long ago, and this time his fists clenched into formidable fists at his sides for a very different reason.

When she revealed her reasons for staying away

from her home, and told him sadly that she could not marry him because she was damaged goods, he had wanted to kill all her dragons and slay any fool unable to see what a treasure she was. At least now he finally knew that he loved her, and how on earth had he kept that secret from himself for so long? The answer was that if ever a man hated the thought of being in love, it was Christopher Alstone, first-born child of his mother's obsessive, one-sided love match to an abusive drunkard.

Then there was the fact that he had never bargained for the advent of a half-naked goddess in his life, which must be an extenuating circumstance. Maybe wanting her so desperately that night had driven the very thought of love out of his head for too long, but now he knew himself better at last and the bravest and truest woman in the world loved him right back! He strode on, torn between delight, fury and fear and tried to sort them into order. How could he be anything but delighted when a woman so much worth the winning admitted she loved him? On the other hand, how could he be other than furious that someone had treated her so brutally, or that her enemies were now working against her once more?

Then there was the dark fear that had ridden him ever since that shot rang out in the bridle-way up on the hills and he felt the blow that hit her just as if it were tearing into his own flesh. Much better if it had—he was tough and tempered by his rough early life and the hard seaman's apprenticeship he had endured afterwards. He rubbed his upper arm as if he would take her pain on his own flesh and paced the garden walks like a captured tiger, full of undirected fury.

Too much was at stake to pace about the place, proving how fierce he was while someone seemed intent on putting a period to his lady's life. He should have known the instant she was hurt that this driven need of her, this fascination with her every word and deed, and the desire to keep her safe at his side for ever, was love. It was true that he had learnt very young not to love anyone except his little sisters, but he wasn't an abused boy now and neither was he anything like his father. Years of taking only the opposite path to the ones Bevis Alstone had staggered down had at least made sure of that.

Now he wished fate had been a little kinder to them five years ago. Of course he had still been the heir presumptive then, the skeleton in the family closet that nobody talked about unless they had to, and then probably only in scandalised whispers. Yet something told him Miranda would have defied the lot of them on his behalf.

Once he unmasked her attacker, then he would have time to make her forget this ridiculous determination to refuse him for his own good, for something told him nothing would do him good again without her. He was just about to resort to his bedchamber to dash off an impatient letter to his friend and business partner when Coppice came through the garden door with the look of a man on a mission.

'You have a visitor, your lordship,' he said doubtfully, as if the old schemer wasn't quite sure if he should bring up such a dubious subject when his employer was busy courting a wife.

'Then either announce them, or tell me where they might be so I can announce myself.'

'If only it were so simple, my lord. The gentleman, for I suppose I must call him so, insisted on settling and grooming his horse before he would go upstairs to the bedchamber I have allotted him, and now he is bathing and dressing himself and will accept no help with that either.'

'Then I know very well who he is and he is very welcome. As soon as the rogue has finished washing and dressing that much thick hide, show him straight into the library and see we're not disturbed for anything less than an earthquake, or another attack on Mrs Braxton.'

'Very good, my lord,' Coppice said with careful self-restraint and returned inside to carry out his instructions to the letter, for much must be excused a gentleman in love, as he later informed the housekeeper.

Chapter Sixteen

Miranda spent the rest of the morning with Leah and what seemed like half the household determinedly dogging her footsteps. Despite the knotty problem of persuading Kit that she couldn't marry him, she knew she was lucky to be alive and it felt like one of the oddest days of her life. Relief at being here to experience it fought with the deep sadness of knowing she had found the love of her life too late for them to be happy together.

Leaving Wychwood would be even more painful this time, when she must leave him behind her along with the home of her childhood, so she played the coward for once and flinched away from the thought of doing so. When the time came she would do it, she assured herself, for Kit's sake. Whatever he might think to the contrary, she knew he would be better by far without her. For now just knowing she must go so soon was quite enough to cope with.

Indeed the very idea proved so painful that she gave up pretending she was as robust as ever and retired to her bed for the afternoon to avoid it. After all, it would take a very determined attacker to reach her with Sukey nodding over her sewing by the fire and a stalwart footman stationed in the hall, enjoying being her first line of defence far too much for Miranda to insist that he went away and did something useful instead. Yes, she would just rest her tired eyes for a few moments and then she would get up and do something.

'Time to get up now, Miss Miranda,' Leah informed her briskly as she woke her mistress as ruthlessly as she had insisted she try to sleep in the first place some time later.

Given that the bed curtains had been rattled back loudly enough to wake a deaf woman, Miranda gave in to the inevitable and sat up to contemplate the fact that she had slept for several hours.

'I only meant to take a short nap,' she protested sleepily.

'You needed more than that after the day you had yesterday,' Leah told her unrepentantly and set about ordering preparations for Miranda's bath with her usual whirlwind energy.

Miranda added the thought of how very much she would miss her old friend to the list of reasons why uprooting herself from Wychwood would hurt even more than last time, when she hadn't even considered it might be for ever. Dwelling on gloomy thoughts of a future of good works and resolute cheerfulness wasn't going to put her in the right frame of mind to hide her torn emotions from Aunt Clarissa and Celia's cold scrutiny, though. Shrugging off the lonely future as best she could, she stretched luxuriously and got out of bed to prepare for another challenging evening with her nearest and dearest.

'There's visitors arrived,' Leah informed her succinctly and when Miranda looked a question at her added, 'that little lawyer for one, and the biggest man I ever did see for another. Mr Coppice says the giant's a friend of his lordship's come to visit, so I suppose he must be right enough. Now hold that arm up, do, Miss Miranda, so me and Sukey can get you undressed and washed.'

Intrigued, Miranda wondered who the mysterious guest could be as she obediently raised her injured arm. She submitted to the inevitable and let herself be bathed as if she was very much younger, for once she was back in Snowdonia such spoiling must end for ever, so she might as well enjoy it while she could. Sitting by the fire afterwards to let her hair dry in the heat, she told herself that she would soon grow accustomed to managing for herself again.

Facing Celia and Lady Clarissa after last night's uproar promised to be an ordeal, especially given the dark suspicions she was beginning to harbour towards them. Putting off the moment until it truly had to be faced might be cowardly, but it was too seductive, she decided as Sukey gently brushed her burnished curls under Leah's stern guidance. She really must have words with Leah about raising the poor girl's hopes of becoming a ladies' maid to such as herself. Miranda frowned at her old friend, who looked serenely back at her as if she was convinced a magic wand would somehow be waved and Miranda would get her happy ending as well. She shook her head, despairing of convincing Leah otherwise just now, and directed her attention to the crucial question of what to wear.

'You need more of a sleeve than usual if you want to hide that bandage,' her stern mentor informed her as soon as Miranda was arrayed in her shift, short corset and stockings.

'Since you will no doubt insist I wear that

wretched sling, I can't see why,' Miranda com-
plained, but she really was heartily sick of the
lilac satin, so donning a velvet gown of a glowing
shade of deepest blue was something of a relief.

Leah added the earrings and pendant Lady Rhys
had insisted on giving her goddaughter on her
twenty-first birthday before Miranda could protest
that a family dinner was far too run of the mill an
occasion to warrant such finery. The single
sapphire, set in diamonds whose clarity contrasted
with such extraordinary depth of colour, fell at just
the right point to emphasise her curves and for that
very reason Miranda did not wear it very often.
Tonight she settled it in place with a certain satisfaction that if she had to sink all her hopes, she
would do so with all guns blazing.

'You'll put Miss Celia's nose properly out of
joint,' Leah remarked with considerable satisfaction and Sukey just nodded under her mentor's
stern eye. 'You be careful, though, Miss Miranda,'
Leah cautioned, with a frown that was part-con-
centration and part-concern.

'If we don't put a stop to this business soon,
somebody else will get hurt and I won't have that,'
Miranda insisted.

'Don't see as you have much control over it,
whoever the rogue may be,' Leah said with a sig-

nificant glance at the eagerly listening Sukey, whom Miranda then dismissed with a smile and a warm thank you.

'Now I think I have,' Miranda replied firmly as soon as the little maid had gone, 'and tonight it's high time I exerted it.'

'You always were one to fight battles that didn't need to be fought, so I'm not likely to stop you taking this one on.'

'True, but if you want to set my mind at rest, you could tell me what Reuben's intentions are, now you're finally home.'

Miranda kept a weather eye on her friend, having no mind to end up with a singed curl or a burnt ear, tonight of all nights.

'I could have told you that days ago,' Leah surprised her by saying complacently, 'and I shall let him make the biggest mistake of his life this time. He's waited long enough to make it in all conscience, just like another person I might mention.'

Miranda considered that statement before coming to the inevitable conclusion. 'You knew we had met before that first day we came back here, didn't you?' she asked, bewildered and furious that Leah had omitted to tell her what happened five years ago when she came out of the dazed state Nevin's drug and her shocked mind had inflicted on her.

'What was the point of you remembering exactly what that animal did to you? And, yes, I knew his lordship was the same man who rescued you from that devil as soon as I set eyes on him again. I decided he'd remind you when he was good and ready, though I never thought it'd take him so long.'

'I don't know that he believed I had truly forgotten at first, then he must have had a good many second thoughts about acknowledging the acquaintance,' Miranda said lightly.

'He's less of a man than I thought if he doesn't.'

'That he isn't,' Miranda said unwarily and saw a wicked gleam in Leah's eyes as soon as the words left her mouth.

'Like that, is it?'

'Apparently,' Miranda admitted rather painfully, for reminding herself how impossible it was to love Kit Alstone didn't actually diminish the feeling in any way.

'Good, it's about time.'

'I won't marry him, Leah. If you hadn't rescued me that night, I would have woken up from that stupor a whore, if I woke up at all. I owe you more than I could ever hope to repay for following me into that hell and dragging me out of it before Nevin destroyed me, but I'm not fit for marriage any more.'

'You owe me nothing, Miss Miranda. You saved me from that worm Sir Horace Ennersley when we were little more than children, and I'd like to know just why Lady Clarissa turned a blind eye to her husband's nasty ways when she's so sharp to pick on anyone else's mistakes.'

Remembering how Aunt Clarissa's husband had lured Leah to the dairy one day when the dairy-maid was ill and tried to rape her, Miranda felt a burn of shame redden her cheeks.

'I have a very odd set of relations, do I not?' she asked ruefully.

'Sir Horace looked odd enough with that pail of whey all over him,' Leah recalled with a grin and they laughed together at the memory. 'And I don't know what you threatened to do to him, but he avoided me ever afterwards.'

'And gave him and his all the more reason to hate me, I dare say.'

'They never needed a reason,' Leah argued.

'I know,' Miranda had to agree as she had never met with the slightest spark of affection from either her aunt or her cousin, and heaven knew she had tried hard to gain it when she was too young to know better.

'So promise me you'll be careful tonight,' Leah demanded very seriously indeed. 'His lordship's so deep in love with you I think he'd go wild if anything happened to you and, when it comes down to it, I suppose I'd miss you myself.'

'It's mutual, so *you* must promise to go and tell Reuben you'll make him happy at last, Leah. It's high time I learnt to look after myself, even if I will miss your nagging after the first month or so of peace and quiet.'

'You'll find it hard to miss me when I'll be living half a mile off,' Leah insisted with a seemingly infallible faith in Kit's ability to overcome all obstacles. 'Now if that's all, Miss Miranda, I have a man waiting for me downstairs.'

'Don't forget to be back in your own bed by dawn, then.'

'It'd be a good idea if you spent the night in his lordship's bed, for both your sakes.'

'And a better one if your mind your own business for once in your life,' Miranda told her with a fiery blush, even as she wondered just how to bring about that longed-for conclusion after all.

With great difficulty if she knew anything about her stubborn love, she decided with a smile, and was so busy considering that problem that she was out of her room and halfway down the stairs before she recalled her steely resolution of this afternoon not to marry him.

'Teaching the torches to burn bright again, Venus?' Kit asked from the foot of the stairs and she felt a very different shiver run through her than the one that had troubled her that first night here when he stepped out of the shadows to inspect her.

This time his gaze was almost like a caress, his smile warm and open. The only similarity to that encounter with a stony-faced conqueror and this Kit Alstone was the desire hot and barely controlled that sang between them with infinite promise, as usual. Maybe those misdeeds wouldn't be so hard to bring about after all, she speculated, a delicious flutter of anticipation making her heart dip then hurry.

'*Romeo and Juliet,* my lord?' she asked breathlessly, and smiled back, unable to resist his potent appeal when he had let so many barriers down.

'I can read, contrary to popular opinion. At sea a captain leads a solitary life when not hard at work, and it helped me pass the time when all I could do was dream of you.'

'At least you knew I was real, while I thought you an unattainable fantasy I tried hard to forget.'

'A nightmare, more like,' he murmured as she finally stepped down beside him and he took her hand.

'Not so—you were my wildest dreams come true, Christopher Alstone,' she whispered and it was the truth, although she should not have betrayed it when she was intent on refusing his proposal.

Heat flashed through brown eyes suddenly velvet dark, and there was even a faint burn of it on his high cheekbones as he accepted what she said—she knew that reckless revelation would have consequences. Still, it was the truth and how could she wish it unsaid? The answer was she must, for his sake, but just for a moment she allowed herself the brief delusion that all might be well after all.

'Sooner or later you'll realise you have no alternative but to accept my offer or burn, Venus,' he told her with such certainty in his deep voice that she almost said yes, until she remembered her past and shook her head.

Once she was away from here, he would have the chance to think about her refusal and realise she was right without the distraction of this sharp need flaring between them. Not that the idea gave her much comfort.

'There is always an alternative,' she told him and forced herself to meet his velvet-dark gaze with only serene certainty in her own deep blue eyes.

'No, I refuse to acknowledge anything but this,'

he challenged back, and bent his head to take her lips with his in a kiss that was all heat and persuasion and certainty.

Instantly her hands flexed in readiness to reach up and draw him even closer, anticipating the feel of warm firm skin and crisp dark curls under her eager fingers with a quiver of pure joy. Somehow she forced them into fists and made them stay rigid at her side, even as his lips on hers made her a thousand heady promises that made her heart race with stubborn joy. In defiance of her will, her feet conspired to raise her on tiptoe so she could return the pressure of his mouth on equal terms, but again she managed to keep part of her resistant and pushed back on to her heels again with a mighty effort.

'You must face the fact that there is a world beyond us and I won't ruin it for you,' she murmured once she managed to duck her head enough to force him to break that kiss, even as her hands almost got away from her dogged will by getting halfway up his back before she ordered them back to lonely isolation.

'You will if you carry on refusing me,' he retaliated, but there was the first hint of uncertainty she had ever seen in his dear eyes as he saw how resolute she really was. 'Nothing will ruin me

more surely than the death of all hope, Miranda,'
he vowed, his words very nearly breathed into her
trembling mouth they were so dangerously close,
and, oh, how she longed to give in!

'Well, isn't this cosy?' Celia asked in an ice-cold
tone from the head of the stairs.

Miranda felt a shiver as if ice-water had run
down her back at the implacable dislike in her
cousin's clipped tones, but Kit refused to hide
what they had been doing and stubbornly settled
a possessive hand on her waist as he turned her to
face Celia's ill will.

'Not noticeably,' Miranda countered, before he
could defend her and make Celia hate her all the
more. At least his show of solidarity gave her the
courage to raise her chin and meet Celia's chilling
scrutiny squarely. 'You should know by now that
the draught on these stairs is never balmy, Cousin.'

'Which makes them an odd place for an assignation, don't you think?'

'An assignation is furtive by its very nature, is
it not, Cousin Cecilia?' Kit asked blandly. 'What
is it that you find sly about Mrs Braxton and
myself meeting at the foot of the stairs in plain
sight?'

'Cousin Miranda has such a genius for misbe-
haviour, my lord, that you might find yourself

totally helpless in her web before you even know it has been spun.'

'How you do overestimate me, Celia,' Miranda countered lightly.

'Really? I don't believe I have ever done that.'

'Then let me reassure you, Cousin, that I never allow myself to be pushed or led anywhere I don't intend going all along,' Kit informed Celia coldly. 'So, having cleared up that matter to our mutual satisfaction, perhaps we should adjourn to the Countess's Sitting Room? It seems boorish to keep my guests waiting while we traduce each other out here in the cold.'

'I would not presume to scold *you,* my lord,' Celia cooed at him and, descending the last few stairs with delicate grace, she seized his arm as if it was her one and only hope of support in a reeling universe.

'How very reassuring,' he said, with an irony Celia chose not to hear as he offered Miranda his other arm.

Tucking her injured one back into its neglected sling, she laid her other hand on Kit's arm partly to annoy Celia, but mostly to please herself one last time. So Miranda sauntered along at his side, telling herself she was amused by her cousin's very obvious ploy and not thoroughly exasperated with her for ruining her grand renunciation of her dear love. Let Celia and her mother goad her into civil war and she would feel she had lost all the advantages holding the moral high ground might give her, and it would also make Wychwood very uncomfortable until she could leave.

'Guests?' she echoed, striving for a suitable distraction.

Miranda had long ago given up on any delusion that the new earl of Carnwood did anything without a purpose. Yet how could he add to the already volatile mix around the dinner table tonight, when some of her darkest secrets might be dragged into the light before the night was over? Whoever was trying to kill her would hardly scruple to fling any amount of mud at her if that would serve their purpose equally well, and she was beginning to wonder if it had not done so very efficiently in the past. She had been completely removed from her home for five long years, after all.

Kit straightened the arm she had been politely brushing with her fingertips and took her hand in his warm one. She could either slink along at his side like an obedient acolyte, while Celia strutted into the room clinging to his arm like a piece of ivy. Or she could show the world how proud she was of the contact he offered her like a lovely promise, however fleeting it must be.

Stepping forward with her chin in the air, she decided to take hold of her courage. This strong and resourceful man believed in her, so it was high time she justified him in that at least by having a little faith in herself.

Mr Poulson, the lawyer, whom she had thought fixed in London and unlikely to be prised away by less than a dozen wild horses, looked resigned to his fate. Next to him was the giant of a man Leah had warned her about, and she was very certain she had never met him before, for once seen she doubted anyone would forget him. His overlong thatch of blond hair was tugged back into an old-fashioned queue and he had donned the dark coat and pristine linen of a gentleman's evening dress, but he wore breeches and top-boots with them in defiance of convention.

Luckily she had already fallen for a damn-your-eyes rogue of the first order, so she was immune to this golden-haired giant's compelling presence, but she noted Celia's gaze lingering in wonder on the giant's very wide shoulders and hastily hid a smile. Her cousin was watching the stranger with an open-mouthed stare of feminine appreciation, something her stern mama would certainly not approve of. Luckily Celia rapidly reviewed his flaws and her mouth turned down at the corners and her eyes grew chilly again, but it was good to see that she was human after all.

'How gratifying to see you, gentlemen,' Kit said benignly, pretending to be a complacent country squire for some reason.

'Kester,' the giant greeted him gruffly, ignoring protocol and brusquely clasping his host by the arm Celia had at last released in what was more than a handshake and less than an embrace.

Miranda could see the affection that bound them together without need for any words, and wondered if they had come up from the streets together. If so, little of their beginnings showed in the speech or manners of either man, not that she would care if it did. After all, she was fiercely proud of her love and he was equal, if not superior, to any man in the kingdom, or outside it for that matter.

'Ben, you're very welcome,' Kit replied, letting Celia support herself for a few more perilous moments whilst he returned the man's mighty grip without wincing.

'This is your lady, then?' the giant asked, and his grey eyes might have seemed guileless without the humour and intelligence he was currently not bothering to conceal.

He regarded Miranda steadily, as if he could plumb her character if he did so long enough. She wondered if he cared at all that Celia had turned from reluctant admirer into his implacable enemy the instant he identified Miranda as Kit's lady. Not noticeably, she decided, as she met his bold grey gaze with a straight look of her own.

'This is the Honourable Mrs Braxton, Ben, and may I present my friend and business partner, Mr Benedict Shaw, to you, Cousin Miranda? Mrs Grant is also a cousin of ours, and I believe you must have already met her mama?'

Kit raised dark eyebrows in polite question, even as his eyes danced at the furtive heavenward glance Ben cast him before bowing with polite coolness in Lady Clarissa's direction, which courtesy received a frigid nod in return. Mr Shaw had evidently been assessed and hastily discarded as a suitable husband for the lovely Celia, and so could be treated as the parvenu Lady Clarissa obviously considered him.

'Coppice gives me to understand dinner has been put back half an hour?' her ladyship questioned Kit's orders, obviously only just holding on to her determination to be civil to him at least.

'Yes, my guests have travelled a long way and needed a little more time,' he said, pretending to be that pompous county squire again, and Miranda cast him a very suspicious glance.

'Then we three seem to have completed the company, unless of course you have asked anyone else to join our delightful little assembly?' she said with a cool look, and all he did was shake his handsome head and grin.

'It was beyond even my ingenuity, sweet cousin,' he replied smoothly.

'I doubt it,' she snapped and freed her hand with a glare for his determined pantomime of the devoted lover, despite her repeated refusal of his proposal.

Seething, she shot him a challenging glare and all he did was turn toward the little lawyer so she must exchange polite greetings with him or look as rude as Celia and her mama, who were intent on pretending he did not exist as usual. Reminded of her own manners, Miranda joined in making the little man welcome, then Kit manipulated her once more into standing with him as if they were in their own little world amidst the sparse chatter.

Not taking very well to manipulation by a master, Miranda quietly attempted to edge on to the fringe of the gathering. The mere caress of one of Kit's long fingers against the sensitive under-side of her wrist where her glove was buttoned was all it took to make her go still and stay exactly where she was. Heat and desire instantly threatened her poise, and that steely resolution not to marry him, whatever he said to the contrary, faltered briefly.

Chapter Seventeen

'Are you ashamed to stand by my side, Miranda?' Kit murmured with just enough hurt in his dark eyes to make his question serious.

'Never!' she gasped from her too-loving heart in return, without waiting for permission from her cooler brain.

'Then what possible reason could you have to avoid me?'

'Well, none, but this is too…'

Miranda lost all grasp of what she had been going to say as the sudden dip of his head toward hers made her wonder if he was actually going to kiss her in front of so many respectable people. Unable to force herself to regard that prospect with the requisite amount of horror, her voice faded away before it got her into any more trouble.

'Too soon?'

'Yes—no, I mean no.'

'How lucid. Isn't it lucky one of us retains even the flimsy grasp on reality I am currently capable of? Later, Venus, you may not be so lucky.'

'Oh, good,' the idiot she became with one touch or glance from him gasped with glowing anticipation.

'Although you may not be quite *that* fortunate, my lovely siren,' he returned with a ruefully intimate grin, before turning her about and back to the formality of Lady Clarissa's furious company, and a very necessary reminder of their true situation.

'I still won't marry you,' she muttered militantly.

When Coppice announced dinner, Miranda was glad not to be seated anywhere near her aunt, for if Lady Clarissa had even a grain of poison in her possession it would certainly have ended up in her soup after Kit's ridiculous behaviour. It occurred to her that he seemed to be deliberately provoking her aunt's fury by making it clear that he preferred Miranda's company to Celia's. Surely he wouldn't be so foolish after the events of the last day or two to try to push any of her enemies into a fury?

She eyed Kit with a militant expression he chose

to ignore. Yet she was sure her look wasn't lost on his friend, for Mr Shaw was watching the company closely, speculation in his acute grey eyes as he summed them up and reached some mysterious conclusion of his own. Nothing much would escape him, she decided, so she should feel reassured with him and Kit intent on unmasking her enemies, for she was quite certain that was why he was here. The reason for Mr Poulson's presence was less obvious to her, but she welcomed it all the same. Something told her she needed all the benign influences she could get on her side tonight.

Never before had the hatred in her Aunt Clarissa's iron-grey eyes been so explicit, especially when not even her ladyship could manipulate matters so that Celia sat next to Kit, in the face of his determination not to be manipulated. Seated at his side as she was, Miranda tried not to let herself dream that Kit could be the rock to build her hopes on after all. Instead, she resolutely turned to meet the shrewd gaze of Mr Shaw on her other side, quite certain nothing that had happened tonight had escaped his notice.

'Have you travelled far today, Mr Shaw?' she heard herself ask inanely.

'I certainly covered a lot of ground,' he replied,

and his smile seemed to hold more than just a polite interest in her question.

'I should imagine that you usually do,' she returned with a shiver she tried hard to conceal.

It felt to her as if they were all playing a game nobody had bothered to explain to her and, if all this was just a preliminary to the real business of the evening, she suspected only he and Kit knew exactly what that might be.

'It comes of being so large,' he explained apologetically, as if all was as serene and correct as it appeared on the surface.

Miranda decided Mr Shaw must make an ideal business partner for Kit. They were evidently equals in stubbornness, dissimulation and arrogant self-assurance and what one did not see through, the other one would. She just hoped she never got in the middle when they disagreed and the sparks flew as sometimes they surely must. They would be like the irresistible force and the immovable object butting against each other, she mused, exasperated amusement threatening her attempts to keep a straight face.

'I dare say it might,' she replied with a stern look he met with such perfect innocence she almost believed he was as harmless as he tried to pretend, for all of two seconds.

'That's why I lack the right build for life aboard ship,' he went on with apparent candour, 'it's really no wonder I swallowed the anchor so eagerly when Kester suggested we make a fortune for ourselves, instead of our fat masters.'

'I should imagine you spent most of your career at sea bent double,' she conceded, wondering how many times he had banged that admittedly handsome head in the cramped space between decks.

'Not quite, but sometimes it felt like it. When a lad begins a life at sea it's not hard to creep about below decks because he is so small, but by the time I was full grown it was like trying to fit a bear into a doll's house.'

Unable to resist the picture of him trying to cram himself into her little sister's doll's house upstairs, Miranda chuckled and forgot her worries for a moment. He was much kinder than he pretended, she decided, and maybe Kit was right to make him privy to some of her secrets after all.

He lifted his wineglass in a toast and, easy with a gentleman's open admiration for once, she gave him a faint nod of thanks and turned away before anyone could think more of his gesture than he had meant. Too late, she met hotly angry dark eyes and saw Kit was furious that Mr Shaw could make her forget her anxiety when he had failed to do so.

Her smile wavered, for how could she explain to him that Ben Shaw might have been a friend if only she was staying, without them quarrelling over the possibility? Kit Alstone was hot-tempered and jealous and far too certain he was always right, and how could she learn not to love him so much that it hurt? If only they realised it, her enemies could threaten the man she loved and hurt her far more than they ever would by attacking her directly. So was it any wonder her tension had wound all the tighter as the evening went on and she hoped and prayed they would never realise it?

'I suppose my sister Kate will have to come home and start attending small dinner parties like this after her next birthday,' she offered as a neutral topic of conversation more or less at random.

'I doubt she looks forward to that with much glee, or the company of the chaperon I must find her before then,' he replied, a glimmer of indulgent humour fighting the storm clouds in his dark eyes.

'She likes her own way a little too well to submit to being seen and not heard as a nascent débutante is supposed to be,' she warned, glad he had taken the trouble of visiting her sisters.

'Her opinions will never be discarded at my dinner table, nor would I try to force her into the mould of conventional débutante, both for her sake and my own,' he assured her.

She believed him, adding one more reason why she should return to Snowdonia as soon as possible. Her sisters would be perfectly safe in the care of their new guardian, and she had no wish to spoil their prospects. She squared her shoulders against the pain of leaving not only her love behind, but also her family, and told herself it was a price she would always have to pay for her folly.

'Would you not?' she asked rather distractedly, realising with another acute dart of pain that he would make some girl a wonderful father.

Her eyes hazed and her heart flipped at the very thought of bearing his children, but she carefully veiled her thoughts before meeting his gaze again.

'It would make her as boring as all the rest of them for one thing, and for another I don't think I could,' he was explaining as she looked at him as blankly as if he had just told her pigs could fly.

Now what had they been talking about? Miranda forced herself off the fluffy cloud she had been drifting on, and reminded herself sternly that they had to have a future before they could start planning it. Ah, yes, Kate—at least her sister's welfare would distract her from building impossible castles in Spain.

'Both my sisters have minds of their own, unless they have changed drastically. So far as I can tell from the letters she sends to Lady Rhys, Kate has some very unusual notions about her future.' And that had been another layer of cruelty on someone's part, Miranda decided bitterly, forbidding correspondence between her and her sisters. At least Kate had cleverly got round it by declaring Lady Rhys an established family friend who could not be ignored even by the junior members of said family.

'Are either of them at all like you, Mrs Braxton?' Ben put in with a smile that won him another frown from Kit and a reproachful glance from Miranda for openly eavesdropping.

'Not in the least, thank heavens,' she replied coolly.

'You are too harsh on yourself and her,' Kit argued. 'All three of you have those extraordinary eyes, and if Kate's hair is more auburn than caramel, she certainly has your height and some of your grace when she chooses to remember it.'

'I meant thank goodness she is not like me, not that I ever thought her less than beautiful,' she told him crossly.

How could he misunderstand her so wilfully when he claimed to want to marry her, despite everything?

'I know,' he told her with a look that told her she was the one who should have a stronger grasp on reality, given that he knew her as well as she did herself, 'that's why you must present her when the time comes, Miranda.'

'I shall be back in Snowdonia well before then. One of your sisters would no doubt make a most suitable chaperon for her,' she said flatly.

'You and no other,' he promised.

If only she could, she would guard them as fiercely as the fabled guard dog Cerberus had the gates of Hades, but surely it was impossible?

'No,' she assured him steadily, 'nobody must speak ill of my sisters, and they would do so if I introduced them into society.'

'Not when the truth is finally out.'

'The truth can never come out!' she gasped, fighting to keep her voice soft and confidential, before she proclaimed her secrets to all and sundry without any help from him.

'Trying to keep things quiet has done more than enough damage to this family,' he murmured implacably. 'Trust me?' he asked with more questions in his dark eyes than she wanted to answer.

'For myself I would do so with all that I am, because of my sisters I must trust only myself.'

'Do you think I would do you less than honour?' he demanded, all stiff pride all of a sudden.

'No.'

'Then accept the inevitable.'

'No,' she whispered steadily.

'I need you, Venus,' he told her implacably.

'And in return?' she asked, stung that he was choosing a public venue for a very private conversation.

'All I am, all I could be if I had you at my side,' he starkly paraphrased her own words and the truth was in his steadfast gaze.

She let her gaze linger on the determined set of his beloved mouth and that stubborn chin, and wondered if he could possibly know how much she longed to give in. He could, if the answering blaze of need in his intent gaze was anything to do by, but he held it mercilessly at bay as he silently demanded that final commitment of her.

'Unfair,' she muttered, for he was forcing her to accept or reject him, before he carried out whatever plan he had for tonight.

'Yes or no?'

'No,' she finally announced on a heartfelt sigh. She knew now he would permit them no illicit affair, no blazing nights in his arms burning out the candles until dawn in each other's arms. There would be nothing but emptiness for her when she left Wychwood this time, but leave it she would. This time the heat and anticipation in his dear eyes died, and, oh, the chill and hopelessness of it all as she tried to pretend she was tasting her dinner and hearing the silly social words about them. For once he had listened to her, and now looked remote and even a little revolted at what he heard.

'I dare say you'll be able to marry whomever you will, once you're in possession of all your grandfather left you and a fifth of his fortune,' he said coldly at last.

The impulse to deny it was strong, but if such a ridiculous idea meant that he took her no and believed it at last, then so be it.

'I dare say,' she agreed lightly enough and got up gladly when her aunt finally signalled the end of this interminable meal.

Not even the company of Aunt Clarissa and Celia could make the evening worse, and the very thought of more of this nearly sent her running upstairs to pack. She stayed where she was, however; if she was not to be a charge on her beloved godmother for the rest of her life she needed her inheritance, for she would never marry now. Pride kept her in her seat, pretending to be intent on her sewing, but it wasn't quite absorbing enough to blot out the triumphant glances Celia sent her when Kit came into the room again and sat down as far from Miranda as he could get.

Shooting him a sidelong look, Miranda saw a reckless glint in his dear eyes and a wildness to his dark hair that indicated he had been enjoying Grandfather's port or brandy a little more liberally than usual. Feeling herself under scrutiny, although Kit had ostentatiously refused to look at her, she raised her eyes to clash challengingly with Mr Benedict Shaw and raised her eyebrows haughtily.

Instead of looking politely away, he mirrored her gesture with a distinct dash of irony and she wondered briefly if she had gained yet another enemy. To her surprise he then smiled and nodded as if making his mind up about her, before moving across the room to take the seat by her side. Surely he wasn't oblivious to Kit's furious looks as his friend put his mighty frame between Miranda and the rest of the company?

'Offended the great lover, have you, Mrs Braxton?' he asked lightly enough.

'I certainly hope so,' she assured him steadily, refusing to pass the matter off as a light social nicety.

'He might be too absorbed in making an idiot of himself to see the wood for the trees just now, but Kester can usually tell a hawk from a handsaw if you give him long enough to calm down and examine them rationally.'

'Thank you for the warning,' she said sincerely. 'I don't suppose you'd care to set up a flirtation with me, Mr Shaw? I have no expectations of marriage, I assure you.'

He grinned and looked impossibly handsome at the same time as presenting a challenge most females would have fought to meet. She decided that together he and Kit must have cut a swathe through the bored belles of the *ton* last year, if only Kit had managed to persuade him into attire likely to see him admitted to the salons and ballrooms they inhabited.

'Sorry,' he said with a fine pantomime of smitten regret that gave her the strength to shrug off Aunt Clarissa's obvious disapproval, 'but I have an odd affection for the impulsive idiot. Not that I wouldn't enjoy a refreshing flirtation with a beautiful creature like yourself under normal circumstances, my dear ma'am, but I've no mind to be invited to eat grass before breakfast by my best friend.'

'Hmm, I suppose it wouldn't serve. I shall just

have to avoid him as diligently as possible during my remaining time at Wychwood.'

'I would wish you luck with that, if I didn't know Kester too well to bet against a certainty.'

'I can't marry him,' she told him, torn between a compulsion to look over at the subject of their conversation and the dread of what she might see in his expression as she outwardly flirted with his friend.

'I think you'll find there's no such word as "cannot" in Christopher Alstone's version of the dictionary. He's his own man, Mrs Braxton, not a product of expensive schools and generations of privilege,' Mr Shaw said seriously, all hint of laughter gone from his steady gaze.

'I know, but I am my own woman too, and wedding a man who will rapidly live to regret it is not my idea of the foundations for a happy life,' she assured him lightly, then sighed with relief as the tea-tray came in at last.

Conversation faltered in the face of that ritual, and Miranda hid her untouched cup behind a collection of greenery for the servants to find in the morning and quietly slipped from the room. At least with Kit's eagle-eyed gaze off her, she could move about the house with a little more freedom, she assured herself, trying not to miss his protective concern for her as she made her way up the stairs.

From the sound of it Sukey was already enjoying the sleep of the just and Miranda couldn't help but envy her innocent slumbers as she gently shut the door to the dressing room and left her to enjoy them. By virtue of contortions that would have had Leah scolding bitterly if she could only see her, Miranda put off her velvet gown with a sigh of relief. Somehow she doubted she would ever wear it again without thinking of the fire in Kit's eyes when he first set eyes on her in it, then the frost that greeted her final refusal as he looked away as if the sight of her pained him.

Luckily her short corset laced up the front and proved less of a challenge, then off with her shift and she could slip on her very proper fine linen nightgown. All she needed now was peace and quiet and a good night's sleep and she would be resigned to her lonely destiny by morning, she told herself. Unfortunately the calm of her room, the soft glow of the banked fire, the security of shutters closed tight and doors bolted against the world as per his lordship's orders had no effect on her chaotic thoughts. Her mind told her she had done the right thing, but she hurt to her very heart and soul at the thought of never having Kit tease or desire her with all the fearsome attention at his command ever again.

'And I never meant to hurt you, my love,' she whispered and had to fight tears at the thought of inflicting pain on the man she loved so certainly she knew it would remain strong and steady in her heart until her dying day.

Impatient of her many bitter regrets when she knew it was the only thing she could have done, given that she did love him with that certainty, she sat up and looked for her usual book. If all else failed, she would just have to read herself to sleep, or wake Sukey and get her to hit her over the head to ensure unconsciousness for a few blessed hours. With a rather woeful smile at the very thought of the little maid's shocked refusal of such a scheme, Miranda bit back a curse at finding no book there to offer improbable distraction after all.

For a while she forced herself to lie back on her pillows and consider the fact that no book would blot out her rather melancholy thoughts tonight, but it was no good. Sleep would not come on top of such turmoil and, if she wasn't careful, she would manage to convince herself she had been wrong.

Kit's bedchamber was only across the other side of the house, which was not nearly far enough away for a decidedly love-sick idiot like her, but she had to resist scratching on his door and begging for whatever he was willing to give—if he heard her at all through the stupor he seemed likely to have drunk himself into. Tenderness played about her mouth as she thought of her love as sore as a tethered bear come morning as he nursed a well-deserved headache, but that was a road she could not go down.

'And you're old enough to know better as well,' she chided herself for so much wanting to soothe his troubled brow, even as she got out of bed and shrugged on her dressing gown and told herself it would serve him right.

Drawing back the sturdy bolt Kit had ordered put on her door, she wondered if her attacker was awaiting just such an opportunity, then dismissed the idea. The estrangement between herself and Kit had been very obvious tonight, even if the evening had got off to an unpromising start for Celia and Aunt Clarissa.

Even now the idea of Celia doing anything so vulgar as carrying out her ill intent herself seemed extraordinary, but Miranda doubted she would put herself into anyone else's power to such an extent as to pay them to do murder. Her cousin had always been utterly ruthless in the pursuit of her own way, but this? Maybe Miranda had been naïve in thinking no woman capable of such ruthlessness. Which was another good reason why she was going downstairs to find something to read, for now she needed distracting from both Kit and her enemies and it would have to be something magnificently compelling to do that.

Shakespeare, she thought, dismissing novels and poetry as well as the might of classical literature in a mental search for a diversion more absorbing than real life. And not the comedies for once, because they were too sunny, at least for the most part. Tonight she needed a lesson in life to show her how fortunate she still was. *King Lear* or *Hamlet* perhaps, but certainly not *Macbeth.* That would be too uncomfortable a reminder of what a woman was capable of in the headlong pursuit of position and power.

Despite herself she shivered, and drew the warm dark wrap closer about her as she stepped out on to the landing in soft-soled slippers. At least she need disturb nobody tonight, she decided, as she crept along the broad corridor and down the wide stairs. From her youthful misdeeds she knew every creaking stair as well as how to avoid the watchful footman in the hall below. Slipping through a narrow door on the half-landing, she used the meagre stair the builders of the house had put in for servants to creep about the house unseen and came out opposite the library door silently as a ghost.

For some reason she held her breath, listening to a silence that felt placid and empty for all her imagination would people it with listeners if she let it. It was a ridiculous notion, she informed herself, and crossed to the open door and stood wondering whether or not to shut it behind her. The moonlight was making the shadows deeper while barring the turkey carpet with silver light as it shone through the tall windows and she paused at the strangeness of it before she felt as much as heard swift movement at her side.

Too late to cry out, she struggled uselessly for a moment as a strong hand clamped over her mouth and Kit's other arm bound her to his side as unshakeably as an iron fetter. Her body knew it was him before her mind caught up, and adapted itself contentedly to every inch of him it could lean into with unmistakable delight as he took his silencing hand away. Trying to repudiate her body's wanton reaction, Miranda forced it to put a bare inch or so of space between them, and managed to stand stiff and offended in his hard embrace.

Chapter Eighteen

'You nearly ruined everything, love,' Kit murmured into her nearest ear and tugged her deeper into the shadows by the gallery steps.

Ruined everything? Miranda silently ranted, then followed up with *love?* as the shock of that endearment sent everything else out of her mind. He hadn't believed her refusal, then? She struggled between despair that it was all to do again, and elation that she hadn't managed to kill his feelings for her after all.

He must have felt her slew round to look up at him with that question on her silent mouth. Instead of explaining himself, he wrapped his arms about her so she stood cradled in front of him, secure and protected and very warm indeed as the intimacy of it engulfed her.

'Be quiet and don't ask questions for once,

Venus, and for heaven's sake stop wriggling,' he whispered softly.

Miranda felt the reason for that last stricture as his very obvious arousal made her more wicked side long to lean back and wriggle to such effect he would stop this odd game and carry her upstairs to their mutual satisfaction. She had tried her best to refuse him for his own good, but she was only human when all was said and done, and just now she felt very human indeed.

Somehow she fought the temptation and felt quiet darkness settle about them again. Kit must be lurking in the shadows of his own library at some ridiculous hour of the night for some reason, so she might as well stand here and listen for whoever he might be expecting. The only hardship would be in stopping herself from twisting round and enjoying the darkness all around them just a little too much. As his warmth wrapped her ever closer she felt her body both tighten and loosen at the same time. It really did have a mind of its own, she decided, as she felt her nipples tighten at the brush of soft linen and velvet when he moved to ease his own evident discomfort and shift her a little further away.

Suppressing a groan of need, she turned her head to look up at him and thought she saw an echo of her own raging desire being leashed by his iron will, as he clamped his jaw shut and shook his head at her in reproach.

'Behave, woman, before Ben and the lawyer see far more than they expect to,' he bent to murmur in her ear so quietly that even the soft rasp of his breath seemed louder than his words.

He must have felt her reaction to his latest warning as she went stiff with embarrassment and his warm chuckle was more a rumble in his muscular chest at her back than any sound at all. Yet it warmed her, and made her see the humour of this extraordinary encounter as she let herself lean confidently back against him once more. Who cared about the niceties of it? She was where she wanted to be and that was enough for now.

Knowing they were not alone in the shadows, she tried to search the darkness for the giant form of Ben Shaw and the much smaller and more rotund one of Mr Poulson in vain. The bright moonlight made the shadows beyond unreadable and she became more confident that whatever they were all up to might succeed after all. She tensed as she heard a soft whirring sound and then relaxed again as the clock on the mantelpiece went through its chimes and ended by striking one o'clock.

How long would they all wait here like a very odd set of marble statues? she wondered, and felt a most unworthy desire to giggle at the thought of all four of them trying not to make sound or movements. Then she sobered as she let herself think of their quarry properly for the first time and shivered. Kit wrapped his arms even closer round her as if to ward off what he guessed was not a physical coldness. Rubbing her head against his chin to signal her silent appreciation, she gallantly fought off an urge to twist round and press a swift kiss on his mouth, and be damned to her relatives and all their works. Then she heard a stealthy brush of a hand against the long windows out into the garden that made her forget even that temptation.

Her heart quickened under Kit's hand and she felt him stand at the ready, even as he pressed close enough to mouth a warning against her ear as the newcomer entered the room. What did he mean by warning her not to cry out, whatever she might see? Did he think she hadn't worked out the idea that two of her nearest relatives were intent on driving her away at the very least and possibly even murdering her. Yet what on earth could Celia have been up to in the garden in the middle of the night?

'Damnation!' cursed a voice she had never

thought to hear again and she knew exactly why Kit had warned her all of a sudden.

Standing with his hand on a swaying bust of some severe Roman emperor he must have carelessly knocked off balance, Nevin Braxton stood in the full glare of moonlight. She might have known that news of his death was too good to be true!

Kit risked the potential of his trap by shifting so his hand brushed her cheek in a gesture of comfort that reminded her how far they both were from that terrible night in a Bristol tavern, when her so-called husband tried to sell her into sexual slavery. No need to fear Nevin would see that stealthy movement, she decided with disgust, and watched him pat the emperor on the head and step away unsteadily. He was drunk as usual. Soft steps hurried toward the library and the library door shut in Celia's wake with the rustle of her furiously swished skirts loud in the ensuing silence.

'I heard you come in halfway across the hall,' she snapped at last.

'And a good evening to you too, wife,' Nevin rumbled in sulky greeting, and this time Miranda nearly jumped out of her soft-soled slippers in shock.

It revealed so much that had been hidden, and yet how deep must Celia's evil go if this was true?

Something told her it was, for there was a cold wickedness in both Celia and Nevin that made them ideally matched, now she thought about it.

'You're drunk again,' Celia accused.

'Of course I am—you would be too if you had to spend all your time locked up in that confounded ruined tower. Why didn't you come to me today?'

'Because I didn't want to,' she informed him with majestic contempt.

'Shall I make you want me?' he offered and Miranda had a job to swallow down her revulsion as she saw her cousin hesitate and then deny herself the sick eagerness for compulsion that obviously bound her to him.

'No, Carnwood put another footman on duty in the hall tonight and I dare say they have been told to check the house every now and again,' she whispered loudly enough to make her refusal penetrate his drunken haze.

'So why the devil did you summon me here?' he asked disagreeably. 'I couldn't believe it when I saw the light in the window after last night's fiasco.'

'I didn't dare come to the tower after that, and I wanted to tell you to stop. There's no point murdering the slut now.'

'Lost your nerve at last, my darling?' Nevin asked

and Miranda could see even by moonlight that he loved Celia's 'nerve', even if it nerved her to murder.

'No, the upstart earl accepted my silly cousin's refusal tonight. I saw that brutish giant from London half-carry him up to bed little more than an hour ago, so I dare say the fool's snoring off his sorrows by now. He'll be desperate for all that money when she leaves, so I'll soon march him up the aisle,' Celia replied.

The combination of contempt and glee in her cousin's voice as she outlined her plans made Miranda feel sick. Somehow she stayed silent as Celia moved even closer to Nevin so they stood side by side, and might as well have been stone for all the feeling in them.

The thought of the unique and wonderful man holding her so securely being locked into such a marriage made her know one thing. She refused to think about any other woman becoming his wife, let alone Celia, so she would just have to do it herself.

'Miranda always was a brainless ninny,' Celia was gloating. 'I've got rid of her this time, just as I did before.'

'*We* got rid of her before,' Nevin corrected sharply.

'Yes, and we only had to do it again because you

let her get away last time, just as you missed your shot the other day.'

'And you wasted the chance to wheedle the old man into leaving you everything, didn't you my clever little doxy? At least I didn't try to stick a knife into my enemy in the middle of my own home, where anyone might have caught me and very nearly did.'

'I got clean away,' she insisted sulkily.

'Only because I carried you to that dank keep you insist on lodging me in and bandaged your feet for you. Confoundedly heavy you were to.'

'I am not heavy,' Celia argued through what sounded like gritted teeth and Miranda wondered if she had that knife about her.

If so, she would be very careful if she was Nevin, for she thought that untrammelled access to the Alstone fortunes would present far more temptation than Celia could resist. With Nevin gone, any union would be legal and suddenly all that had been odd about Celia's marriage became clear. Grandfather had known about that as well, and Miranda wondered if she had ever really known him at all. To conceal such a crime as bigamy in the defence of the family name was taking pride much too far, especially after the way he had punished her for a lesser sin.

Shivering, she leant into the embrace of the one man to stand with her every time she needed him to. At last she knew family pride and fear of scandal were as nothing beside true love, and he had known it far sooner than she had. Kit's arms pulled her yet closer and past present and future slotted into place in the most extraordinary fashion. Nevin didn't matter and nor did Celia; nothing mattered but this man and the family they would make together, once they had dealt with the minor annoyance of having a potential murderess in the family.

'I think we have heard enough, don't you my lord?' she heard Mr Poulson say from his hiding place, as coolly if he was back in his chambers discussing some dry point of law.

'Aye,' Kit agreed tersely, and freed one arm from about Miranda to reach out for the loaded pistol he had laid ready on the gallery steps.

Stepping forward, he stood shoulder to shoulder with her, his left arm about her narrow waist and his eyes hard on the pair frozen in the shaft of moonlight.

'More than enough,' Ben Shaw's deep voice added from another dark corner and it was he who stepped forward to thrust a taper into the dying fire and kindled as many branches of candles as it took to banish the shadows.

As he too held a deadly-looking pistol in his other hand all the while, neither Nevin nor Celia showed much inclination to move, but even from here Miranda would see that her cousin's eyes were wild with fury. If she had possessed a firearm, no doubt one of them would have been dead by now. As Miranda stepped into the light, she had little doubt which one.

'God, how I hate you,' Celia hissed at her, her small, capable hands clenched in impotent fists.

'I don't think God has anything to do with it,' Kit said in an icy voice that made Miranda shiver, despite the reassurance of his arm warm about her waist. 'So we have enough this time, Poulson?' he went on without taking his eyes off their prey once.

'More than enough, my lord. With the proof of their marriage your agent found in the Gretna register, it is obvious they have both played the bigamist without so much as the hint of a conscience. Indeed, I dare say we already had enough to hang them before they damned themselves. With our testimony it will all be wrapped up neat as ninepence,' Mr Poulson said triumphantly.

'You won't prosecute me,' Celia defied them confidently.

'I will, you know,' Kit returned implacably.

'And see the precious Alstone name dragged through the mud, and your whore's name along with it? Never!'

'Just for naming your cousin so I would now, even if I felt the ridiculous regard for a mere name your mama and grandfather seem to have shared. My name got dragged through the mud by my father before I was even born, it means very little to me if it is pure as snow or black as midnight.'

'You're just a commoner,' she spat the words at him contemptuously.

'Maybe, but I still hold most of the cards, don't you think?'

'Then think again,' Nevin sneered and grabbed Celia so she made a screen for his body. 'Commoner or not, you won't shoot a woman,' he said confidently and began to back toward the long window where he came in.

'No, but I will,' Miranda told him and seized the pistol from Kit's lax grip and aimed it steadily at Celia's heart. 'As soon as I shoot her, kindly despatch Mr Braxton for me, please, Mr Shaw,' she added without looking away.

'It will be a pleasure, ma'am,' he said with an irrepressible laugh in his deep voice that didn't make it sound any less dangerous.

'How reassuring,' she returned ironically and

challenged Celia with an unflinching gaze. 'Give me one reason why I shouldn't pull the trigger, Celia,' she urged coldly.

'I am your cousin.'

'Not much of a recommendation, and a couple of shots now will save a very public trial, so you see, citing the family name won't work on me either.'

'Then go on and shoot me, you'll have it on your silly conscience for life and that'll be revenge enough for me.'

'I really think you are mad.' Miranda felt the same sort of pity she might for a rabid dog.

'And I that you are stupid,' Celia spat and tried to shove Nevin aside in order to run past him into the night.

He was too frightened of Ben Shaw to let her do so and they grappled like ill-matched wrestlers until Kit and Ben pulled them apart and proceeded to bind them with stout cords they no doubt considered essential equipment for a gentleman.

'The strong room, I think,' Kit said to his friend as if they were discussing something perfectly trivial. 'Luckily it has some ventilation so they won't stifle and cheat the hangman, then in the morning the local magistrate can have them with my blessing, for I'm heartily sick of the pair of them.'

'Aye, aye, cap'n,' Ben said cheerfully and shoved Nevin along with a none-too-gentle push in the small of his back before he picked up Celia and threw her over his mighty shoulder as if she weighed no more than a feather. 'Come along then, Sir Lawyer, can't you see that we're very much in the way? You can bother them about their settlements another time,' he said cheerfully and led off his procession as if it was nothing out of the ordinary.

Miranda recalled that most of her important meetings with Kit Alstone had taken place in this room, and this promised to be the most important of all.

'What are you going to do with them?' she asked at last.

'I want information, and a night contemplating their fate at trial will make it easier to extract. Then we will see,' Kit replied.

'But what useful information could Celia possibly have?' she asked, puzzled by such an unlikely prospect.

'None, I suspect, but Braxton is connected to the business that took me to that tavern in Bristol one fateful night five years ago.'

'So what *were* you doing there, my lord?' she asked stiffly.

'Searching for the butchers who took one of our ships and murdered the crew. I traced the ship's master to that dive where we met, and then I let him slip through my fingers. Now I want to know everything Braxton saw and did in that tavern, for he may know more than he thinks, even if he wasn't involved, which I have yet to be convinced of.'

'I'm surprised your mysterious rogue let Nevin live,' Miranda objected.

'Yet the world, apart from his wife, has thought him dead for nearly five years. If I were in his shoes, I would want to disappear again at the double.'

'So long as he takes Celia with him, I for one will gladly see him go.'

'I think we will make that a condition of his freedom, don't you? I can think of no better punishment than to inflict them on each other for life,' Kit said with a satisfied smile that looked rather implacable.

'So long as they are not allowed to conceal their connection ever again, for don't forget poor Lieutenant Grant was their victim as surely as I was. How very annoyed they must have been when he was killed before he inherited the family fortune, although I wouldn't have given sixpence for his life once he had. And I should hate to think of them trying their disgusting scheme on some other gullible little fool like myself.'

'Not a fool, my love, just a romantic child with a head full of poetry and tall tales,' he admonished gently, making her stupid infatuation with Nevin the irrelevance it should have been.

'Yes, and the tallest one of all was you,' she said, trying to keep a catch out of her voice and the stars from her eyes, perhaps a little too successfully as it happened.

'I'm not sure whether to be flattered or disappointed at that conclusion,' he said with a vulnerability in his dark eyes that made her heart miss a beat.

Who would have thought Kit Alstone, Earl of Carnwood, and a considerable power in his own right, was insecure about his own desirability?

'Flattered,' she reassured him with a wicked smile. 'I don't dream about every passing rogue I meet for five years afterwards, you know? Especially as I only set eyes on you that one time and wasn't even in my right senses at the time.'

'Well, it was a memorable occasion,' he assured her huskily and she had little doubt he looked back on their first meeting with fondness.

Despite the horror of her situation so did she, now love had joined the terrible wanting and the curiosity that had burnt through her at their first meeting. Then she had too newly emerged from the horrors Nevin had inflicted on her to fully appreciate the fact of Kit Alstone, survivor, fighter and the strongest and most noble man she had ever encountered. That had not been their time, but at last she knew without the slightest doubt that this was.

'So memorable that I couldn't even recall it?' she teased.

'I don't think you would let yourself do that, Venus. I'm not being vain in saying I appealed to your wild side, and just then you didn't trust it one iota.'

'How did you know?' she murmured, marvelling at such understanding and wishing above all that he would stretch that intuition and kiss her until said wild and very real Miranda was rampant and in control.

'When I first saw you standing at the bottom of the steps, all I wanted to do was have you in my bed and at my mercy for a very long time. Then I came to know you and could tell nothing was as it had seemed that night. Instead of a goddess who played with human fools for your own pleasure, you were kind and beautiful and very human. You were also very responsive to my shameless advances, even if your susceptibility to them plainly shocked you. I soon decided you would make me an ideal wife, my love, but I didn't let myself see how empty my life would be without you until I nearly lost you. If I had any sense, I would have fallen on my knees that first day on the carriage sweep and surrendered, but I'm too much of a fool to have recognised my fate the instant I met it again.'

'I don't think you're a fool at all, but are you certain?' she asked painfully, for if he was not it would rip the heart out of her now.

'Idiot,' he chided, 'do I look uncertain?'

She allowed herself the luxury of gazing into his eyes with her own feelings naked in her own and, no, he really didn't look uncertain at all. In fact, he looked exultant and ardent and very, very certain.

'No, you don't look as if a doubt ever entered your handsome head, my love, which is a very good trick and some day you must teach it to me,' she teased him, and rose on tiptoes to kiss him.

After a very heated few minutes he finally forced himself to let her go and held her at arm's length.

'So, are you going to make an honest man of me after all?' Kit asked and she was amazed to see how nervous he was of her answer.

'Yes, for I think you really do deserve me,' she

said with a smile of such gloating joy he picked her up and swung her in a dizzy circle.

'Ah, but don't I?' he said with exultant complacency. 'In fact, I think we deserve each other, Miranda mine.'

'Yes, I am, aren't I,' she replied with a self-satisfied smile that belied all her stern resolutions that she would manage her life alone. Her life without Kit Alstone in it would be no more than an existence. 'There will be whispers,' she managed to caution him, as if he didn't already know it.

'Considering you are noble, lovely and rich, as well as soon to be possessed of a very handsome husband who is completely besotted with you, why would there not be? You can write it down to jealousy,' he told her with an arrogant grin.

'*Very* handsome?' she asked, looking up at him consideringly. 'Hmm, I dare say all that feminine attention you enjoyed during your London Season has gone to your head, Lord Carnwood. Your features are a little too decided to be considered classically perfect, you know?'

'Witch,' he chided and ran his hand down the side of her cheek and over her own features as if testing a theory, 'you may carry the palm for both of us then.'

'I will very soon have to hand it on to my sisters,' she said lightly, but knew he was trying to give her back a part of herself she had come to hate.

Knowing her looks had been a hair shirt to her these last five years, he was letting her see how precious a gift they would be between husband and wife. Husband! Now there was a possession she never thought she would have.

Chapter Nineteen

'What if it comes out about that I was never really wed to Nevin?' she asked as doubt suddenly rocked the foundations of her lovely new certainty.

'If it does, the full tale will soon turn you into a heroine, love. An established beauty of three and twenty schemes for her secret husband to elope with her innocent young cousin, so she can work on their ageing grandparent to leave her his fortune, or maybe even out of plain spite. And she has a husband so disreputable even her lecher of a father couldn't stomach him as a son-in-law, and died in mysterious circumstances very shortly after he discovered their marriage and hushed it up. Most daughters would have spurned Braxton and denounced him to the world, but Celia wound herself ever tighter into the web of sick need they seem to have for each other. Then the cold-hearted bitch decided public humiliation wasn't enough and tried to murder you, her rival for my most noble hand in marriage. No, somehow I don't think the tale will leak out through your cousin or your aunt this time.'

'Speaking of my aunt, what is going to become of her?' Miranda asked.

'You, my darling, are far too soft-hearted for your own good. I suppose you would have me hand over the Dower House because she failed to make your life a misery?'

'I'm not that stupid,' she defended herself, although the thought of even Aunt Clarissa becoming an outcast made her uneasy.

'Good, because if she comes within fifty miles of Wychwood ever again I will have her arrested,' Kit told her with a little too much understanding in his dark gaze.

'What for?' she protested. 'The most I can accuse her of is being in my room the first time and spoiling my letters and my desk. She didn't actually hurt me.'

'Only because she's too much of a bully and a coward to have the courage to do more than first throw mud at you and then try to scare you off. No, she is one good work I refuse to let you indulge in, my love. Save your compassion for those who deserve it and God knows there are enough of them.'

'But I know the Ennersley heir refused to house her when Sir Horace died, because that was her excuse for bringing Celia to Wychwood.'

'Wise fellow,' he said approvingly, 'she will just have to get used to living in less state than she considers appropriate, and she's not having your house in Bath before you even suggest it. You're going to let that at a proper rent, my love. I don't want you to feel dependent on me when we're wed and you're as much your grandfather's heir as I am myself. He plainly wanted this marriage nigh as much as I do.'

'In that case, what about Celia?' she protested.

'What about her?'

'He left her in the running for the Countess of Carnwood stakes, which was very wrong of him when he knew she was already married.'

'I dare say he thought that it would keep her in line while she tried to charm me into the biggest mistake of my life. He must have known I would only need to set eyes on you to fall head over ears in love.'

She blushed and felt warmth steal through every inch of her, but nobly persisted in trying to divert them both from all the possibilities a moonlit room behind a closed door offered lovers.

'Well, it seems to me to be a ridiculous scheme and one that nearly got me killed,' she insisted.

'True, but at least the old man tried to set things right,' he replied, sounding more than a little distracted, as if those possibilities had occurred to him as well and were occupying at least half his attention.

'Yes, I suppose he did his best.'

'Belatedly, but now can we please talk about our wedding before I go mad with frustration? It should be very soon if those daughters we discussed are to be born at a respectable time.'

'I thought you had that all arranged.'

'Offended, Venus? If you only knew what that termagant look of yours does to me, you might be a little more wary of aiming it my way.'

Blushing as she guessed some of it from the hot look in his intent dark eyes, Miranda let him pull her into his arms because it was so much where she wanted to be and why deny themselves after so long a courtship?

'So what do you propose doing about it, my lord?' she asked with a provocative look.

Annoyingly his self-control was superior to her own, for he put a little distance between them. 'I shall set off for London as soon as it is light, so I can bring my sisters back in time for the wedding,' he told her in a voice so husky with longing she knew he was finding it harder than she dreamt to resist her silently offered invitation.

'You do expect to be here for it yourself, I hope, my Lord Carnwood?' she joked in an attempt to lessen his tension.

'Oh, yes, Venus, I shall be here, and then you can expect no mercy.'

'Maybe I'll stay after all, then,' she whispered provocatively.

'You'd better—try to run away this time and I'll hunt you to the ends of the earth, my love,' he vowed. 'There's no chance of escape for you.'

'I should hope not,' she said severely, 'a lady can only wait just so long to be swept off her feet by her dashing rescuer, you know? Five years is an excessive time to wait for that.'

'But in three weeks' time you'll discover it was well worth it.'

With an infuriated growl she hit him half-heartedly on one broad shoulder and tried hard not to sulk. Given that every inch of her was longing for a deeper intimacy than she had dared dream of until now, he had better be right.

'I would have liked Godmama to be at our wedding,' she said and tried to keep her regret that it couldn't be out of her voice.

'Lady Rhys is on her way,' he admitted.

'How can that be, my lord?' she asked with dangerous sweetness.

'I thought you might be pleased to see her,' he told her with a suave innocence she didn't believe in for one moment.

'She will badger you unmercifully until she is convinced you will make me a suitable husband, whatever the rest of the world thinks of our match,' she warned him with a vengeful smile.

'Then I shall just have to charm my way into her good books.'

'You can certainly try.'

'Yes, if riding back and forward to London doesn't rid me of some of this desperation for you, at least being under her sceptical scrutiny will make me behave like a gentleman for once.'

'You are the greatest gentleman of my acquaintance,' she endorsed disgustedly, 'and very inconvenient it is too when I want to be swept off my feet by my pirate with the eyes of a fallen angel. After all, you did buy me, my lord.'

'And in three weeks I will collect my dues. I am a very patient man.'

'No, you're a very annoying man,' she told him with pardonable frustration.

* * *

Three weeks later Miranda faced the new Lady Carnwood in the mirror while Leah brushed her shining curls until they lay soft and heavy over her scandalously sheer night attire.

'Your lord's sister has good taste,' Leah informed her with a sage nod.

'Has she? I think she was robbed myself. There isn't enough fibre in this whole ensemble to clothe a gnat, let alone a grown woman.'

'You're just feeling fretful because his lordship's been away,' Leah said knowledgeably, having been married herself for a whole week.

'I'm fretful because he's a high-handed, secretive, scheming deceiver,' Miranda corrected her acerbically.

'And he refused to stay here and bed you?'

'There's that as well of course,' Miranda admitted grudgingly.

'He thinks to honour you.'

'I know,' Miranda said with a sigh, 'and I had far rather he just wanted me.'

'You deserve patience after what that miserable worm did to you.'

'Maybe I do, but perhaps it would have been better if we had just got on with it, Leah,' she admitted finally. 'I'm so nervous now that I fear he may get a very bad bargain for his new wife after all.'

'He'll know just what to do to make all right, you only have to look at him to see that,' Leah reassured her. 'You chose very well that night you first set eyes on him and that's a certainty.'

'He thought me a man-trap,' she replied indignantly.

'None so blind as a man in love.'

'Or a woman,' Miranda muttered darkly and felt tension winding itself into knots in her stomach and elsewhere.

'Never mind, my lady, his lordship's a man of experience,' Leah offered by way of comfort as she finally satisfied herself that Miranda was as ready for the night ahead as she would ever be.

'Perhaps that's what I'm afraid of.'

'Don't be; this one will make you happy,' Leah assured her softly, then hastily left the Countess's Bedchamber as Kit came in.

'I don't feel like a countess,' Miranda greeted him crossly.

'Good, I don't feel much like an earl just now.'

'Oh, Kit, I don't know what to do,' she admitted and spun round, ready to rip up at him if he dared to laugh at her.

'Luckily I do,' he told her with an admirably straight face.

'You know perfectly well what I mean,' she snapped, sincerely hoping he did, for she wasn't in any fit state to explain it.

'Yes, you have never truly made love before, Venus, which is quite something, considering your namesake. That rat you ran off with just rutted, and you're afraid I might do the same.'

'No! You could never be anything like him; it's just... Well, it's just that you might be disappointed,' she admitted on a ridiculous blush.

'With you, my love? Never,' he promised on a predator's purr of satisfaction as he drew her very slowly into his arms.

'How can you know that?' she asked, despite the shiver of arousal that shook her at his very touch. 'I never felt the slightest spark of desire for Nevin once that first time was over and I knew what it would be like—surely I should have felt something?'

'Yes, revulsion and fear. Now stop trying to make yourself out to be an ice maiden, when we both know you take fire whenever we are anywhere near one another.'

'But I'm not a maiden of any sort, am I? You deserve better.'

'No, I deserve you, Venus.' With that he closed the last inches of space between them and held her close for long minutes of utter contentment. 'I dare say I could just hold you without going completely mad for one more night, if you would like me to, my Miranda,' he finally murmured into her shining curls.

'That I wouldn't,' she whispered back, some of her old courage returning with the heat that scorched between them as he promised. 'If you stayed sane, *I* would end up as demented as my not-so-dear aunt.'

'We can't have that, then,' he murmured and trailed kisses along her collarbone that made her melt from the inside out.

'I love you,' she gasped as he worked his way up her neck towards her ear, and who would have thought such a workaday part of her could hold such magic as it did when he finessed kisses into the hollow between her jaw and her earlobe?

'I didn't want to love you, Miranda,' he whispered, and all her senses concentrated on that lucky ear. 'I spent nigh on five years hating you just for putting the idea that I might into my head.'

'I suppose that's honest,' she gasped distractedly.

He raised his head to look down at her with incredible warmth, his dark eyes heavy lidded with desire as he met the dazed ultramarine heat in her gaze and seemed to glory in it.

'I promise to always be so with you, Miranda. We both put up an armour against the world and I dare say we will have need of it, but with you mine will always be laid down.'

Suddenly that honesty was better than a thousand comfortable lies. 'Good. Then if you have quite finished slaying my dragons, it's about time you attended to your marital duties, my lord.'

'Certainly, my lady.' He gave her a wolfish grin and laid his mouth against hers at last.

Just the brush of it against hers as he soothed and teased against her lips and she was lost. Impatient of his gentleness, she opened her mouth greedily under his and demanded the passion he was holding back. She felt him shudder and the fine control he had been holding himself under snap as she boldly tangled her tongue with his. Now his hands were urgent as he moulded her to him so every inch where they touched was hot and explicit, one against the other.

'I love your honesty, Kit,' she gasped as his arousal nudged her with an urgency she guessed was fast outrunning his self-control.

'And I love you, Miranda,' he told her, with such sincerity in his passion-rasped voice that she let go of the past she had not even known she was holding on to and just trusted him.

'Prove it,' she teased unsteadily, and since they were so close to the marriage bed anyway she gently pushed him backwards on to it and followed, to crouch over him and squirm her way up his mighty body.

Suddenly Louise Kenton's taste in night-attire seemed infinitely practical after all as she felt the heat and tension of him under her exploring hands and all she had between her and her goal was a few ells of gossamer. Would that she could say the same of her lord, she decided militantly, and set about the task of undressing him in a way that would have sent his valet screaming for his portmanteau and civilisation.

'Did you think I would run away screaming if you came to me all but naked?' she asked impatiently, as she finally tugged off his cravat and unbuttoned his shirt.

'And if I did, what a mistake that would have been,' he replied with a rather satisfied smile and pushed her away momentarily, so he could shrug off coat, waistcoat and shirt with one disrespectful heave.

Agreeing absently, she ran a wondering hand over his exposed torso. She hesitantly admired

the satin of his skin over rigid muscle, then drew
away in wonder, only to gently flex her fingers
against the freedom of touch, the liberty to
wonder. Moving on to the light dusting of curls
that shadowed his chest and made a faint line
down which her other hand could follow, she
fumbled with buttons that would at last let her
closer to the glory she could feel pooling between
her own legs in anticipation.

Letting her feel the emphatic reality of his
roused state, Kit lay and watched her, dreading
her hesitation, longing for acceptance. With
hawk-like concentration on every nuance of
feeling, he saw a flush of colour tint her cheeks
rosy and fought like the devil to hold back his
need to lay her flat on her back and take and take
until they were both sated and helpless. She licked
her sharp little tongue over lips already dewy
from their kisses and he impressed himself by
becoming even more aroused than he had thought
possible.

His Miranda wanted him nigh as badly as he did
her! Boldly and delightfully, she caressed his
aching shaft where it thrust towards her delightfully arched body as if that was his magnet, which
indeed she was if she did but know it. All of her,
not just the goddess's body and fabulous face, but

every contradiction and contrariness in her stubborn, wonderful mind as well.

'I don't know how much of that I can stand without going demented,' he cautioned and she just smiled that secret smile of hers, before sitting back on her heels and looking at him with a wicked curving of her delectable mouth.

'I am Venus, don't forget, husband,' she told him arrogantly, 'and if I say you will bear it, then that is exactly what you will do.'

As she then straddled him and promised Elysium, who was he to argue? He just lay there and waited for the next outrageous demand his goddess might make. Sending out those exploring hands of hers with an instinctive hesitancy that clutched at his very heart, she ran them up to his tight male nipples and rubbed experimentally, even as her mass of caramel-coloured curls swept heavy silk over even more sensitive areas and he bucked under her restraining legs.

'Do you like that?' she asked wantonly, her eyes sparkling with mischief and satisfaction.

It was a rhetorical question and they both knew it. He reached out and pulled her closer, so her nipples danced down to rub against his.

'Can't you feel the answer for yourself, wife?'

he demanded with sultry certainty that she very definitely could.

'Yes,' she gasped, seeming impatient with their game now she was open to the promise of his rampant need against her very aroused femininity. 'I want you inside me,' she gasped and at last he knew the past was forgotten and this was just for them, only for now.

'Far be it from me to gainsay you then, my lady,' he growled unsteadily and thrust up, even as she sank on to him and let out a long moan of satisfaction.

Silk and wet softness enwrapped him, his unique lady love rode him, and five years of waiting for this moment melted away in a second. Control he had never thought he could offer in such extremity held back the roaring need to take over and drive them to ecstasy. For her, for love, he could fight the relentless drive of desire and let her have the tentative delight of being the controller and not the controlled.

With a soft moan of satisfaction she sank down and took all of him. 'Oh, Kit, how can a person experience such incredible pleasure and still live?' she asked in wonder.

'Because it's life itself, or it is when true love is

involved,' he murmured back, wondering if that fine control he had just congratulated himself on would hold out for much longer after all.

She was so beautiful, so extraordinary as she surged forwards and began the race for fulfilment she still didn't fully understand, that to resist her seemed almost inhuman.

'Then it's new for you, too?' she whispered and, as she stayed the fabulous dance of their entwined bodies to wait for an answer, he knew it was vitally important to both of them.

'So new that I can't find words to describe it, my darling.'

'Good, then we might as well just get on with it,' she said with delicious practicality and his hands reached out and urged her to do just that.

The feel of his strong, urging hands against the softness of her neat derrière sent Miranda into a novel reality; suddenly she was steady where she had been tense, sure where the last remnants of fear had haunted her. Glorying in the power of her own body for once, she concentrated on the incredible feeling of her husband and lover stretching her and filling her. Here and now they could share more than she had ever dreamt of, for this was the heart of love. The place where they could express everything they were to each other, and give all to gain all.

His sure touch beckoned her on as she rose and fell, gave and took, and whatever he asked there was always more than she had dreamt of to offer in return. Now the gentle learning of their beginning this wonder was a frantic striving for something even more incredible. She gasped and cried beyond words as he rose and fell with her, as active in their dance to whatever headlong goal they were flying towards as she was.

'Kit, I love you!' she gasped out as she let go and flew, arching back as her eyes rolled back *in extremis* and her body bucked with his as convulsion after convulsion of unknowable delight soared through them.

Through them! That was the joy of it, the wonder and delight of it, and there weren't enough words in the English language to go round when it came to describing what they were to one another as their bodies spasmed with ecstasy, until she felt hollowed out and yet full of golden promises.

'Love, you were so much worth the waiting for,' he gasped in return and at last her vision cleared and she sank down on to his broad, heaving chest to look straight into his velvet-dark eyes.

At last there was nothing to hide between them,

nothing left to be hidden, and she put all her own love and trust into her adoring, well-loved and rather incredulous blue eyes. They were still joined and she loved the connection of them, the fact of them and was reluctant to give up the wonderful completeness, the fabulous sense of having been stretched and delved and adored by every inch of him.

'And that's just the beginning,' she told him confidently, taking on her siren's role and loving every second.

'You will probably kill me before daybreak,' he teased, but the evidence between them was emphatically giving him the lie already.

'No, but I might be tempted to torture you a little, for all the years we were not lovers!'

'You were only seventeen, my love, so I'm mightily relieved I managed to leave you alone long enough to let you grow into the wondrous woman you are today.'

'I grew up very fast under his control,' she said sombrely, not willing to even mention her tormentor's name at such a time, but still regretful that he had not been so careful of her tender years.

'Then you needed time to heal and grow away from what he had done, and I should have killed him when I had the chance!'

'That you should not, for I have no fancy for living in Newgate; anyway the best revenge is to live well, is it not? And we should spite them by doing that to the very last second of our allotted span, don't you think, my lord?'

'Oh, I do, Venus, I do. Now come here and let me love, my darling, for I think we have a few hours left us before dawn. I intend to make full use of them, before your maid or one of our relatives decide to rouse the household at some unearthly hour just to keep us on our toes.'

'They wouldn't dare,' she murmured as she traced the strong line of his cheek with fingers that seemed addicted to the feel of his firm features under them. 'If I am Venus, then you are my Mars, and I fully intend to be faithful to you unto death; unlike my namesake, who really isn't a very flattering creature to liken me to,' she told him with mock severity.

'I can't help it; from the first instant I met your eyes across that stinking dive you had my heart and by the time I actually found out your name it was too late to think of you by it all the time. Once we became better acquainted, of course, I learnt to love Miranda even more than my wild goddess, but you'll have to excuse me if I recall that moment now and again, and can't help saying how fabulous a being you are to me.'

'I suspect I had best treasure that admission, for I think it was hard won when I recall my first days back here, but I won't always be young and in my prime, you know, Kit? One day I will grow old, God willing.'

'And I mean to make the best of every one of them with you, for time won't change the way we feel, Miranda. I have known enough of infatuation and just plain lust to tell the difference. Yet will you watch me grow old before you and wish you had wed a man of your own age? I am ten years your senior, after all.'

'And I would not have you a minute less, you are tried and tested and proven, love. There is no other man for me and you should have believed me the night we got engaged, for I swear there never will be.'

'You're right, I should have, and I do, and if you've quite finished rebuking and traducing me, will you kindly be quiet and let me show you how much I love you back?' he asked with the wicked glint in his eyes she recognised from his piratical days.

'I might, but as you were crass enough to mention being infatuated with and lusting after other women on our wedding night, I might not,' she teased.

'Only so you would realise no other woman exists

for me, lover. Now I think it really is time I took over this enterprise for the rest of the night. We haven't done enough to insure making a good start on those daughters we promised each other yet.'

'And a boy or two as well,' she said dreamily, the idea of carrying Kit's child making her feel languorous, hot and very demanding all at once.

'Anything to oblige my lady,' he told her with a wicked smile and flipped her over on to her back so they could begin the task straight away.

'We countesses are slaves to our duty,' she informed him primly, then forgot to breathe for a moment as Kit's lusty attentions took their love-making to another level altogether.

* * * * *

HISTORICAL

LARGE PRINT

THE VIRTUOUS COURTESAN

Mary Brendan

Gavin Stone discovers on his brother's death that, to
inherit his estate, he must also take on his mistress!
Sarah is horrified – she never thought she would be
passed on as if she were a chattel – but what choice does
she have? And Gavin will expect a practised seducer –
when in reality she is as unschooled as a debutante…

THE HOMELESS HEIRESS

Anne Herries

Runaway Georgie is disguised as a boy, living life on the
streets after fleeing her scheming aunt and uncle. Cold,
hungry and desperate, she is forced to pickpocket – but
she thieves from the wrong man: the dashing Captain
Richard Hernshaw! And the consummate Captain
very soon discovers the grubby boy is actually a
pretty young woman…

REBEL LADY, CONVENIENT WIFE

June Francis

Driven from her home by accusations of witchcraft,
Lady Anna Fenwick embarks on a dangerous quest. Her
reluctant protector is darkly brooding Jack Milburn, a
merchant venturer with a shadowed past… Jack exists
only to exact revenge on the man who killed his lover and
his son – but slowly Anna teaches him to feel again…

MILLS & BOON®
Pure reading pleasure™

HIST1108 LP

HISTORICAL

LARGE PRINT

MISS WINTHORPE'S ELOPEMENT
Christine Merrill

Shy heiress Miss Penelope Winthorpe was only trying
to escape her bullying brother. She didn't mean to wed a
noble lord over a blacksmith's anvil! And Adam Felkirk,
Duke of Bellston, had no intention of taking a wife. But
Penelope's plight moved him. Now the notorious rake
has a new aim: to shock and seduce his prim and
proper bride!

THE RAKE'S UNCONVENTIONAL MISTRESS
Juliet Landon

Miss Letitia Boyce didn't begrudge her sisters the pick
of London's available bachelors. She'd chosen her own
path, and knew that book-learning and marriage rarely
mixed. Lord Seton Rayne, one of the most notorious
rakehells in town, had every heiress hurling herself at
him. So his sudden kissing of unconventional Letitia
took them both by surprise…

RAGS-TO-RICHES BRIDE
Mary Nichols

Impoverished beauty Diana Bywater must keep her
circumstances secret – her job with Harecrofts depends
on it! Then an unwanted marriage proposal from the
younger Harecroft son threatens everything… Captain
Richard Harecroft is suspicious of this gently reared girl
who has turned his brother's head. But the closer he gets,
the more the mystery of Diana deepens…

MILLS & BOON®
Pure reading pleasure™

HIST1208 LP

THE SHOCKING LORD STANDON

Louise Allen

Rumours fly that Gareth Morant, Lord Standon, is to be wed. He cannot honourably deny them, but he won't be forced into marriage. Encountering a respectable governess in scandalising circumstances, Gareth demands her help to make him entirely ineligible. But he hasn't bargained on the buttoned-up Miss Jessica Gifford being such an ardent pupil...

HIS CAVALRY LADY

Joanna Maitland

Alex instantly fell for Dominic Aikenhead, Duke of Calder, even knowing he would never notice her. To him, she was Captain Alexei Alexandrov, a young man and a brave hussar! Alex longed to be with her English Duke as the passionate woman she truly was. But there was danger in such thoughts. What if Dominic ever found out the truth...?

AN HONOURABLE ROGUE

Carol Townend

Benedict Silvester is a rogue and a flirt! His skill as a musician means he is always travelling...and he charms women wherever he goes. Now he is on a special mission: to accompany Rozenn Kerber to England. Rose is frustrated by Ben's frivolous behaviour – but on their travels she begins to suspect that Ben is more than he appears...

MILLS & BOON®
Pure reading pleasure™

HIST0109 LP

HISTORICAL

LARGE PRINT

SCANDALISING THE TON

Diane Gaston

Lydia, Lady Wexin has been abandoned by her family
and friends, and creditors hound her. Her husband's
scandalous death has left her impoverished, and the
gossip-mongering press is whipped into a frenzy of
speculation when it becomes clear the widow is with
child. Who is the father? Only one man knows:
Adrian Pomroy, Viscount Cavanley…

HER CINDERELLA SEASON

Deb Marlowe

Lily Beecham has been taught that pleasure is sinful –
now she is determined to find out for herself! Freed from
dowdy gowns and worthy reading, Lily charms Society –
except for the cold, aloof and wildly handsome Mr Jack
Alden. At the end of the Season Lily must return to
normality – unless the wicked Mr Alden can save her
from a future of good behaviour…

THE WARRIOR'S PRINCESS BRIDE

Meriel Fuller

Benois le Vallieres, legendary Commander of the North, is
ruthless in battle. But when he rescues Tavia of Mowerby, a
feisty yet vulnerable maid, she gets under his skin like no
woman before… When her royal blood is discovered, Tavia
has his protection and his passionate desire – but will she
ever melt his frozen heart?

 MILLS & BOON®
Pure reading pleasure™

HIST0209 LP